THE PLAGUE BARRENS

ENORA ONLINE: BOOK THREE

ARLO ADAMS

PROLOGUE

The conflicts in the Eastern Kingdom of Lau erupted in violent light shows of magical warfare. When news traveled across the Great Sea, the Western Kingdom of Rubal shuddered. In response, King Constance Luttrell imposed sanctions upon magic casters in a foolhardy attempt to protect his kingdom from a threat he didn't understand.

The tyrant suppressed magic users and created a registry of those advanced in the ways of combat and magic so any who grew too powerful were kept under his watchful eye. In an ironic turn, adventurers turned from the dungeons and disappeared into the hills, while casters formed a secret coven, swearing to one day return and bring an end to the Luttrell edicts.

Whether by virtue or curse, the cleansing of my memories left the notion I was but a simple Elven woman of the woods. I could not quantify the passing of the years, for repetition blends the days into a blur with the absence of new sights and sounds to measure their passing. Aided by a magical ward on my back that softened the violent dispositions of predators and men alike, my life in the forest was all but guaranteed to remain quiet.

Long after the casters of Rubal spread across the continent or joined across the sea, my last several years in the Dark Wood passed in long days, endless eves, and lingering nights. The forest chirped and hummed in a continuous drone as I stared at the stars under the watchful eye of a magical treant cast to be my protector by Zhara, the Matron of the Wood and my bloodline.

When my sullen life overflowed with a boredom I could no longer stomach, I plotted to carve out a smidgen of freedom from Zhara and the army of treants she bade watch me.

Deep root systems restrained sentient trees like my beloved guardian Magellan, so only their gazes could follow me beyond the reaches of their branches. When Magellan used magical root-based communications with his lesser soldiers to track my movements, I began to use my knowledge of their locations, mapped in my mind over the years, to evade them.

Then I covered my ward of protection with the beautiful red robe weaved by Zhara, the magical being who claimed to be my aunt but was actually my mother. I sampled a life she'd gone to great lengths to protect me from.

The bright exhilaration of my rebellion brought a new energy to my existence as I learned to conceal myself in the low branches of thick trunks, to move undetected in underbrush, and to step silently over dried, fallen leaves. I lived new adventures of my own machination as I spied the habits of deadly forest predators, competed for the skins of their prey, and traded in the nearby town of Brumhill. But my childish games one day bore the spoiled fruits of a dark imprisonment that would change my life forever.

With my ward covered and unable to protect me, I was captured by the minion of a demon underlord. Empowered by his demon master Caym, Crohl controlled my body to rule his slaves in the tunnel depths for months. But an unknown destiny born decades before beckoned anew as a traveler from another realm loosed the bonds of both my captor and, just days ago, my ignorance.

When I learned from a mage named Prantu that I was the victim of one of King Luttrell's greatest offenses—cloaking the memories of magic wielders who did not fall in line with his new edicts—my simple perspective of the Old World shone in a new light.

My man, Gemini Fowler, would have been miffed to know of my dreamy ruminations. I stood outside a heavy door waiting for the guard to return and give me leave to enter. Gem—that's what I called him—would curse my lack of focus in such a precarious situation, but all I'd learned about my past in just the last two days had set my mind to wander.

And the more I learned, the more questions arose.

I imagined with a slight smile how Gemini's face would shrivel into a scowl if he knew about my lapse in focus, how he'd admonish me for losing sight of our mission—our quest for Roshan.

My ear twitched with desire to hear the low drawl my friend applied to the Common tongue as I leaned toward the ajar door. Instead, the guard addressed her.

"It serves no benefit for you to refuse food, my lady." He spat the term of respect as if it poisoned his tongue. My friend was a foreign woman of the East, and the lone reason he lent her courtesy was that she was the property of his patron—Zane, the Governor of Knall.

"We enter the Plague Barrens tomorrow and will reach his lordship's domain in a week's time. If you arrive at Millbury Peaks composed of skin and ribs, he might consider you lost and feed his dogs what few scraps remain."

This bastard underestimated his quarry. Roshan was as likely to flinch at his threats as gouge her own eyes from their sockets. She traversed life as if floating on winds blown by the divine, and her captor's words would penetrate like sand against iron as long as Roshan held Solara close.

Which she always did.

"I would sooner be the food of dogs than a wet place for your governor's violations. I am promised to another, and for him I save my fruits, fool. Begone and keep your poison."

My lips stretched into a smile that tugged at my ears, but I suppressed it when his jangling armor signaled movement. If the guard opened the door to discover me eavesdropping, he might engage the use of his sword to render my grin permanent, carved by blade. I was but a servant come to deliver nourishment to a prisoner, and if a smile drew his attention to my otherwise shrouded features, I'd fail my mission. Then he'd slit my throat for the second time, with the same blade he'd used in an inn room in Brumhill.

"You eastern types are hardheaded, huh?" The guard laughed. "That's fine, my lady. I've dealt with thick ones. Your food is coming, and I suggest you eat it, lest I force it down your gullet."

The thump of metallic boots approached and prompted me to jerk away. I held the tray close and bowed my head so my hood shadowed my brow.

When the heavy door swung open, his disdain for me came clear in his tone. "You're new, aren't you?"

I nodded and bowed deep, hoping to convey the subservient demeanor of a chamber servant, though I didn't know how such a laborer would behave. Relief washed over me as the guard waved a dismissive hand.

"Leave the food on the table inside." He peered over his shoulder, then leaned to a conspiratorial distance to mutter in my ear. His breath stank of under-cooked meat. "Maybe you could have a word with her. Give her a woman's softness, eh? Get to her to take a few bites so we can collect our bounty, and there's fifty silver in it for you."

"It would honor me to bring the lady nourishment in exchange for your coin, my lord," I said with a deep nod.

"Good luck," he grumbled. As his boots struck stone, he muttered, "Sometimes I think the lot of you are more trouble than you're worth. Give me a good ol' Trowlsby whore and..." his voice trailed off to indecipherable mumbles that echoed off stone walls as he descended the stairs.

To imagine the plights of the poor prostitutes who would suffer the stinking weight of this man who'd spilled blood from my neck not five days earlier filled me with empathy. I enjoyed a brief fantasy where I'd grab the pommel of his jingling sword from its scabbard, run the bastard through, then kick his ass so he careened down the stairs, splattering them with his stinking blood. But I served a higher purpose than revenge.

Heart thumping against my ribs, I hurried into the room and eased the heavy door closed with my rump.

The figure standing in the room's center twisted her fingers as she peered out the arched window of the massive keep and across Trowlsby's governmental district reserved for official council business. Glossy black hair flowed midway down her back across the same green and yellow robe she'd worn when last I saw her. I longed to embrace my friend and scream with excitement, but I paced passed her instead, set the tray on the stone table, then turned. Weighty enthusiasm coursed through my veins as I reached for my hood.

"I told the guard," her words came in a low tone, but her drawl was clear enough, "I will not take sustenance just to become the slave of his wretched master. Take it away or leave it to rot."

As the hood slid down, I stared into the oversized sienna irises of the beloved friend for whom I'd traveled and battled for what seemed an eternity, though it'd been mere days. After so many years in a forest devoid of companionship, it hadn't taken me long to absorb this woman into my soul, and I planned to take her with me.

My heart swelled as her stern expression weakened, her jaw relaxed, and shocked eyes locked with mine. Rushing forward, she threw her arms around me.

"Priya! How you bless me!"

"It is I who am blessed again by the sight of you, alive and well." I squeezed her until my shoulders protested.

Roshan pulled away, holding me at arm's length. Her head swiveled to the door.

"This is not safe!" She lowered her voice. "They will catch you."

"Gemini has devised a plan to reunite you with your destiny, Roshan." My smile cast more confusion upon her features. "Trust me. Can you do that? We are short on time."

"Undeniably." Her hushed voice croaked as a tear welled in her eye.

Her full cheek was soft and warm as I planted a kiss and drew my lips close to her ear.

"Gem is near. Watch for him to walk away from the bridge in a few minutes. He will signal, but your freedom will come only with great faith."

She set a hand on my breast bone as her eyebrows raised in gratitude. "I'm a Priestess of Solara's Light. Faith is my strong suit."

The door swung open with a wall-slamming bang and the guard who'd once taken my life entered with another dressed in a suit of chain.

"Stop in the king's name!" He stomped toward us, his sword unsheathed and erect.

"So much for explanations. Watch your interface and recall the promise made in the wood," I whispered. "You must emulate what you see."

"I do not understand!"

"Your interface. Your attribute points. Trust. Emulate."

I wheeled around and sprinted toward the open balcony at the opposite end of her stony quarters. Metal rattled as the guards gave chase. Though it was higher than it'd appeared from a distance, I struggled onto the stone ledge overlooking the lower parapets and gave silent thanks to Solara for every tree I'd climbed in my former forest home.

The guards stopped on the terrace and glared. My murderer wore the twisted scowl of a man intent on repeating his dastardly act of days before.

"Okay," the bastard said. "Time to come on down, lest you fall from there and turn yourself to mush. The game is over."

"The game has but begun, you ass." Raising my hands into claws, I cast a spell. "A gift for you."

A blue progress bar across the top of my field-of-vision

filled and, as the guard realized my intent, he covered his face and stepped backward. I unleashed my energy spell. My target convulsed as a mana-fused orb of lightning slammed into his chest and the subsequent lightning ball jumped to his companion. His face scrunched in pain as he let out an involuntary curse. His lower level partner left his feet and slammed into the stone wall behind. As his partner slumped to the floor and my former killer fell to his knees, I raised my middle finger.

"Fuck you."

Gem would be proud.

Men filed through the door behind Roshan as he struggled to his feet and lunged. Roshan sped toward me as I threw my arms out to my sides, squeezed my eyelids shut, and leaned back into the cool air of the open city.

"No!" Roshan screamed. "Priya!"

Though I knew all would be well, an airy fear inflated my lungs as I fell through space.

1

The castle blended with the rock face reaching toward the cloudless azure sky. A two-story draw-bridge centered on the high wall crossed a moat of crystal-clear water.

The gargantuan structure housed the city's council of elders. Given the recessed state of technology in Enora, I reasoned that magic must have carved the massive facade.

What I'd learned in the two days I'd cased Trowlsby was that the elders inside were little more than figureheads who stood at the ready to pass down the will of the Governor of Knall, the king's regent who couldn't be bothered to live in the city. In casual conversation with vendors and townspeople, I'd learned the leader lived four days' journey to the north in a fortress founded as a reward for his loyal service to the king decades before. Knall was the eastern region of the continent called Rubal, and his fortress was centered on a place my map labeled Millbury Peaks.

Maybe someday I would pay that fortress a visit. It invited trouble to swipe the regent's eastern prize from his grasp a second time, and defense wasn't my style. First, I had to get Roshan out of the city.

For days I'd alternated between worries about whether we would catch up to Roshan in time and whether our levels would be high enough to free her from the governor's kidnapping bastards. Though the quest granted by Lucera—the A.I.'s extension into Enora's physical realm—recommended level sixteen, the guards in the castle were ranked more than twice that. I suspected the quest design intended I catch the governor's men outside of town and fight to free my companion, but for once I would do things my way, using good old human ingenuity.

I planned to cheat.

Priya, Desini, and I had counted guards at the keep and the northern gate. Then we waited for the men to appear with Roshan in tow, but she'd remained in the room often reserved for dignitaries for two days. She spent hours on the terrace in her green and yellow robe, taking in the sight of the city. Seeing her so close but out of my grasp tested my resolve. When my patience wore down to a thread after a single day, my companions grew weary of my bickering and sent me to explore the town.

I'd tried to invite her to a party, but the system returned error messages.

This entity is not eligible for party chat.

Cheating-assed game.

The previous evening, I bought a stocky laborer an ale in a local tavern to loosen his lips and learn what I could about the region's ruler and the guards who patrolled the city and manned the gates. A few drinks later, he spoke of the governor exclusively in whispers and gave the impression the aforementioned fortress in Millbury Peaks was the center of a feudal system where the governor oversaw the true center of his wealth instead of wasting his time in a city that delivered the taxes to him.

I learned that "Governor" wasn't a title born of elections. The bastard who'd had my companion torn away from her family in the East had been appointed by the current King Luttrell's father in reward for his service as a hired henchman, and he'd served the crown for decades now with little oversight or supervision from the disinterested monarch.

When a demon invasion across the sea prompted the grandfather, King Constance Luttrell, to absorb the mage university of Warrington into the royal government, many magic wielders took understandable offense. Long had the university served as a place of refuge where citizens born with mana pools could learn to control their gifts of magic in service to society.

The henchman Zane oversaw the suppression of the mage revolt and introduced the process called lavation, where rebellious magic wielders had their memories shrouded and were sent to serve the monarch's lords across the Kingdom of Rubal. They became nothing more than blank slates to be molded.

Priya had been smuggled out of Warrington after she'd gone through lavation, but before they could send her off to be a slave.

Resistors who weren't captured, killed, or exorcised of their memories had formed a group called The Shadow Coven and vanished.

I sniffed corruption in much I'd heard about government in my first days outside the Dark Wood. But at least the people of the city didn't go hungry. Trade was steady, with carts forming endless streams at the southern and eastern gates, and stone buildings housing businesses enjoyed a consistent stream of foot traffic. I took a little credit for the traffic at the southern gates, since I was responsible for clearing the mercenaries who'd terrorized the road from Trowlsby to Warrington, and from there to Brumhill.

About a hundred people queued across the drawbridge to make requests of the city authorities when I approached. There were all kinds here, from those wearing loose, home-spun rags to the straight-backed business people whose clothes expressed exquisite tailoring. I didn't know if the people of Trowlsby observed lunch hours per se, but the line was longest when the sun was highest overhead. I planned to use that to my advantage.

This might have been the first time in my life I considered a long line good luck. I didn't want to reach the front of the queue where warriors in full plate to their shoulders scanned petitions. The crowd served my purpose divinely.

Just before stepping onto the bridge, I waved a few people by as they approached. "Please, after you."

"How very chivalrous of you, my lord." A woman cradling a small child bowed her head.

"Not at all." I waved my arm toward the line with a gallant flourish.

But it wasn't chivalry at all. One more body between me and the other side of that bridge served as another cushion that allowed me time to get my work done.

I stepped behind the woman as she bounced the babe in her arms and opened my interface with a combination of right and left eye blinks that had become second nature, I doubted others would notice the subtle gesture. I no longer had to scan the tabs, just a thought brought me to the pane I wanted.

Companions.

I skimmed past the alphabetical listings of Click, Desini, and Priya before Roshan's profile appeared. A film of gray washed over the image of the copper-skinned mage with flowing black hair spilling over the shoulders of a green-and-yellow caster's robe.

"Still out of range," I muttered. "Shit. C'mon, Priya."

My heart thumped at the thought of my half-elf companion up there, somewhere inside that castle, in a constant state of danger. Every moment inside increased the chance we'd fail.

When we cased the castle after I'd come up with the new plan, a shorter servant girl had wandered past the guard without a word, crossed the drawbridge, then followed the western road out of the valley and into the city proper. After following her for a few minutes, I knew her robe would be a perfect fit for the height-challenged Priya. I'd considered using my stealth ability to trail her further, but the high-level guards in Trowlsby wouldn't have had any problem spotting me. My last desire was their attention. So, I'd pursued her the old-fashioned way by sticking to the shadows of the enclosed stone structures and keeping my distance.

Desini was guarding the servant while Priya used her robe with a royal insignia patch to gain entry. The last thing I wanted to do was injure an innocent, and we proved lucky in that she quietly surrendered at the sight of Desini's sword. Adorned in the servant girl's robe, Priya had garnered little more than a glance from the guards as she'd stepped off the other end of the drawbridge with her hood up then passed him by.

A man further up the line pointed toward the rampart high on the face of the castle. I focused beyond the image of Roshan in my interface and followed the direction of his finger. My heart nearly burst into my throat as a figure in a servant's robe climbed onto the wall. Even beneath the haze of the high sun, the crackles of light bursting from her fingers were clear. An energy orb exited her hands. I felt no pity for its target.

Utterances of disbelief sounded across the bridge as the queued became spectators, all heads turning in that direction. Mumblings crossed the drawbridge as orders barked by the guards at the other end echoed in my direction.

Their orders wouldn't matter. There was nothing they could do. We were putting on a show today, one I suspected would be the talk of the town—and Millbury Peaks—for some time to come. Priya raised her fist and thrust it out. I was too far away to see the finger I knew was raised.

That's my girl.

In my HUD, Roshan's image still wore a gray film.

"Come on..."

Priya held her arms out to her sides and fell backward as if part of a trust exercise. The air filled with screams as her body careened through space. I cringed as gravity hauled her toward the foot of the castle. Though I knew Priya would resurrect a few blocks away in the shop of one of Desini's allies, the inevitable, permanent image of her impact on the stone at the bottom of the four-story drop didn't hold much allure, so I averted my gaze and turned my attention back to the image of Roshan in my interface.

It bloomed into full color. My breath hitched in my chest. The short form of her stats flashed into sharp text beside her picture.

Roshan

Human
Level 10 Light Priestess
*Strength: 4 **
*Dexterity: 4 **
intelligence: 19
Wisdom: 10
Constitution: 11
*Charisma: 14***
Roshan has four attribute points available.
With a disposition of beloved, you may distribute four attribute points for Roshan.

One point. At any other time, I might have dropped it into Constitution, but today hit points were the enemy, lest she plunged those four stories and survived. Sure, it was unlikely, but Enora could be a real bitch and my manipulation of the quest objective rang as dishonest. But fuck that. I wanted Roshan back, and something told me Enora wanted me to have her back. They'd brought me to this world for a reason I didn't yet grasp, but I suspected my priestess was part of the plan.

Since her spells benefitted most by Intelligence, I focused to tick that attribute up by one point. Text zipped onto my screen.

Warning:
If you spend more than five points on this NPCs attributes, she will be bound to you.
Binding an NPC to you means that if you fall in battle and re-spawn, the NPC will re-spawn with you, should she fall.
Binding is not to be taken lightly and cannot be undone.

While bonds can be broken when two NPCs share a bond and one dies, this human-to-NPC bond is permanent.
You may only break this bond by killing the NPC by your own hand.
If you have a garrison or pay for a room at an inn, you can leave the NPC behind at your choosing, but you will still be bound.
Be aware: There is no limit to the number of NPCs who can be bound to you, as long as they are of endeared disposition or higher upon binding. You may bind a non-player of endeared or higher disposition without permission.
This bond can only be broken when the non-player is killed by your own hand.
Binding cannot be undone.
Are you sure you wish to spend further attribute points for this NPC and permanently bind her to you?
Yes/No

With my pulse thumping hard in my ears, I focused on *Yes*.

Roshan, Clan Fortwan has been soul bound to you.

I clinched my fists as excitement surged through my arms and shoulders. I itched to pump them overhead.

Touchdown, bitches!

Hmm, perhaps that wasn't the best metaphor considering the way Priya had just plummeted to the ground.

After confirming the soul binding and adding two more points to Intelligence, I dropped the last point into Wisdom to increase the rate at which she recovered mana, because why the hell not?

Roshan

Light Priestess
Level 10
*Strength: 4 **
*Dexterity: 4 **
Intelligence: 19
Wisdom: 10
Constitution: 11
*Charisma: 14***

Done.

I turned toward the outside of the bridge so the guards would be less likely to spot me as I paced away from the crowd. When I peered over my shoulder and up at the place where I'd last seen Roshan, I counted three guards staring down over the ledge. Then she appeared, just on their right. An airy swell filled my chest at the sight of her.

She scanned the foot of the castle, a hand covering her mouth, then turned her attention to the crowd on the bridge as if to escape what she'd seen. I was pretty sure they fell on me when I became the lone pedestrian who crossed the threshold onto the cobblestone walkway while everyone else stared over the side of the bridge. Although I took solace that the guard standing next to her hadn't yet noticed his charge's appearance since his attention was focused below, I wished she'd get on with it.

After I'd positioned myself so the guards on the drawbridge wouldn't spot me beyond the crowd, I raised my arms high and waved them a single time. Roshan raised a low hand in greeting so I knew she'd spotted me. I extended a finger, pointed toward the stone to which Priya had fallen, and then I pointed at her.

My expectation was that she'd stare for long moments,

fret over the decision, then maybe not jump at all. A spine-tingling thought passed through my mind—she might not have received my directions. But then Roshan clambered onto the wall. The bottom hem of her robe fluttered in the breeze and the glossy black strands atop her head swayed. She turned, said something I couldn't hear to the closest guard, and repeated the gesture Priya had used before jumping.

That was all I needed to see.

2

I trusted nothing. A constant inkling of doubt itched in my brain—that my splattered companions would join all the other lost souls of the dead wherever Enora deposited them for eternity. My seed in Priya's belly was the source of great contention when we'd devised our plan to recover Roshan. Something about her plummeting two stories to her death rubbed me wrong. Call me crazy.

But Desini's tail and the cute little ears atop her head wouldn't go over well in the castle's vicinity. Prejudices born of a beast invasion and ransacking less than twenty years before would bring undue attention to her attributes. She also stood nearly six feet tall and her discernible fiery red hair wouldn't help. She'd be like a flashing stoplight... in a world where stoplights didn't exist.

Since my hours of recon had revealed no male chamber servants when I'd cased the castle, Priya had insisted she would do it, without or without my leave. I'd argued that at just over five-feet-tall, blonde, and beautiful, she would stand out, but I could call Priya many things, and stupid wasn't one. Rebuffing my sudden cowardice had proven easy for my half-elf lover.

Priya was bullheaded about her people. Roshan, Desini, and I were her people.

Desini zipped past me on the street, mocking my lack of stamina in her mishon accent as her tail swung high behind her. "You run like a cow, but slower."

"Fuck you, kitty!" I barked as she sped off.

She hated being called that, but I knew the middle finger she raised like a flag in response wasn't out of genuine offense. That all three women had raised their middle fingers in spiteful salute within the last five minutes warmed my heart.

That's a hat trick!

But her confident demeanor had degraded by the time I arrived at the shop. Her toes aligned with the threshold as if she didn't want to risk the ruination of resurrection magic by stepping inside. She was one member of my group who'd never witnessed the second coming of a resurrected soul or lived through it, herself. Desini had the fewest reasons to believe.

In a rare display of physical affection, she interlaced her fingers with mine as we stared together through the open doorway. With the light foot traffic of midday on the back-street, Desini couldn't have picked a more secluded shop.

"It is taking too long," Desini said. "She should've been here by now."

"And how would you know that? Last time we rezzed, it was hours later." I suspected NPCs would instantly resurrect if their bound players hadn't died, because it would suck to have to wait for them. It would be a major strike against the game. But Enora had a way of doing things, and they didn't always add up.

"I trust nothing."

"It amazes how alike we are, sometimes." I squeezed her hand. "It's okay. She'll be along. They both will." I tried to project confidence, but the inflection of my words relayed little. The final words came out like a question. I expected her keen intuition would stamp that shit out.

"I am unconvinced by your words. It sounds like you don't trust yourself."

Bingo.

"Be patient." I squeezed her hand again.

"This is an odd way for us to bond, master." She returned the squeeze, anyway.

I accepted the whole "master" thing since she used the word like she would with a respected teacher.

We threw up our free hands in sync to block the glare of a white flash. When we lowered them, a transparent, huddled image faded into view. Then the solid form of a slight woman materialized, tangled curls twisted in all directions, like a blonde medusa. She wore the slight wraps of starter clothes around her curves. Her hips quivered in the shadows.

Gods, I forgot. The servant's robe wasn't soul bound. That means it's sitting at the base of the castle, maybe Obi-Wan Kenobi style!

We raced inside.

Desini won. She set a hand on Priya's shoulder to steady her as I ran my fingers through her wild hair and tilted her face upward, toward mine.

"Gem?" She blinked and her knees buckled.

I swept her up and sat on a wooden platform between stacks of folded garments and cradled her across my lap.

"I'm here."

"My beloved!" Desini planted kisses on Priya's neck. "I

feared it was a myth and you would not return to me... I mean, us."

I grinned at the Freudian slip.

"Forgive me, master. I forget myself."

"It's fine." I threw her a wink. "And it's me you forgot."

I inspected Priya to staunch my worries.

*Priya Skyy**
**Pregnant*

Relief washed over me. Then the fact that relief washed over me cast my mind in heavy surprise.

"It was much easier to die that way." Priya rubbed her temples. "There was no pain. No blood." As if in contradiction to her words, she shuddered and leaned back.

I held her steady. "Thank you." I wore my best fake smile as I clutched Priya's hands. "I know that wasn't easy."

"Are you kidding?" she asked, still shivering. "That was fun. I cast Lightning Pulse on that bastard who slit my throat in Brumhill, and I might have killed his compatriot."

That was strange. Priya's Lightning chain only did 60% damage on subsequent jumps. I'd have to check the battle log for companion combat data.

"The fall was... cool. I could hear the awe of the crowd. I guess they'll be looking for me!"

"Doubtful. Your corpse lies splattered at the foot of the battlements. They're scraping you off the stone as we speak." I was so proud of my genius plan.

"The notion of my Priya's broken form is anything but humorous, master. You should apologize."

"I'd be glad to apologize, but I'd be unsure who I was apologizing to. Priya, for making light of a twisted body she no longer occupies, or you for engaging your overactive imagination."

"Both," Desini said. "You heartless fucker."

My head jerked back. "You wield foul language like a seasoned pro." My pride beamed brighter and I let it show on my face.

"It is not like you invented the word, master." She wagged a finger. "Don't change the subject. You owe apologies."

"Thicken your skin, woman." I waved a dismissive hand.

"Thicken my skin, indeed, master." Desini squinted an eye. "Someone begs a duel when his tongue forms such edges. Perhaps we should take to the street, Gemini." One side of her lips ticked up. The mishon had a two-level advantage over me.

Now it's 'Gemini.'

"Yeah, yeah. You wait until I catch up to you. I plan to give you a good throttling."

Desini kissed Priya's cheek and replaced her arms around the shorter woman's neck. Priya clutched them.

"You know she's sitting in my lap, right?"

"Yes, master." Desini shrugged.

"You will have to let go, eventually."

The mishon slid her arms under Priya and raised her up. Then she carried her across to the shop's counter. Her tight, wiry muscles flexed but her face showed no strain. "It wasn't until you left that I realized I lacked belief. Now that I have seen this miracle born of Solara, I am shamed by my lack of faith in you both. Now, I understand. The two of you are my destiny. Long shall we serve together."

With that, I agreed.

"Priya, how's the sickness?"

"Sickness?" Desini asked, standing straight and drawing her hands away to bunch up Priya's hair. She tied the locks into a makeshift pony tail.

"I guess I didn't mention that. Yeah, we got a little sick last time we resurrected. Supposedly it gets worse each time. It's part of the reason I wanted to take on the task instead of Priya."

"It's terrible," Priya said. "My head throbs at the temples." She rubbed them to illustrate. "My stomach begs to lurch. White spots dance before my—"

A second blinding flash filled the space. The ghost standing where the light receded wore the green and yellow robe in which I'd last seen her as she faded into existence. I skittered across the shop before she formed so my face was the first thing she saw.

Roshan's irises flashed with the brilliance I recalled as she merged into focus. We stared at each other as a stupid grin wrinkled my face. When her shoulders shuddered, I flung my arms around them and pulled her close.

"You're okay." I rubbed fast circles across the back of her robe. "The chills and visual discomfort will pass in a couple minutes. Just rest easy."

"Gemini? Am I really here?" Her arms slipped around me and her weight fell against me. I squeezed her as close as two people could get.

I forced my reply through a tight, quivering throat. "You're here, Roshan."

"You came..."

"Did you expect I'd leave my healer behind?"

She shuddered again, but the chills had little to do with it.

3

T hough the shop sat at the tail end of a back alley near the eastern wall, pedestrian traffic filed by a few minutes after I yanked Roshan into a long embrace. Though she hadn't recovered from her own resurrection sickness, Priya slipped in and the three of us held each other.

"We're back," I said.

I never planned on letting Roshan out of my sight again.

When we relinquished our embrace, Desini's trading partner returned to reopen her shop, as if on cue. I thanked her and dropped a few gold pieces into her hands for her trouble, which she accepted only with debate. It dropped our reserves to twenty-six gold and change, but in my current state of elation, I might have given her the entirety of our stash, found a box into which we could all fit, and slept in an alley that night as long as it meant I kept my party together.

"Oh, how I have longed for the two of you," Roshan crooned.

A new airiness filled my chest at the warm timbre of

Roshan's voice. She set a gentle palm on my cheek. "I had faith you would come for me and that the Light would rejoin our paths."

"Faith seems to be the theme today," Desini said from behind me. "I was reminded of its value moments ago after I lacked it."

Roshan stepped toward her. "My master once told me that our failings to keep to the goddess's will also ensures balance in the world. Rejoice in your return to devotion and the lesson you have learned." She half-bowed and extended her hand. "I am Roshan, Clan Fortwan."

Desini extended her own and stepped forward.

"I have heard so much about you, priestess. It is as if I have known you for years. My new friends have longed for your return. As you are part of this family, let us embrace as sisters."

Before Roshan could answer, the taller mishon had pulled her to her chest. Roshan shot me a look and her cheek nestled against Desini's shoulder.

I threw her a shit-eating grin.

Desini took a step back but grasped her hand. "We will need to put your robe in Gemini's bag and outfit you before we leave so that we might slip out of the city, unnoticed."

When Roshan peered at me, I nodded. "That's the plan. They shouldn't expect to see you or Priya since your bodies were, um, you know. But I sometimes have shitty luck."

"Hmm. Yes." Roshan nodded with enthusiasm, a gesture I remembered from our time in the Dark Wood. "I recall this tendency, but you always somehow weather Hokhram's storms." She clapped her hands together. "I am just so overcome with Solara's energy to be with my new family again! I can barely contain the Light bursting from my pores!"

And yet beads of sweat covered her forehead. Her teeth chattered.

"Well, maybe you can burn it off casting some of those warming heals, baby, but we need to haul ass."

Somehow, the form-fitting leather pants and tight blouse hadn't been my idea of inconspicuous, but Desini had insisted that those who shrouded themselves in a city of experienced guards appeared the opposite.

I pulled my attention back to Roshan. Desini dropped a wide-brimmed, finely woven hat atop the Light priestess's head to shade her face and round out the outfit. Then we hustled along our predetermined cobblestone path to where our cart waited near the northernmost gate of Trowlsby.

Though we didn't run, Desini reminded us to slow our excited pace several times as we strode to the cart. As we came to the final turn leading to the dusty lot set aside for carts of traveling merchants, Priya caught my eye. She glanced down, and I followed her gaze to find my white-knuckled death grip on Roshan's hand.

Oh, gods. I'm hurting her.

I loosened my grip.

She squeezed my hand, shook her head, and pulled me closer. "Never further than this will you be from me. Never again."

I focused on a flashing indicator in my HUD I hadn't noticed.

Quest Updated:

Rescue Roshan

(Recommended Level 16)

Recover Roshan from the clutches of her captors—Complete
New Objective:
Smuggle Roshan through the city gates before she is
discovered—Incomplete.
Reward: 18,000 XP
25 Gold

New objective? What the hell?

So much for my daydreams about the glorious XP reward the quest offered. The revelation of a new requirement washed a crawling sense of foreboding across my neck and shoulders in a cold shiver. I wondered if the new objective was a punishment for not taking Roshan by force as Enora might have intended. To overcome obstacles was the whole point of gaming and the A.I.'s tricks would hinder my path for the rest of my life.

I'd better get used to it. Hell, I should've expected it.

The absence of the new objective until we completed the first one meant *she could string these quests out forever*.

I stopped next to the cart, and my boots scratched up puffs of dust. Then I swept Roshan up into my arms.

"Gemini!" she bellowed. "What on Enora are you doing?"

I used a low rail for a step and set her on the riding bench of Desini's cart.

"Carrying you across the threshold." Sure, it was corny, but I didn't give a shit. "Or dumping you across it, I guess." To complete the effect, I leaned forward, cupped her cheeks gently in both my hands, and kissed her. Her warm lips were so soft and full that I didn't want to relinquish my suction. "We're bound now, which makes me yours, and you mine. So, I follow tradition."

"Tradition?" Priya asked. "How do you know..." The

hints of crow's feet beneath one temple alerted me to my mistake.

As far as Desini and Priya—and too many others, for my comfort—were concerned, I was a *Shénhuà*. A mythic being with no memory of an existence before Solara conjured me. Priya had caught onto my absent-minded slip about tradition. The emotions pouring out of her across the airwaves of our Elven-based bond removed any remaining inkling of doubt.

My mother's voice echoed in my mind from across eternity.

It is better to keep your mouth shut and appear stupid than to open it and remove all doubt.

My mom would've *really*, really liked my half-elf sweetheart. For all her faults and the ways she suppressed my activities as a child out of fear I'd come to harm, my mother was a snarky one, like Priya. In a good way.

Priya's vibes softened, calm passed between us, and she showed me a slow, gentle smile. She whispered, "Whatever that was, it warmed me."

"I dig you," I said.

"And I, you. Noob."

"Ugh!" Roshan interjected and jerked us out of our soft moment. "My language scratches at her Elven lips like cricket legs on a calm night. It is good I have returned, for I will teach her how to say *noob*."

"Maybe we should take our priestess back to the castle from which I plunged in service to her," Priya squinted.

"I would as soon you come and press your lips to mine, elf, for I have missed thee."

One of Desini's cheeks twitched, but then her gaze met mine, and I threw her something between a squint and a glare. Color flooded her cheeks, and she bowed her head in a short nod.

Good. We have enough fucking problems without jealousy.

I climbed onto the bench next to Roshan and held the split canvas to one side. "Climb in the back. We've joined a couple crates for you to hide in until we're through the gate." I cocked my head at the metal structure in the distance. As Roshan climbed through, I turned my attention on Priya. "You too, little lady. We can't have anyone seeing you after you splattered—"

"Shut it, Fowler," Priya said. It was the first time she'd called me by my surname. The face *of a woman I'd* gamed and shared a bed with in my old world flashed through my mind.

Desini threw me a death stare as Priya mounted the bench. "I warned you of such jests. We will duel at our first opportunity and I shall throttle you soundly." She finished with a mutter as she mounted the bench like a thousand times before. "Hmph. *Splatter.*"

Priya patted my cheek and stuck one leg through the opening. "You should've known better. I see bruises in your future."

I smiled. "I might even get a skill point or two."

Desini settled on the bench next to me, and I leaned in so our shoulders bumped. When she faced me, I pinched her narrow chin between my thumb and forefinger.

Cocking my head toward the cart, I whispered, "They did their part. We can throw down later if you desire it. Help me get them away from here, and I'll duel you all night long. No distractions, no more joking around. Just like we discussed. If the blades have to come out, we cut every bastard between Roshan and freedom. It's you and me now, Desini."

Though I'd somewhat expected her to peer down in defiance at the fingers grasping her chin, I found only the characteristic focus and tight-cheeked determination from my mishon companion. Her reflective slice-of-lime irises never so much as twitched as she absorbed every word.

"It will be as you say, master. Even if I must fall to ensure they escape, ride out into the night without me. I will catch up with you."

"We all escape together or we fall together." I shook my head. "I don't want them having to suffer res-sickness again, so let's make it the former. They're putting on brave faces, but let me assure you, the sweat on their brows isn't from the heat. They're weakened back there."

Desini and I had discussed the logistics for our flight at length, and she'd decided the best way to go was south, back toward Warrington. But I had different ideas, and she'd been all-too-happy by the time I was finished explaining.

The night we'd met, the cat-like goddess told me how her people were forced from their land by the denizens of Warrington and Trowlsby, only to be driven north through the deadly Plague Barrens. Many died in the Exodus, and the rest were driven from their new home a couple years later. I'd been intrigued by the story of how they formed a small, nomadic community to the northeast and rotated between camps as the surrounding foods of the changing seasons appeared in each region.

Like Earth's hunter-gatherers.

I wanted to find them. Desini had adored the idea. My suspicion that she'd longed to see her family again had proven out. I also had an inkling her new status as an adventurer played no small part in wanting to reunite with her people, but I'd never suggest it aloud. First, we needed to go to ground. Hide out for a bit. Keep our heads down.

By Desini's descriptions, the Plague Barrens sounded like a vast wasteland of torment and terror, which sounded to me like a perfect place for a party of four composed of two DPS, a healer, and a tank, even if our average level was a bit low for the area. After talking to my drunken new friend at the bar about the history of the governor and his feudal domain, I'd snuck off to a map shop and spent fifty silver on a crude map of the barrens and, sure enough, I'd found the perfect place for adventurers to lie low while staying productive.

A dungeon.

Near the corner where the southern and eastern borders of the Plague Barrens converged, the red mark wasn't labeled, but the shopkeeper ensured me it was what I wanted. It was time to get this show on the road. If things went according to plan—which they almost never did—we would camp a couple nights out in the wilds, then continue north into the Plague Barrens.

The map I'd purchased depicted a small town near a crossroads halfway between Trowlsby and the black mass of territory labeled Plague Barrens. Hopefully we could bind ourselves there and, if anything went wrong, we'd have a spawn point to regroup.

Party time, people!

My excitement waned as we pulled up to the gate. I gave Desini's knee a clutch and a curt nod. Beyond the line of people, carts, and horses lined up to leave the city, two guards stood on the driver's side of the cart. When we drew close enough to make out their features, my heart sank.

The figure in the shining plate on my side of the cart wore a face I'd never forget. My hands reached back for my daggers before I realized what I was doing, but Desini clutched one arm. My face warmed as I ground my teeth so hard an ear popped. My hands dropped back into my lap and grasped the reigns.

Last I'd seen those features, they'd twisted into a sneer as the bastard opened the carotid of the Elven woman huddling in the cart behind me. I longed to open his arteries in the same fashion and watch his life source paint the ground. The conjured mental images of his blood pouring into the sandy road beneath his boots fed my soul.

Turning from the cart in front of us, he shook his head at the other guard, who waved them through. Then it was our turn.

Only strenuous mental determination relaxed my features. Though the guard next to him spared me only a careless glance, the shit head's gaze lingered. I didn't bother trying to smile or be cordial. Such a vain effort would've just aroused suspicion.

"Say," the mother fucker said after a long gander at me and the mishon next to me on the bench. "Do I know you from somewhere?"

Brazel Snead
Level 13 Human
Fighter

My heart thumped with both the desire to murder him and the need to get my team out of this city in one piece. The conflicting emotions tossed my mind like a salad and I had a hard time gathering the simplest of words.

Die, you son of a whore! I longed to scream as I plunged my instruments of death deep into his eye socket.

Then a calming wave rolled over my shoulders and

down, into my chest. My shoulders dropped and my jaw relaxed.

Priya just intervened.

With a furrowed forehead and my mouth twisted to one side in contemplation, I leaned toward him. "No, I think I'd remember a face like yours."

"Where are you headed?" He squinted and scanned me high to low.

"To burn a swath of destruction across the Plague Barrens." It was the truth.

The guard laughed, but it caught in his throat as it dawned on him I was serious.

"Ha!" the mother fucker blurted. "You and what army?"

I tilted my head to the woman seated next to me. "This army."

"Bah," he waved a dismissive hand. "It's your funeral. You sure I don't recognize you from somewhere?"

I shrugged.

His stupid face bore down on me for a couple heartbeats longer before he smirked. "Yeah, you must have one of those faces." He poked a finger toward the cart. "Gonna need to check your cargo. We have a fugitive on the loose."

Fugitive? "Oh. Well, we're always happy to help the law." I stared at his chain armor. "But where is your insignia, sir? Are you a member of the city guard?"

The asshole squinted at me. "You getting smart with me?" He gripped the pommel of his sword.

No, just buying time for the women to hide in back.

I stared him down, but didn't reach for my weapons, as much as I wanted to.

The man next to him pointed at his shoulder patch. "I'm with the guard, and he's working with me. So, submit to a search so we can move the line, eh?"

"The guard can search, but we're messengers and due to security reasons, we can't allow douche bags near the cart." It was juvenile, but since my daggers weren't an option...

"What's a douche bag?" the guard asked, shaking his head. The asshole's face turned an interesting shade of red as the guard stepped up, poked his head through the side of the canvas, then stepped back. "No one in there. Any reason to hold 'em?"

The ass turned and shook his head at the guard. "Though he'd do well to watch his tongue if he ever sees me again."

Even if they don't know what a douche bag is, I guess my tone gave me away. One day, I'm going to bleed this guy out.

"A warning best heeded in both directions," Desini muttered.

"Does the beast have something to say?"

"Move along," the guard said, stepping between us. "Safe travels."

As the wheels of our cart rolled off the gravel and onto smooth soil, I ventured a final glare over my shoulder to find the governor's task boy watching us go. With a tug of the reigns, I faced front and clicked my tongue a couple times.

"Who was this man you so wanted to kill?" Desini asked.

"What, you feel my emotions now, too?"

"Even though I've known you for only days, your hide your ire poorly." She raised her shoulder in a half-shrug.

"He's the one who slit Priya's throat at the Brumhill Inn."

Desini's hand clutched my leg and her head swiveled so fast and far, I envisioned a cheesy ancient movie called *The Exorcist* where this possessed girl's head spun around. "This is the one? Where is my sword! I will slit necks, too!"

She was crawling over me before I knew it, and I had to throw both arms around her to keep her on the bench. I received a face full of breasts for my trouble, which wasn't all bad.

"Gods, woman," my muffled voice pleaded into her chest. "Calm the hell down! Imagine my restraint! I saw it happen!" She fell back onto the bench and crossed her arms. I leaned toward her. "Nothing would give me greater joy than to go cut him with you, but this isn't the time."

"Oooh, how I would like to throttle this one." If not for the underlying emotion, the way her face scrunched with pouty lips would have been hilarious.

"Save your energy for when I teach you not to threaten me with duels."

She leaned forward and pressed her lips to mine for a long moment. My eyelids flared with surprise. She patted my knee.

"Go in the back now and tend your lovely mage. You have longed for her return, and your time together is well-earned." I pulled back the tarp, and she stayed my hand. "Oh, and tell Priya I would welcome her company in an hour or so, when we are clear of Trowlsby. Only if she is feeling better." Desini winked.

I slipped one foot through then stopped. "Hey, you're not going to dismount and go after that guy, right?"

"Master, it is not I who deceive with regularity, but you."

"Okay, good. Hey! What the fuck does that mean?"

Arms flailed around my neck and yanked me into the back of the cart. The wind fled my lungs as I was twisted in the air and landed on my back. Blinking rapidly, I grinned beneath the smattering of kisses Roshan planted across my face.

"You came for me!" she blurted. Kisses flew between words. "You. Pull. Me. From. Horror. After. Horror." A longer kiss, and then she continued. "With no concern for yourself. You will be thusly rewarded, as promised the first time, my love." She threw a glance at Priya. "I must ask you for the same leave you once asked of me at your aunt's tree."

Aunt? Wow, she's missed a lot.

Priya giggled. "And I would give you the same answer. It is not mine to give leave for you to enjoy that which belongs to you as much as me."

"I think Desini's sword is under my back, pressing against my daggers."

"Or perhaps you are just happy to see Roshan," Priya said with a toothy grin.

I shook my head. "That's not how that joke works, hon."

"I'm sure you will teach me, in time, *master*." Priya pulled open the tarp and climbed out onto the bench.

"Don't even think of starting with that shit!" I called after her.

Desini welcomed her ahead of schedule. Then the half-elf peeked back between the slits in the canvas. "That same man guarded Roshan. They moved him to the gate. This seems important."

I nodded agreement over Roshan's shoulder. "They might have stationed him there as punishment."

"You see only what you desire. What if our corpses vanished like the squirrels you showed me?"

Shit. I hadn't even thought of that! They might not have had to scrape Priya and Roshan off the stone at all. That would raise suspicions, for sure.

The fruits of our labor lay atop me, planting kisses all over my neck as if trying to suck Chicklets off my skin. My hand bumped something as I reached up to embrace her and I peered over to find her scepter leaning against the inside of the cart.

Definitely a woman after my own heart.

"It is my strongest urge that you enjoy the pleasure I promised you in that horrid place, my three-time savior." Roshan rolled off and unfastened her leather pants.

"Though I want nothing more in the world," I grasped her hand, "I'm not deflowering you in the back of a horse-drawn cart."

Roshan's lips parted and her forehead wrinkled. "You do not desire me?" She pulled her hands up to her chest. "What has changed? Has this blonde minx ruined you for love?"

"Hey!" Priya barked from the front.

"Roshan, your skin is gray. You have resurrection sickness. We should wait and make the first time special."

Her gaze bore into me for a few heartbeats, and then she sighed. "Thank Solara for your patience." She dropped her weight onto my chest and settled her head on my shoulder. "Perhaps a nap, then we will play."

"Play, sure. But I'm still not deflowering you in the back of a cart."

4

As Roshan snoozed with her head on my shoulder, I glared at my interface in befuddlement.

Quest Updated:
Rescue Roshan
**Recover Roshan from the clutches of her captors—Complete*
**Smuggle Roshan through the city gates before she is discovered—Complete*
New Objective:
Hide Roshan from the governor's men.
Reward: 18,000 XP
25 Gold

What kind of crap was this? Couldn't I complete the quest already? Was Enora going to carry it on until Priya and Roshan were at the recommended level, too?

My excitement at entering the world and experiencing its dynamic quests had all but dissipated. My molars grew sore from all the clinches.

Priya's head poked through the canvas and one side of

her mouth stretched upward as she took in Roshan's sleeping form. She whispered, "Might I take the other shoulder?" I glanced down at Roshan, grinned, and waved her over with my free hand.

She climbed through and crawled onto the furs. When her head rested on my free shoulder, a long sigh blew warm air across my chest.

I shot up to the sounds of thundering hooves. Pickney whinnied in distress.

"Yield in the name of the king!"

Never a moment's rest in this freaking world. I swear it.

Roshan rolled away and sat up. Still adorned in her red robe, Priya rolled the other direction and got to her knees in one agile motion. I shot up and patted around for my dagger belt.

Roshan reached for her blouse.

"Go for your robe." I pointed. "In my bag."

She nodded without a word and shot across the cart as it slowed beneath us and I bumped into Priya. We recovered without a word. It occurred that my soul bound bag might be inaccessible to Roshan, but then her hand withdrew clutching her robe. Maybe our binding entitled her to access, but I didn't really care why. Priya clutched her staff. When Roshan reached for her scepter, I shook my head. "You got an upgrade, remember?" I withdrew the staff from my inventory and held it out.

Staff of Endless Bounties

Level 8

Slot: Hand

Type: Light-imbued Staff

Damage: 10-14

Light magic +3

This staff increases the chance you will find magic items
by 9%.
Intensifies the power of light spells by 2%
Automatically binds to caster until death

It was a testament to Desini's quick thinking that she brought the cart gradually to a halt, which allowed us time to prepare for what waited outside. I would be sure to commend her for the quick reaction. She appreciated that sort of thing.

I shook those thoughts away as I donned my stealth boots.

"Priya, step out and leave enough of a gap so I can slip through, unnoticed," I whispered.

She nodded and crawled forward on her fists and knees, her staff clutched in one hand and Desini's sword and sheath in the other.

I tapped Roshan's shoulder, lifted the side panel of the adjoined crates we'd engineered, then I gestured inside. She glared at me and shook her head.

I nodded.

She shook her head.

I pressed my mouth close to her ear and whispered, "No one can know you're alive. Let the three of us show you what a team we've become. If things get hairy, you can bring your new staff and heal."

Roshan pressed her lips into a white line but relented, tossing her scepter in ahead of her and crawling into the narrow space. I snapped the panel into place, activated my stealth ability, then followed Priya through the slit and onto the bench.

Where I might have put Priya in the box with her again, I wanted her offensive capabilities available if shit got hairy.

I suspected who I'd find when I passed through that canvas and I was bracing for conflict, if it came to it.

Desini stood on the narrow road with her hands raised. Two men in leather armor held swords at their hips as a third who wore plate dismounted.

The one closest to Priya gestured with his sword. "Stand right there next to the beast woman."

Jurnal Plunt
Human
Level 13 Fighter

"Of course, my lord," Priya cooed in her most demure voice as she slipped off the bench and stood next to Desini. "Have we offended the king somehow, m'lord?"

I counted five horses when I leaned to peer around the cart. The last man to slide off his horse as he stepped forward brought warm blood to my neck. Two men remained mounted, in the back. Thirteen was the highest level of the group, the other three were twelves.

Brazel Snead
Human
Level 13 Fighter

Snead stepped forward. "You can stop with the games right there, little miss. I never forget an epic pair of tits, and I remember opening your throat. Something smells foul around here."

Priya's chin dropped and formed eye slits. She spoke to Desini. "This is him. The man who murdered my sister in cold blood!"

Wow. Nice gambit. She's quick.

Snead's head cocked back. "Sister?"

Priya eyed the other man. "I accuse this man of murder! Why, you heard him confess! You must take him into custody and administer the king's justice, or I will report you for dereliction of your duty!"

Man, she poured it on thick.

The guard stepped forward and backhanded Priya.

Priya Skyy
-7 HP

Now, that pissed me off.

"Keep your mouth shut, wench. If we want to hear your blather, we'll beat it out of ya."

Priya raised two fingers to her nose and touched blood.

Snead threw a suspicious eye at Desini and stepped in her direction. He scanned her form and spread his lips into a smile that reminded me of a Batman villain. "Well, for a beastie, you're quite the eyeful, aren't ya?" He reached for her chest, but she slapped his hand away before he could touch her.

Snead chuckled and shoved her with both hands as he hooked a boot behind hers. Desini tumbled to the ground and Plunt stepped forward, leveling his sword at her, keeping her in place.

Priya sneered. "My friend and I are merely messengers."

Snead laughed. "You should join one of the traveling troupes, little one, with lying skills like that. Only problem is, I saw your body disappear after you jumped from the castle today, blood and all. Stood up after you shocked Willem Shunt—and killed my friend, I might add. Looked over the edge of the bridge and watched your mess of a body vanish, leaving only your disguise behind."

Ah, the Kenobi.

Then he slapped Priya again, causing her to stumble back a step.

"Now, tell your friends to come out of the cart."

Priya raised her fingertips to brush the flesh he'd smacked. Then she lowered her hand and smiled. "No one inside, m'lord. You're welcome to check."

He stepped closer, his fingertips gently brushing the wrapped hilt of his sword.

"Plunt, if she lies to me again, kill the mishon."

That was my queue. I slid off the opposite side of the bench and circled around the back of the cart. Then Roshan called out.

"I will come! Do not hurt anyone!"

I cursed silently at the sound of canvas rustling.

"Ah!" Snead barked. "So, you were lying, after all, little one!"

I circled to the two men on horseback and sized them up. Though swords hung from their sheaths, they carried no ranged weapons, so I passed them, sneaking toward the third man standing behind Snead. Roshan stepped off the bench as I came up behind him.

Steven Zane
Human
Level 1 3 Fighter

Snead unsheathed his sword and cocked his head toward Roshan. "I don't know what trickery is at hand, but you won't have another chance to defy the governor. Step to the back of our line there, mount up, and drop your stick on the ground."

Roshan eyed Priya, then looked back at Snead. Then she raised her scepter in the air and it flashed a blinding white light against the dark night.

"Bah!" Snead raised a hand to guard against the glare.

She brought the scepter instead of the staff! Awesome move!

Priya's fingers crackled purple, and Desini kicked the legs of the man above her and rolled away. Her captor swung his blade wildly toward the earth as she rolled forward, spun, then tackled him.

With a quick Spine Snap, I slammed my dagger into the back of Steven Zane.

Critical hit!

Mortal wound!

Zane's knees buckled, and he folded to the ground with a thud. I lowered myself with him and twisted the knife before yanking it out. Something inside gave a satisfying *pop!* I assumed it was his spine.

A pulse of electrical energy slammed into Snead's chest and ricocheted over my head.

"Gah!" A scream echoed from behind me. A glance over my shoulder revealed the tumble of a horseman from his saddle. His body seized as he hit the earth, and his back arched before he settled.

Desini pounded her fists wildly down onto the face of the man who'd tripped her. Roshan kicked Snead as little electric waves crackled across his body.

"Evil man! Evil, evil bastard! Solara's justice finds you this day!" She shouted a word per kick. "You. Cut. My.

Friend!" Again and again, she kicked him in the stomach, and I thought I heard a rib pop but couldn't be sure. "Kicks in trade for all your groping, you evil, evil bastard!"

The final man on horseback glared around at the scene. I launched in his direction, but I was too late as his horse jumped past me and circled around, galloping down the road and away. I raised one of my daggers and flung it at his back, but I missed. By the time I cast Vine Entanglement, he was out of range.

"Shit!"

Priya's casting bar filled again on my party interface, and I wheeled around. "Stop, Priya!" Judging from the sneer plastered on her face, I didn't think she had any intention of listening. Desini stopped pounding Plunt's bloody face and glanced back at her. Roshan stopped kicking Snead and stepped away.

The light surrounding Priya's hands dissipated and dimmed. Her casting bar emptied.

I swung around and pointed. "Cast on the runner. Use Ice Storm!"

"He's out of range," she replied.

The man I'd stabbed in the back writhed on the ground instead of being a good boy and dying, and his sudden movement caused me to jerk. But I didn't care. Zane wasn't going anywhere. I stepped on him with one foot and over with the other.

"Desini, take Plunt's sword."

She complied and held it over Plunt as I paced to Snead. I glanced at the orange bar drawn above his head by the A.I. He'd lost about sixty percent from the lightning spell and a flashing eyeball icon showed he was still partially blinded by Roshan's scepter. I placed a hand on my mage's shoulder. "Heal him."

"What?" she asked in disbelief.

I turned my gaze on her, adopted a calm expression, then nodded. "You heard correctly. I won't let them take you again. Heal the bastard."

"Only because it is you who asks." Roshan raised a hand, and its aura glowed against the dark of night.

Flash Heal
+40 HP

"Now, again. Get him nice and full."

Flash Heal
Critical Heal!
+ 76 HP

"Good. Now you're topped off, Mister Snead. Stand up."

Snead sneered as he struggled to his feet. He eyed my daggers but relaxed his arms.

With a quick check on the man Desini had been beating, I smiled.

Jurnal Plunt
Human
Level 13 Fighter

She'd beaten nearly half his health off with her bare fists. Desini didn't take well to people messing with any of us, even less Priya.

"Desini?"

Her cat-like irises gleamed green in the night as she leveled them on me. "Yes, master?"

"I need for mister Snead here to understand we mean business." I jerked my head toward her prisoner. "Please kill Mister Plunt."

A disturbing wide smile crossed Desini's face as she wheeled around. "Of course, master."

Plunt raised his hands in the air above his head, but Desini secured a double-handed grip on the pommel of his sword and sliced right through them as she slammed the wide blade down, into soft flesh between his neck and chest.

Roshan flinched at the violence. "Gemini. This is…" her words trailed off.

I thrust a finger at Snead.

"Welcome to the Wild West, Roshan. This is our life now. These people need to know we play for keeps or they'll never stop. You're just going to have to trust me."

Your decision to have Desini kill an unarmed soldier has displeased Solara.
You have lost 30 points of Light.
Alignment: Light + 437
Alignment: Good

I was finished with the nice guy shit.

As Plunt shimmied in his final death throes, Desini circled back to us and stood behind Snead. Her natural tendency toward intimidation carved out a soft spot in my heart for the mishon.

"You're all going to die for that," Snead said. "You're nothing but a bunch of animals." He sneered at me. "Governor Zane has a special way of dealing with animals who defy him."

Snead spat on my boots.

I slammed my dagger into his stomach. "Have a seat, asshole."

Snead slapped both his hands over his guts as blood poured from his wound, and he involuntarily complied with my order. His mouth gaped as his knees broke his fall with a crack.

"Ah! Ah! Gods, it hurts! You son of a bitch!" Falling onto his side and curling into a ball, he cursed me as I scanned the road in both directions.

"Roshan?" I asked.

When she didn't answer, I turned. Her head shook side-to-side, her eyes narrowed to slits, and she pressed her lips together. I gripped her hand. "My love?"

Her eyelids slowly raised. "Yes. Gemini?"

"Please heal Mister Snead."

"But why?"

"Because I need information."

She sniffed. "Are you sure this is the path you wish to follow, Gemini?"

"I have never been surer of anything in my life, Roshan. They took you from me, tried to murder Priya and me in cold blood, and planned to do it again tonight... right after they kidnapped you. Again. I'm walking away from this in the know."

Without words, she gave a single nod. Her hand glowed, and she cast heals until Snead was at full health.

I stood over him with the handle of my remaining dagger pressed against one hip. I was pissed that I'd have to go find my other one. "Here's the thing, Snead. I made you a promise when you cut my beloved's throat at the Brumhill Inn. Do you remember what I said?"

He didn't bother to answer.

"That's okay, I'll remind you. I promised that I would

kill the both of you. Your friend isn't here for me to fulfill my promise in full, but I'm hoping our paths cross again someday. Meanwhile, all I have is you."

"So why don't you quit your posturing and do it, boy?"

I chuckled at his goading. Then I turned my smile on Roshan, but she didn't share it. Priya's cheeks stretched with pure hatred as she glared down at the man who I now recalled had squeezed a breast before slashing her throat. Her anger bit as it surged through my veins, and I had to restrain myself from slicing this bastard into something like pulled pork.

"It's a good question, really," I said to Snead. "I figure the guy that got away will have your men on my tail in a day or two, at most."

"You can count on that."

"So be it." I shrugged. "Now, how many men does the governor have in Trowlsby?"

"Ha! Fornicate with a gruel, you shit! You'll get nothing from me!"

I was fuming, but I'd recovered my Light priestess, and prudence dictated I push to the north and get her as far from the Governor of Knall's grasp as possible.

Governor Zane. Wait a fucking...

I wheeled around and eyed the man whose back I'd stabbed when I broke stealth. The fellow I'd so casually stepped on as he had lain dying.

Steven Zane
Human
Level 13 Fighter
Dead

"Oh, shit."

"What is it?" Roshan asked.

"Roshan, raise him."

"Who?"

"Who? The guy I'm staring at." I pointed. "Resurrect that guy!"

"I find both your disposition and your methods questionable, Gemini. They are not expressive of a creature of the Light."

"You have to trust me! Do it!"

Our glares met as a silent battle of wills passed between us. She finally relented and, knowing Roshan's typical determination, I counted myself lucky.

"I shall try..." Throwing her arms out to the side, Roshan stood over the corpse. I watched her casting bar as I glared through my translucent interface at the scene.

Nothing happened.

"I cannot resurrect this man. Nothing is happening."

I found the reason in my combat log.

Raise can only be cast on companions or party members. **Steven Zane** *cannot be resurrected.*

"Ha!" Snead barked. "Seen it a bit too late, didn't cha? Now you did it, didn't cha? Ha! The governor's own nephew! You're gonna pay for that one, boy! You'll have 'em on ya for the rest of your short-lived days! There'll be no running! There'll be no—"

I kicked Snead in the face. "Shut the fuck up."

"Uh-oh," Priya said.

"Unfortunate tidings," Desini agreed.

Since these fighters had chased us up this road for hours once Snead finally placed my face, I knew how the governor desired his Eastern prize. After all, the trip across the sea was a treacherous one, and he'd gone to great expense to bring Roshan across. This was his domain. He was a feudal lord and the king's own regent. It went without saying the power-hungry dick would not take lightly someone traipsing into his territory and stealing what he perceived as his.

Swipe his concubine, kill the bounty hunters who kidnapped her, and murder his soldiers? That all seemed bad enough. But now I'd killed his kin and raised the stakes to a new height. Way over my head. This could make things... suck.

Any hope the Governor of Knall might write off his losses and consider Roshan not worth the trouble vanished the second my knife slipped into his nephew's back.

I'd screwed us. Nothing we did here would improve that position. But I still had a decision to make.

The mother of my child wanted revenge. I felt her hunger for it surging through me. Roshan was the very picture of inner-torment at the treatment of our prisoner. When he cut Priya, he thought he'd ended her life. When he stabbed me through the neck and shoulder, he'd thought the same.

Roshan had been there. She'd seen it. Yet she stood here in doubt.

I read the message about my loss of Light Disposition again and nodded. The chasm between the two women's attitudes toward the situation had to be reconciled. Ultimately, I reminded myself Roshan had been through the wringer and the reason Zhara wanted her in our group was now crystal clear to me.

She was our moral compass.

"Well?" Blood poured from Sneed's lips from where I'd kicked him in the face. He hunched from his seated position and spit two teeth onto the ground. His sneer revealed a gap in the top row, and his words came on a lisp. "You gonna thtand there all day with your cock in your hand? Or doan ya have the ballth to do it?"

"So, this Governor of Knall, Zane," I said. "He's a pretty harsh guy, right? Pretty brutal fellow?"

"You crawthed the wrong man, boy. Heath gonna pull out your fingernailth. Then heath gonna rape your women. Then he'll path them around the barracks for hith men to take turns."

"Right. If you think the governor's gonna come for me, what do you think he's going to do to you when he finds out you brought his family out here to be slaughtered?" I sheathed my dagger.

Horror washed across our captive's face. "You don't mean..." His eyes darted around our little circle. "No! You're gonna kill me, right?"

"Priya, put him to sleep."

"You can't just—"

I was almost blown backwards by the rush of her cold emotions as my dark caster turned on me.

"What?" she growled.

"Cast sleep."

"You jest!" Priya stepped forward. "He slit my throat. He snapped your spine! He took Roshan! We have suffered endlessly at this man's hands!"

I sighed and forced my shoulders to drop. With a glance at Roshan, I let the emotions ooze out of me in Priya's direction so she might understand my conflict. Sure, I wanted to cut the guy. I'd wanted to send a message just moments ago, but then I'd killed the family of the man to whom the communication was intended. We didn't need to say any more.

Priya's features softened, and she nodded. "You're

right." She pressed a hand to my chest. Then she turned to Roshan and pressed her lips to the taller woman's cheek. "I'm sorry, my beloved companion."

"You have nothing to apologize for," Roshan said, giving Priya's shoulder a quick squeeze. "Darkness is a difficult adversary."

Priya turned and paced to Desini. I scanned my party members in-turn, pleased we could come together and make a decision we could live with.

"You people are the truest form of evil," Snead said.

A wave of utter darkness slammed into me and my breath caught in my throat. "Priya! No!"

She grabbed the sword from Desini's hand, drew back, and decapitated Snead in a single, wide, brutal swing. His head thumped to the earth as blood and spinal fluid erupted from his neck.

My jaw dropped.

But she doesn't have sword skills.

Priya dropped the sword onto the road, clapped her hands together, and then she kicked the head like a soccer forward. It rolled off the narrow path and into dark soil.

Roshan shook her head and muttered, "I cannot heal that."

5

I tensed a length of reigns between white-knuckled fists. My neck burned with anger while Pickney plodded past the lone town between Trowlsby and the Plague Barrens. The concept of companions was a conspicuous difference between the last game I'd played and Enora. Although they weren't new concepts in games, what Enora had done with its evolutionary world building took the concept to new heights. My new friends were partners, lovers, strategists—everything one could want. But with Enora's ingenuity came a new twist.

Companions don't always obey.

Though she'd peered directly at me and experienced the intensity of my sympathy for Roshan, the half-elf had not only misled me by suppressing her emotions, but she'd even apologized to Roshan in advance of the murder.

It'd been damned devious. Companions didn't do stuff like that in games!

Her casual stature as she'd paced to her mishon companion, swiped her sword, then separated Snead's head from his shoulders in a single, brutal blow replayed in my mind. On one hand, I shared her hunger for revenge, but its execution came at the price of my trust.

It was early in the morning hours and the sun wouldn't rise for a while yet, so the cart and clopping hooves of the horses we stole from the governor's men drew no attention. There were no guards posted outside the huts of the sleepy little town. I guessed the threats of the Barrens didn't come this far south.

From the lack of emotional connection to the half-elf mother of my child, I knew she slept. Though dreams were part of Enoran existence, the Elven bond didn't cross sleep's barrier.

Gods forbid my anger and disappointment from keeping her awake.

When the burning torches of the town were but blips in the distance, I peered over my shoulder to where Roshan rode a horse about five lengths of its impressive body behind the cart. Her jet-black hair was almost invisible in the night, except for where it flowed over her robe.

Her disappointment had been palpable as we'd looted the bodies of the fallen, and I didn't need an emotional bond to know how she felt when she'd chosen to ride separately so soon after we'd reunited. Though she'd claimed she simply missed riding horseback, the fact she denied herself much-needed sleep spoke magnitudes. My mind jumped back and forth between anger over Priya's betrayal and wonderment as to Roshan's contemplations. I blinked in succession as I focused on her.

Roshan
Human
Level 10 Light Priestess
Strength: 4 *

Dexterity: 4 *
Intelligence: 19
Wisdom: 10
Constitution: 11
Charisma: 14**

Combat Skills:

Melee: 7
Ranged: 1
Unarmed: 4

Defensive Skills:

Resist Magic: 20
Dodge: 2

Weapon Skills:

Swords: 5
Staves: 15
Scepters: 23
Daggers: 9

Spells:

Outer Illumination

Level 5
Affinity Required: Light Magic
Projects a ball of light that floats above the caster for 10
Minutes
Mana Costs: 45 Mana

Inner illumination

Level 5
Affinity Required: Light Magic
Allows the caster to see in dark environments
Mana Cost: 35
Cooldown: N/A

Minor Heal

Level 7

Affinity Required: Light Magic
Heal over time (HOT) spell
Mana Cost: 40
Cooldown: N/A
Heals injuries for 10 to 15 hit points per second for 10 seconds
Potency dependent on the Intelligence of the caster, and Light Skill level
Maximum yield: 150 hit points

Flash Heal

Level 8
Affinity Required: Light Magic
Instantly heals 50-79 HP
Cost: 45 Mana

Raise

Level 10
Affinity Required: Light Magic
Raise a KO'd ally, swiping them from the jaws of death.
Mana cost: 100
Cooldown: N/A

Occupational Skills

Not to be confused with combat professions, occupational skills allow people to earn a wage, run a business, build garrisons, or create weapons, armor, and potions to supplement adventuring.

Carpentry: 10

Rank: Beginner
Tool tip: Carpenters use wood as their primary ingredient to construct structures, tools, weapons, and furniture.

Forestry: 19

Rank: Apprentice
Tool tip: Foresters are lumberjacks skilled with axes. They

also make excellent field hands and use scythes as their secondary gathering tools.

Skinning:21

Rank: Adept

Tool tip: Skinners remove hides from vanquished animal beings—and sometimes humanoid ones—for raw materials used by leather workers, clothiers, blacksmiths and other professions. Leather working is often selected by skinners as a secondary occupation.

Cooking: 31

Rank: Journeyman

Tool tip: Yum! Cooks use myriad ingredients to concoct tasty dishes to feed the hungry, boost morale, and provide buffs to tradesmen and adventurers, alike.

Gemology: 43

Rank: Expert

An expert in identifying valuable and/or magical gems, gemologist can also shape gems and precious stones in jewelry.

Mining: 40

Rank: Journeyman

Affinities:

Light Magic: 100%

Nature Magic: 100%

Languages:

Fortwan

Common

Disposition: *Beloved*

I focused on the last line. I'd already confirmed Priya's disposition toward me hadn't changed. Both of their disposition meters were maxed. That surprised me, considering how the half-elf must have detected my sheer rage after her betrayal.

Roshan clicked her tongue, and the horse trotted up next to the cart. Only then did I realize I'd been staring back at her the whole time I'd been lost in thought, and I had to work a crick out of my neck. With an agile grace born of someone who was no stranger to a saddle, she kicked one leg over and reached out. I grasped her hand and she hopped onto the cart. The horse fell back to pace with the others.

"Hi," I whispered.

She gripped my hand. "Hello, my beloved." She pressed her lips softly to my cheek then pulled back to turn my face toward her. "Perhaps our reunion has not gone as you'd hoped."

"I should mold you a trophy for understatement."

Her lips twisted to one side of her mouth, then her eyebrows twitched with understanding. "Your humor reflects your adaptive nature. I know how you must be burning inside."

"Two trophies."

"But I want you to know," she squeezed my hand tighter, "I appreciated your restraint with that evil man. You responded to my discomfort. I'm accustomed village life where my emotions held little sway over others. The respect you showed me and that you endured against the dark desires that tempted you prove the Light guides you." She kissed me, her full lips warming mine as she gently turned her head. "You gave me much pleasure earlier. I am glad we've waited. I want the memory of our bonding to be equally rewarding."

"Me, too." I relaxed my shoulders.

She kissed me again. "I will sleep now." She set a hand

on my knee. "Try not to let your anger linger. It serves only to feed Hokrahm's will, and you are a soldier of the Light."

She kissed me a third time before I could respond then disappeared into the cart.

The canvas rustled behind me a moment later, then Desini's head poked through. "Might you enjoy my company, master?" Like Roshan, the mishon beauty we'd rescued on the side of the road outside Brumhill had been true to me since the day we met—promises of a throttling aside.

"Your company is the best kind."

Desini slipped through the canvas, throwing a quick glance over her shoulder before allowing the cloth to fall back together and seal Priya and Roshan in. I wondered if her new acquaintance with Roshan was part of the reason she'd exited, but I wouldn't make her uncomfortable by asking. Desini had a way of letting me know if something was on her mind.

She sat so her hip pressed mine and wrapped an arm around my waist. A short skirt I hadn't seen before covered her legs to the knees.

"Your priestess nestles with your mage. A scene of forgiveness. I see why you labored to return her to our party."

The smile I wanted to give in response to Roshan's generous spirit was tempered by the suspicion Desini was trying to goad me into forgiving Priya. I turned my head up and away, peering across the shadowy hills to the west. "Not yet. I need to sit with it."

"It's unsurprising you're disturbed by the events of this past evening, and I wouldn't presume to interrupt your contemplation. Priya revealed... dispositions unknown to me with her actions. I see why you said your priestess's influence is critical." She tightened her grip around my waist and scooted closer so our legs touched all the way to the knees. Her head leaned on my shoulder and a soft purr vibrated my bones. The weight of her was comforting.

"I'm sorry, Desini. I mistook your intent."

Her voice came on softer than usual, the low grumble replaced by a feminine hum. "No, I apologize. I relinquished my sword, master."

Since Pickney required little guidance, I dropped the reigns and slipped my free arm around Desini. "You're as loyal as they come. Priya didn't leave you any choice."

She raised her head. "You lift weight off my back, master. I know I jest about duels and pour my affections on Priya more readily, but don't think I hold you in low regard."

"Thank you, Desini. I'm fond of you, too."

Desini raised her head. Her bottom lip pushed out as she blinked. "I fear you misunderstand me, master." Her voice was barely discernible over the clops of the horse hooves and the rickety sounds of the wheels as they popped rocks beneath. "As you know, my experiences with the men of your race have proven hazardous. Though they speak of me as if I were a simple beast of little redeeming value, they would then take to me in private or follow me and try to persuade me to give in to their low desires."

"I'm sorry my kind has shown such dark appetites and so little restraint."

"You have shown much patience since we met these days ago, master." Her gaze continued to jump from one of my eyes to the other. "You shared with me Priya, one of your great loves. Your unending determination to recover one of those bound to you displays a fierce loyalty for which I have much respect." She laid her cheek on my shoulder again and, as she exhaled a long sigh, her tension seemed to melt away on the wave of a long purr. "Thank you for bonding with me, master."

Desini's head remained perched on my shoulder when the sun rose, and her even breaths told me she slept. My arm tingled with the lack of circulation, but the way her purrs rumbled softly against my neck, I didn't want to wake her.

The canvas rustled, and I turned to find Roshan's wider, tan face peering at us. After taking in the full scene, her lips stretched into a soft smile, and she planted a kiss on my cheek.

I held a single finger to my lips, and she nodded before sitting on the bench next to me. She wore my black shirt that clasped in the front, her long, tan legs visible in all their muscular glory. Since Desini snoozed with her head on my left shoulder, Roshan whispered into the opposite ear.

"You draw females of all races to you. Pray tell they will not keep you from my own furs." She chuckled a little.

"A friend. We don't, you know."

"Oh, I see."

"She's been through things that would darken your mood."

"It's a miracle of Solara I've stayed intact in a world filled with men of such insatiable and impure appetites. But you haven't taken advantage. You have such patience. Women are not held in such high regard where I am from."

A louder purr escaped Desini's chest as she turned her head on my shoulder. Then she threw a leg over and straddled me. He fiery hair flew back.

"Surely you expected me to ride him like a wild beast, priestess." She ground her hips down in a sudden, shocking illustration and my lower parts sprung to life. "That I would fill myself with him and unleash my wet will upon my handsome master?"

Okay, what the hell is going on here?

I muttered, "Somehow, calling me master in this context seems wrong."

"We all need release from time-to-time," Roshan said, playing along with Desini.

"Oooh." Desini peered down, raised her skirt to look beneath, and then glanced at Roshan. "It seems our words have awoken our companion's hungers."

"Ugh, stop screwing with me, woman. Get off." I smiled.

Desini cackled and dismounted, returning her backside to the bench.

This world's casual approach to sex still left me off kilter at times. The reservations of sexual discussion in my old world seemed almost wholly absent. But knowing what Desini had lived through, her sudden looseness with me caught me entirely off guard. Apparently it showed in my expression.

Desini grinned. "I'm sorry, master. I was just having fun at your expense." She pecked my cheek. Then my neck. Her cheek settled on my shoulder. With a purr, her body settled as she dozed again.

We rode in silence for a few minutes before Roshan spoke again. When she did, it came on a low drone I could barely hear over the crackling rocks beneath the cart's wheels and the steady clop of the horse's hooves. "The hardships you endeavor for your women."

"You said 'hard.'"

Roshan chuckled rarely, but when she did, it was like a soft tune plucked on the strings of my soul. "You are terrible."

What my Light priestess friend didn't realize was my joke masked my true feelings. Desini hadn't just come out to bond with me that morning, but to calm my anger and help me to relax. The unexpected physical intimacy had taken me completely by surprise, and now the speculative side of me burned like an ancient ship's boiler being overfed coal.

In recent days, the mishon hadn't just gained friends who respected and trusted her, she'd gained a family. When taken in context with her experiences, the trust these gestures expressed weighed tons. That she added the brief bit of sexual playfulness, while surprising the hell out of me because it was so out of character, exposed her faith in me even more. To take advantage of that and have any kind of sexual relationship with her would be as wrong as wrong could be.

"Your frown betrays your jest," Roshan said.

Busted.

"I was just thinking about what a lucky bastard I am."

6

The four of us squeezed onto the bench with Desini at the reins and Priya sitting on the opposite end from me.

"How long before they regroup?" Priya asked.

The slight upturn of Desini's lips seemed plastered there. "I think it depends on how many men they plan to bring. A hunting party requires preparation. It will be tomorrow morning before they've caught up. But when they see how far north we have gone, they dare not follow. It was wise to ride straight through instead of camping, master."

"Why would they not follow?" Roshan asked.

"In a matter of minutes, you will see for yourself, priestess." Desini pointed ahead, to the top of an incline. "Just there."

Roshan nodded, but I took the twisting of her features for nervousness. I had to admit, Desini's foreboding tone tweaked my nerves, as well. My imagination ran rampant, painting a dark image of chaos filled with all manner of beasts I'd encountered in my earlier gaming life. Giant serpents crept from the earth in my mind, bony wights swung rusted swords, and boars gaped with long-fanged jaws.

We all leaned forward as the cart crested the hill, and our mouths fell agape at the sight of the sprawling valley of death that stretched as far as our eyes could see. The lush green of the flatlands we'd traversed for a day ended as if an invisible barrier kept this new blackness at bay. An instant chill filled the air. All three of my companions folded their arms across their chests and shrugged against a sudden gust of wind.

Roshan shook her head in disbelief. "Blight."

A scent like spoiled berries rode the breeze. While it wasn't enough to nauseate, I didn't adjust to it as quickly as I'd have liked. My Adam's apple bobbed hard as I swallowed the dry air.

Instead of the land being populated with imagined enemies, it was charred and barren. Desolate. Dull black trees bent as if under hurricane-force winds. The sand-covered earth appeared volcanic. Jagged black crystals jutted across the blighted land. They ranged from the size of our horse to the size of an eighteen-wheeler on Earth.

"The Plague Barrens," Desini whispered. "The largest known example of evil's wrath in the entire Kingdom of Rubal. It is said the goddess herself abandoned this place long ago when the minions of death rose from their shackles and breached the surface to rain blight across the entire region."

I squinted against the morning sun and spotted larger square structures in the distance I'd mistaken for ill-shaped stones. They were buildings the blackness had crept over and painted black like a reflective mold. Toppled and degraded beyond repair, they littered the hillside in neat rows like a town frozen in time.

Somehow, this wasn't what I'd imagined when Roshan used the word 'blight' to describe the demon wars in the Eastern Kingdom of Lau. "Was it populated when the blight came?"

Desini nodded. "This city marked the dawn of advanced civilization. It was the root of intellectual traditions. Traders came from villages far and near to deal here. Many races lived in peace under the shelter of the Elven stronghold."

"Elven, huh?" Priya asked.

Her curiosity tugged at me and reminded me of our connection. Our adjoined feelings when my own were at least slippery left me off-balance.

"Indeed," Desini continued. "Your forebears founded the City of Ninn. They fled back to the forests of their own heritage when the grootslang rose up and murdered millions."

Roshan set a hand on my leg. The wrinkles crossing her forehead illustrated her distress. "These are the same creatures who blighted lands in the east when Arturus read his dark incantation. Was such a dark tome read here?"

"Its history amounts to nighttime tales told to the children of my people," Desini said. "But the demons reigned over a millennium ago. The elves are certain to possess annals about such happenings." She turned her chin toward Priya. "But they hold knowledge close to their vests. My mother believed they bear dark secrets best kept from the more violent races."

"Like humans." I nodded.

"Perhaps," Desini said. Then she leaned in nudged her nose in short strokes across my cheek. "But not all humans."

The mishon was definitely warming toward me. As the slightest smile creased my lips, a flash of dark emotion caused me to tense. My gaze shifted to the half-elf. Although she wasn't wearing the full scowl and one eye was only half-squinted, I recognized the dim sentiment radiating off her. Priya didn't seem to curry to Desini's affections, given our current dispositions.

Well, tough shit.

I resisted an urge to check her disposition toward me.

After turning and grabbing my bag from behind the tarp, I pulled out the map I'd purchased in Trowlsby then spread it out on Desini's lap so Priya and Roshan could see. I tapped the marked spot.

"How far is this? I can't tell by the map in my interface. Can you?"

She blinked in succession as she checked her own interface. "It's not far, master. Just minutes from here, at most. Does this place hold importance?"

"Damn right." I smiled all around, even at Priya. "That is our first real dungeon."

Jaws dropped. Shocked, excited expressions were exchanged. Desini rubbed her palms together. There would be nothing like working as a team to bring us together during trying times.

"Time to kill some shit." I leaned forward, needing to tamp down the negative emotions passing from Priya. "What do you think?"

Priya nodded and gave a blood-hungry scowl. "Kill some shit, indeed."

The switch of her emotions to an outward aggression directed less at me would have to do, for now. Maybe I could learn to restrain the communications of my own passions—or at least suppress them.

You have discovered:

The Plague Barrens
These three hundred square miles of desolate, blighted lands
are home to vile beings untold.
Discovery XP: 725

"One thing is for certain." Desini tapped the red X. "The governor's men will not follow us there."

"That's what I hoped."

She pointed down the lingering hill to the outer edge on our left where an ancient stone structure of a flattened city full of them stood like a lone monolith of the Stonehenge monument. Unlike the crumbling walls of black stone lost millennia earlier, the entryway's smooth granite frame was devoid of the influences of blight. It almost gleamed in contrast.

"I believe that's the location marked on your map."

Pickney's powerful haunches dragged the cart across the glassy sand shards with little trouble, but all four horses communicated in nervous nickers the further we stepped from the narrow trail. The chill bit harder every few yards.

A spiral of light swirled in the opening at the center of the granite frame. To one side stood a waist-high stone with four flat sides that merged into a diamond point on top. When we dismounted and approached, I found a runic symbol of wavy lines glowing on the front face of the diamond.

You have discovered an instanced dungeon!
The Plague Gates
Discovery XP: 1,000

A golden flash enveloped Roshan, and victory music

trumpeted inside my head as the light funneled into the air above her.

"Yes!" I yelled. "Level 11!"

Priya and Desini pumped their fists in victory. Roshan blushed and gave a slight bow. The mage seemed... softer than I remembered.

"The gifts of your companionship continue to avail themselves my friends."

Roshan
Human
Light Priestess
Level 11
*Strength: 4 **
*Dexterity: 4 **
Intelligence: 19
Wisdom: 10
Constitution: 11
*Charisma: 14***
Roshan has four available attribute points.
*With a disposition of **beloved**, you may distribute four of Roshan's attribute points.*

I continued to scan my interface to allay a suspicion. I found the answer beneath Roshan's Experience bar, in the form of a slimmer, purple bar with no numerical value attached to it. When I focused on it, it read:

Rest Bonus
When players and their companions rest in a major city or a location built upon a Foundation Stone for over one day, they achieve a rested state. Adventurers with rested bonus achieve

XP increases of 20% for up to two levels. To display a rested bonus icon on your primary interface, focus here.

When I focused on the spot indicated by a red arrow, a small icon of a bed appeared next to each name in my party interface. I wanted to smack my head.

I need to read the fucking manual.

Priya leaned toward Roshan and muttered in a low voice, but since Roshan stood on my other side, the half-elf intended the words for my ears.

"Don't even ask for strength. He won't give it to you." She cocked her chin toward Desini. "Seems she's the only one who gets that around here."

Roshan chuckled. "Solara entrusted Gemini with these powers, Priya. We should trust in the goddess's judgment that our leader knows what is best, no?"

Without speaking, I flashed a glowing smile at the eastern mage.

"You people are no fun," Priya said. "Though I admit I sometimes forget the father of my child is a mystic."

I cringed as something occurred to me just a second too late.

Roshan's jaw dropped and her neck craned forward as if her spine had failed. "Father of... What?" Her head swiveled. "You are—?"

Priya's angular cheeks flushed red and warmth rushed into my own.

My thumb and middle finger found their ways to my temples. "Not how I planned on breaking that small bit of news," I muttered.

While the all-over-body cringe seized my muscles, Priya grinned mischievously and nodded.

Roshan jumped forward as if she'd leave her boots and

flung her arms around the half-elf. She bounced up and down. Relief washed over me.

"Blessings from Solara! This news fills me with hope for our future, Priya!"

Priya bounced with her as they turned in a circle like soccer players who'd just scored a goal. Tears streamed down both faces.

A smile stretched across Desini's face as she rubbed a circle in my back. She slipped and arm around me and I returned the embrace. She leaned in.

But, single-minded dork that I was, and seeing there was a dungeon entrance right behind us, I focused on her for a moment.

Desini Sherre
Mishon
Level 17
Fighter
Attributes:
*Strength: 24**
*Dexterity: 19**
*Intelligence: 7**
*Wisdom: 6**
*Constitution: 29**
*Charisma: 42**
Combat Skills:
Melee: 14
Defensive Skills:
Dodge: 44
*Melee Defense: 47**
Weapon Skills
Swords: 19

Unarmed: 14
Blunt: 14
Bonuses:
Resist Magic Attacks: 5
Resist Charm Effects: 10

Affinities:

Languages:
Common
Dwarfish
Elvan
Gnomish
Mishon

Occupational Skills:

Not to be confused with combat professions, occupational skills allow people to earn a wage, run a business, build garrisons, or create weapons, armor, and potions to supplement

Stonework: Skill Level 13
Woodworking: Skill level 11
Horsemanship: Skill level 22
Swordsmanship: Skill level 7
Cooking: 50

Magic

Light Magic: 20%
Dark Magic: 15%
Nature Magic: 55%
Disposition: Beloved

Desini leaned in and whispered as Priya and Roshan settled into a motionless hug.

"Maybe you will bless me in this way someday, master." She rubbed a circle against her bare midriff.

Aw, Jesus.

Twenty-four hours ago, Desini and I had been closer to colleagues. Now, she was bleeding affection in place of her sometimes gruff, other times shy demeanor. I wondered if her new disposition resulted more from Roshan's return or Priya's constant glow.

Maternal instinct? A cat in heat? No, that's terrible.

Desini's arm slid away.

I read disappointment in her slack expression. I tugged her arm back to my waist and shook my head. "Sorry, Desini, my head wanders sometimes. Don't take my delay as a response, okay?"

The mishon's tail rose over her shoulder and waved back and forth. I wasn't sure what that meant from a body language perspective, but her weight shifted against me. "Yes, master. I just assumed you would want to expand your influence to serve Solara's will, that Light be spread across the land. If I hold no attraction..."

"No, no. You're every bit a part of this family as any of us, and if Solara deems that we will sire children together, I'm sure it will be so." I did not understand what the fuck I was saying or where it was coming from, but I surged forward as I channeled the thought. "I don't know how I will handle one child, so it's a challenge to think in bigger terms. It has nothing to do with you. You're a sexy goddess."

Desini flexed her left arm, a taut bicep popping up. "So virile and strong is your seed, I'm sure, master. Many warriors shall you, sire. I can wait until you're ready for me." She cackled.

Is she screwing with me? Maybe she's screwing with me.

I gulped. Roshan's and Priya's mouths hung agape.

"Oh, winding fuck widgets," I whispered. I didn't know what that meant. They were just the right words.

Roshan clapped her hands. "Now it is time for you to bless me!"

"What?" My eyes shot to her flat belly, imagining a little Gemini there.

One of Roshan's eyebrows arched. She followed my gaze to her midsection, and her full lips twisted into the smirk with which I'd become familiar in our short time together in the Dark Wood. "Be serious, Gemini. Must your mind always follow a path to its basest desires?"

"Huh?"

"I've adopted a simpleton." Her head craned forward, and she peered at the sky.

Priya chuckled. Desini threw me a glance of confusion.

Roshan huffed. "Let me speak slowly for you. When I said you should bless me, I was referencing my attribute points." She shoved my shoulder. "I gained a level only seconds ago!"

"Oh!" I grinned with relief. "Right! Right!"

Roshan gazed skyward. "Dimwit." She muttered the next set of words. "Blessed by Solara to empower others, yet all he thinks about is planting seeds."

A droplet of sweat rolled into my eye, despite the chilly air.

For the last week, I'd been staring at Roshan's grayed-out image in my Companions tab and gazing at those attributes, fantasizing about how I would improve her at her next level. I ticked off two points in Intellect, added one in Wisdom, and dropped the last in Constitution. She clutched the open blouse she wore for a moment then she bowed.

"Thank you for this gift." Turning to face the sun, her lips moved silently, ending in a slight bow of her head.

When she finished her prayer of thanks, I kissed her cheek. "You're welcome."

"How shall we deal with our bounty?" Desini's hand lingered at her bare, muscular midsection.

"What?"

She gestured back at the four black horses hitched to her cart.

I needed to deal with this Priya thing. It had me all flustered. "We should pull them all inside with us." I peered over my shoulder at the wide, stone-framed entrance. "Your cart will fit. We'll leave them at the entrance."

"Will they be safe?" Desini asked.

"How would I know?" I raised one shoulder in a half-shrug.

"You lend little confidence." She stroked Pickney's shoulder and muttered something in sweet tones in his ear.

"Don't worry. We'll clear the initial areas to ensure they're okay."

Hopefully there wouldn't be enemy re-spawns inside. It would suck to kill monsters, leave the horses, and come back to find their guts splattered everywhere. Or eaten.

"We will cleanse the demons from this dark place!" Roshan raised her scepter high.

"No, you will equip your staff and make use of its upgrades," I ordered.

Roshan frowned as she returned to the cart. After withdrawing her staff, she returned.

When the mishon's cheeks remained taut and uncertain, I walked over, rubbed Pickney's neck, and smiled, hoping to set Desini's mind at ease. "Leaving the horses at the entrance inside is better than out here, in a place called the Plague Barrens. I mean, call me crazy, but..."

"Your humor is simple-minded but effective, master."

Desini cackled and slapped my chest. "Fine. We will bring our possessions inside."

"Let's drink, eat to get our stats up, then head inside."

A deep voice behind us stopped us in our tracks. "You will not be going inside."

We wheeled around. Roshan raised her staff, and I reached for my daggers as I pivoted.

A hooded figure stood between Priya at the rear of our procession and the horses and cart.

A blob of black and orange splashed into my arm. A sliver of my mind reserved for autonomic thought awaited pain, but was instead filled with a speedy, crawling numbness engulfing my muscles from shoulder to fingertip. Then my black shirt turned gray as my arm hardened into a hard slab so heavy I feared it would rip my shoulder out of its socket!

The women fanned out in a semi-circle and reached for their weapons.

My knee hit the black sand as I growled my complaint. "Ah! What the hell?" I clasped my arm, which was now hardened rock from the bottom of my bicep to the tips of my fingers. My shoulder struggled under its weight, so I tilted sideways lest it separate. "I can't feel my arm! What did you do?"

"Who are you?" Priya growled, forming her fingers into claws.

The figure reached up and pulled his hood back, revealing a youngish face topped by curly blonde hair. I'd expected a wrinkled old man, so his youthful appearance came as a surprise.

Jing
Human

Level 15 Shadow Mage

"It is of little consequence who I am," the young mage said. He replied absently, as if we were of secondary consideration, if any. "I am here to collect a bounty." He tilted his own noggin to one side and blinked his eyes in succession. His head pivoted, and his gaze jumped around as if seeking a landmark.

My hand twitched for my bow.

He raised his own. "Hold your weapons. They will be of little use."

"Cocky much?" I asked. "You're only Level 15."

"I tire of your voice." Jing's face stretched into a wide smile as his hands glowed. He swept his arms in wide circles and his cheeks stretched so his smile morphed into a maniacal grin as the wide sleeves fluttered in the breeze, but then his expression morphed as his jaw dropped. The light surging through his arms dimmed and vanished, and he crumpled to the ground in a heap.

Priya's casting bar stopped halfway through a spell and the electric tendrils forming an orb above her palm crackled and dissipated.

In the space behind the mage, clutching a dagger coated with blood, was a wiry being with long white hair and elongated, sharp features.

"Guiles?"

My back-alley weapons trainer from Brumhill.

"It is I, come to render aid in your time of need." One arm crossed his waist, then he bowed.

"What? How did…?" I shook my head. "What?"

"I have taken our mythic by surprise. I will boast to my grandchildren." His tone dripped with sarcasm.

Desini laughed nervously. Roshan gaped. Priya nodded a greeting.

"Very funny," I said to Guiles. "What are you doing here?"

Pins and needles crept through my arm as the stone softened, my sleeve transitioned to cloth, and my flesh reappeared. I wrung the arm with my opposite hand as I spoke.

"I have answered this query."

"How did you get here?"

"I stole a horse, which I stabled in the town you passed to the south. Then I rode on the back of your cart."

"So, what you're saying is, you've been following us?"

He glanced at each party member, then shrugged. "Yes. I almost lost you in Trowlsby. Luckily I discovered where you'd parked your cart."

"Why follow us?"

"It's clear you could use the help." He nudged the mage with the toe of one boot. "So, I followed."

"Wait," I said, flicking a finger toward him. "Are you saying you've been trailing us since Brumhill?"

Priya snapped her fingers. "You're the one who killed the men at our cart as Desini and I slept... when Gemini went to fetch water!"

"I must confess my guilt, sister." Again, he bowed.

I can't act surprised. It was what I suspected.

"So, you've been watching our backs." It wasn't a question.

"Aye, I have. I'm impressed with how you've done so far, though I regret the rider last night escaped my grasp. I was lingering near the head of the mishon's horse." He considered the mage at his feet again. "Unfortunately, gold coins shone in this one's eyes, and I feared he would use *this* again before you could respond." Guiles held up his hand, which clutched a small, crooked rod I hadn't seen before. He tossed it.

I snatched the item from the air and scanned it. It was about the length of my forearm with a red gem, a couple shades lighter than a ruby, notched in its center.

Grim Wand of Stone
Level 13
This wand temporarily turns animate beings' appendages to stone, disabling them.
**Has no effect on creatures of stone such as rock elementals.*
Type: Wand
Quality: Rare
Durability: 70 of 70
Damage: 27-39 Earth Magic Damage
Effect Duration: 20 seconds
+9 Shadow Magic spell damage
+5 spell resistance

"Well, hell! Looks like a little elf friend of mine got an upgrade!" I tossed the wand to Priya.

She missed it and smirked at me before bending over to pick it up. "You could've warned me."

"You could be less clumsy."

"Bite me, my lord."

I loved Priya, even if she pissed me off. "Hey, you got that expression right. Congrats."

She squinted and her lips strained to suppress a smile as she raised the wand.

The return of the emotion I recognized as love was a welcome respite from the tentativeness all morning.

She scanned the wand. "Oh, my."

"A well-timed boon for someone who plans a little instance grinding, I think," Guiles said.

"I'm sorry," Priya said. "What will I be grinding?"

Desini eyed my pants, and I remembered how long I'd stayed at attention as she snoozed on my lap that morning. Enora's women were buckets filled with hormones. Players would dig it. Just to screw with her, I twisted my lips to one side and winked. She blushed. A sensation like *victory* swept over me.

"Grinding is an expression for gaining experience points, Priya." Guiles explained. "We kill our enemies to advance and call it *grinding out levels*."

"Oh. Well, that makes sense, I suppose. *Grinding*. I like this."

"I know you like grinding," I said. "Desini also knows you like—"

"Stay your tongue, fool." She pointed with the wand.

I threw both hands up and cringed. "Don't point the wand at people until you know how to use it!"

Priya's face turned crimson as she dropped the wand.

Roshan clicked her tongue in derision, threw a hand on one hip, and wagged a finger with the other. "You will stay close to me at all times." She lurched two steps forward and swept up the wand, shaking it sideways at eye level. "This is not a toy. You will be careful where you point it, you will not use it until you learn how to wield it effectively. And you will never, ever point it at your companions!"

Damn! I guess Priya got told.

Priya accepted the wand and lowered her head in a half-bow. "I'm sorry."

"Fool." Roshan pecked Priya's cheek.

The half-elf smiled.

It was poorly-timed. I jutted a finger toward Priya. "Be careful with your fucking weapons."

My little blonde demon woman threw me a sideways grin. A vibe slammed into me, but instead of the irritation I'd expected, the sensation came softly. Her gaze meandered to my pants.

Priya wanted make-up sex. I wasn't there yet.

"Gemini," Guiles said. "The Plague Gates is a five-person instance."

I turned and stared at the swirling light of the entrance. "For some reason, I thought it would be a four-man deal. Not sure where I got that."

"I'm happy to offer my help, since I've never had the pleasure."

"Oh, you've never run this one?"

"Alas, I have not."

"But you're a Level 50 rogue. Wouldn't our XP get dwarfed by your presence?"

"I think perhaps you mean *'elfed.'*" He stared at us each in turn. "No? Anyone? Elfed by my presence?" He sighed. "Humorless twits."

"I got the joke, Guiles," I said. "It just wasn't funny."

All three women turned their heads, covered their mouths, and giggled.

"Now, experience penalty? Yes or no?"

"You have much to learn about Enora, mystic, and the time has come for me to teach you."

Though his tone reeked of superiority, the concept of a century-old elf divulging my ignorance of the world around me caused a giddy surge in my veins.

7

Guiles walked over to the pedestal near the entrance and set his hand on the rune. A red glow shone between his fingers as he blinked to activate his interface.

"The max level allowed is twenty, but this prison is level-adaptive."

I'd seen games where higher-level players could party with lower level friends in dungeons because the game system scaled them down so their stats were the max possible for the instance. But it was the other word he'd used that snagged my attention.

"Prison?" I asked.

"This is why death surrounds us." He raised his hands with their palms up to gesture around our party. "After the blight consumed the land here, Solara drove the minions underground to live an existence of eternal captivity. The level cap in the prison regulates their advancement."

"They can't go higher than Level 20?"

"Correct. But their hunger for blood and power causes them to turn on each other inside, which means we'll encounter some beings of lower levels. When they fall, creatures re-spawn after sometime, returning to the level they were when Solara first imprisoned them."

So each dungeon run varies. That's cool.

Desini shot me a look and then turned it on Pickney. "How fast do they re-spawn? I'm worried about our horses. We'd planned to take them inside."

"There will be a safe area warded off at the beginning. They will be quite secure there. But you should know the answer to your question, anyway. Usually they will not re-spawn until a day has passed, so adventurers rarely encounter the same beings twice."

It's amazing how lore can suspend disbelief. This set of explanations flies in the face of reality. These are dungeons. They're made for players who want challenges and gear.

"Our goddess is wise, and I understand she has prisons like these throughout the world. Unfortunately, the underworld's grasp on these places is equally strong. Darkness controls the inside, and Solara has left the demons and unruly beasts in the prison to rot for eternity. The eternal war between our goddess and Hokrahm rages on."

Roshan nodded. "The East has these places." She breathed a cleansing breath. "Though magic users are not allowed in our lands, soldiers of different warlords use these places as training grounds. Battles are also fought over access to these portals."

"People fight to own dungeons?" I asked.

Roshan nodded. "But you focus on the wrong thing. Our goddess contains this evil so it might not blight the rest of the world. The power of Solara's Light is the epicenter of Enora's beauty. I am humbled by this."

"You will be more humbled when you encounter the bosses of places such as these," Guiles said. "They are wretched creatures who rule over their domains with vile curses and traps." He shrugged, and his tone became lighter. "But you'll see when we get inside, as experience is the finest teacher." He nodded at me. "If the traveler has no objection to taking an old rogue along."

"Fuckin' more-the-merrier, I say. Even if you're capped at Level 20, your company's a gift. We all agreed?" I peered around to enthusiastic nods. "Welcome to the party, Guiles."

"Speaking of parties," Guiles said, "please shoot me an invitation."

"Oh, right." I focused on him. Guiles nodded, then the head of his avatar appeared at the bottom of my party list. His health and mana bars came into view, as well as a new yellow bar which, when I focused on it, was labeled, *energy*. This was the bar he'd told me rogues receive when they adopt the profession at Level 20. It fed combat maneuvers in place of the stamina reserves assassins used. Just seeing it and thinking about how it would free up my stamina resource tempted me to go that route at Level 20.

"Shall we?" Guiles asked.

"Hold on just one second." I stepped up to the dead mage and analyzed his robe.

Robe of the Night Caster
Level 13
Type: Body
Quality: Rare
Durability: 47 of 50
Magic Defense Bonus: 35
+10 to dark magic spells
+15 to dark magic spells after sun fall and in dark areas
Renders the wearer impervious to sleep spells

"Looks like a double-upgrade, Priya."

"I shall not wear the bloody..."

I held up a finger to delay her comment then doubled over to untie and remove the garment. When I held it up to the sunlight, the blood was gone. Something told me it would fit Priya like a glove. I tossed it to her.

Priya snatched the garment from the air and eyed it with suspicion. "Then she pushed out her bottom lip. "I like my robe."

"We talked about this. Upgrades are crucial to survival as you reach higher levels. I'll keep your old robe in my bag, and if we can update it somehow, we will. Meanwhile, the Robe of the Night Caster is badass, and you will rain hell down on your enemies."

"You think I am so simple that when you say—" she raised her hands and splayed her fingers for dramatic effect, "—'Rain hell down on your enemies,' I will just swoon and become so excited as to forego my emotions."

I crossed my arms across my chest and smirked. Then I threw in a challenging squint, for the added effect.

Priya dropped her shoulders and sighed. "No. You're right. 'Rain hell.' I love it." She turned her back to Guiles and slipped off her robe.

Warmth replaced the Plague Barrens' chill at the sight of her ward as it glowed to life. My knees quivered, and my jaw dropped. Guiles hunched over and clutched his knees as he glared in wonder. Roshan raised a hand to her forehead. Desini took a clumsy step backward and fell hard on her ass in the black, sandy shards.

Then Priya dropped the new robe over her head, shrouding the ward. The chilly air crept its way back into my bones. A collective sigh of disappointment followed. She whipped around and scanned our faces.

"What?"

The rest of the party peered at each other and smirked.

"Oh!" She covered her mouth. "The ward. Hmm. I should remember that."

Guiles shook his head. "I wish you wouldn't. The world is so much brighter, if only for a moment."

I nodded, my voice sounded distant in the wake of the effect. "It's like a slow, less-messy orgasm." I realized I had never made love to Priya from behind. I wondered what that would be like, with that glowing beauty shining on my soul.

Roshan nodded. "A boon of Solara's warming love." The priestess had a gods damned way with words.

Desini was silent, but her hand had returned to rub circles in her exposed midriff. The gesture made me nervous.

"Well!" Priya said, raising one shoulder. The combination of her toothless smile and an emotion I didn't recognize gave me pause. I sought out words for the feeling as it washed over me and it snapped in place like a puzzle piece.

Mischief. She activates that ward on purpose. I'm going to ask her about it, one day when we're not fleeing into a dungeon to hide Roshan... and ourselves.

"I'm glad it pleases you all," Priya said.

"It does," absolutely every one of us said in perfect sync. Then we all nodded at each other.

The new robe fit her shoulders perfectly and ended at her ankles. She peered down and threw her arms out as she twisted, taking it in. "Doesn't do much for my figure, does it?"

"Rain hell down on—" I began.

She dropped her arms and tilted her head in exasperation. "Yeah, yeah. Shut it, already."

Things were starting to feel normal again.

"Okay," I said to Guiles. "You said we can bring our horses in with us?"

Guiles nodded. "If this mage predicted your path and took on the expense to portal here, it's logical to assume others might. If they don't find your cart or horses, they might assume you've moved further north." He waved a hand along the black, glassy sand we'd crossed from the road to arrive here.

Scanning the path we'd trudged, I saw no signs we'd come that way. I raised my boot and peered down to watch as the shards caved into my footprint.

"Excellent." My curiosity got the better of me. "What expense are you talking about? Portals cost money?"

"Yes. His level was only fifteen. He didn't have portal spells, which means he had to pay to have another mage open it for him. Luckily, that mage didn't come."

"Yeah, that might have been bad," I agreed.

Guiles continued. "In either event, a bounty has been placed on your head. You must be cautious. Tell me you understand the weight of this Gemini."

I nodded. "I get it. I'm going to have to kill the Governor of Knall."

Guiles's head jerked back and he huffed. "I wouldn't have gone that far. I was merely suggesting a low profile."

"Meh, I don't like to hide."

"Said the assassin," Guiles quipped. His gaze made the rounds, but no one laughed. "You all need to learn how to relax. I foresee boring lives."

I prattled on, undeterred. "But hey, if a low profile is prudent until I'm powerful enough to do the deed, so be it. I'm just tired of this bastard trying to take my shorty from me." I wrapped an arm around Roshan.

"I am quite tall for my people."

Roshan stood five-and-a-half-feet.

"It's a term of endearment," Priya explained. "I've tried to get him to stop saying it, but he's relentless and unchanging."

"You're my shorties."

I shrugged.

Desini stepped closer. "You will not call me this. Ever."

"Do you people take anything seriously?" Guiles rolled his eyes.

"You're the one who said we needed to lighten up," I replied.

"Hmm. I concede the point." He nudged the mage's half-baked corpse with his shiny boot. "A shame. So young. So stupid." He raised his gaze. "Shall we proceed?"

"Right!" I faced the entrance. "Gear up everybody. Time to kick some bad guy butt."

We transferred into the instance in a flash. There were no loading screens, no countdowns between two worlds. I passed through first and was treated to a sprawling, dim room with ivy-covered stone walls. In its center sat a glass fountain that climbed to the ceiling with clear waters somehow recirculating as they filled a pool at the bottom then cycled back up glass tubes to flow from a box at the top. It gave off a dim azure glow, matching the water.

That's not glass, it's some kind of crystal.

I jumped as Guiles spoke beside me. "Step away from the entrance, lest you get run over by the cart."

I stepped to one side and focused on a flashing exclamation point.

Welcome to your first Enora Online instance!
Ruins of the Plague Barrens 1:

Plague Barren Gates
Levels: 12-20
Difficulty: Normal
Grand Bosses: 1
*All party members with levels above twenty will be synced upon entry.
*XP is equally distributed among party members, regardless of level.

Talk about power leveling! If Level 20s brought a Level 10 in and gained droves of XP, that Level 10 could shoot up the ranks! Of course, the lower damage or healing output of a Level 11 might get them killed.

I read on.

A new Raid Tab has been added to your interface. Using the **Raid** tab allows you to organize raid members into smaller groups.
Note: Raids are not available in **Ruins of the Plague Barrens.**
Party member maximum: Five
You have discovered:
Fount of Healing
This blessing of Solara replenishes all essential life pools when touched.
Health: Full replenishment
Mana: Full replenishment
Stamina: Full Replenishment
Energy: Full Replenishment
Fury: Full Replenishment
Spirit: Full Replenishment
Shadow Mana: Full Replenishment
Founts of healing also serve as **bind points** for players and

their party members. Party members who fall in combat will be returned to this place for resurrection. Only players can bind to the fountain. Non-players in their parties will also resurrect if they fall in battle.

When you bind to a fountain, it removes all other bind points unless you have marked a preferred location and have a teleportation crystal.

Unbound non-players who venture inside without players are not resurrected and their souls are consumed to serve the dark lords of the dungeon in beast or demon form for eternity.

Now *there* was a cheerful thought. Nice detail, too. But there was a lot of new stuff here. Spirit. Shadow Mana. Fury. Teleportation crystal. Healing fountain. I needed to read the fucking manual.

Desini navigated the horses and cart into the space.

"It's always a wonder to gaze upon a first-time adventurer," Guiles said next to me.

I peered at him through my translucent window. I was anything but a first-time adventurer, but I silently acknowledged he had a point. In Enora, all new players might as well be.

Guiles patted my shoulder. "Don't worry, my friend. I believe our destinies will carry us all well beyond this place."

He'd misinterpreted my expression.

"I'm fine," I said. "Just reading about the fountain."

"Ah, your Analyze skill is powerful. I should not be surprised."

Roshan and Priya entered the instance together, hand-in-hand, and paced to the fountain as Desini settled the horses. As they released their grips, I realized from the remnants of an emotion Priya held that they'd stepped in together like that out of uncertainty.

Their first Instance.

A prompt with a golden ribbon appeared as flashes ensued.

Priya, Desini, and I were surrounded by golden light and triumphant tympani filled my head as two sets of numbers flashed before me and zoomed into the distance.

You have completed the quest:
Rescue Roshan
Rescue Roshan before the guards can deliver her to the Governor in Millbury Peaks.
Reward: 18,000 XP
25 Gold
A foundation stone
**Recover Roshan from the clutches of her captors—Complete*
Smuggle Roshan through the city gates before she is discovered—Complete
Reach the Plague Barrens before the Governor of Knall's men catch up to you—Complete
Find somewhere to hide Roshan until your trail goes cold —Complete

It's about time!

"Congratulations to all of you!" Guiles said. "The road ahead shortens!"

I shook my head in derision.

"What is it?" Guiles asked. "I spy a question in your gaze."

"I completed a quest, but I don't understand why."

"Ah. Share the details, and I will look with you."

"I didn't realize I could share details." I switched to my

quest tab and peered at *Rescue Roshan.* Then I focused on Guiles and he nodded.

The interesting part was that Guiles had knowledge my companions didn't. I wondered if advancing levels unlocked more of the interface for NPCs.

After scanning the quest, he nodded. "Ah. I see." He winked off his interface. "This place is instanced. If anyone outside your party tries to enter, they will enter a different existential plane. They cannot follow you here. Since your charge is now out of the reach of the governor, your quest is complete. Hence, the trail—as the quest so eloquently dictates—may go cold."

Not only did that make sense, but it displayed a kind of genius.

"Thank you, Guiles." I gave a slight bow.

Another realization dawned on me.

If Guiles has never partied with a player yet had reached Level 50, did that mean he'd never fallen in battle?

"Guiles, have you lost many friends in these instances?"

"Wise adventurers always bring scrolls of resurrection or a class with the power to resurrect us if we are rendered inactive."

"Of course!" I barked out loud. "Scrolls, resurrection spells."

His forehead wrinkled at my outburst, but he nodded as he muttered.

"Yes. There was a challenging instance around Level 30 where we brought a priest but didn't bother purchasing scrolls. After a fierce battle with the über boss, the priest's mana pool depleted, then the boss cast a debuff that slowed his replenishment. As a result, the blood stopped flowing through a companion's veins so the spell didn't work by the time his mana refilled." He shook his head as he peered at his boots. "It is a source of sadness each day I think of his corrupted soul having transformed to live out his days doing the bidding of a demon underground."

Did that soul appear in every instance of that dungeon, or just the one in which he died? Are instances always conjured anew with fresh code?

Having taken an interest in the conversation, the women gathered and gave Guiles their rapt attention.

Roshan nodded sympathetically at his sentiment.

"Yes, I imagine that's terrible to live with."

I pushed past the trip down memory lane. "When scrolls or priests and priestesses are used, is there an attribute penalty duration, and do you have to wait in that same spot where they fell?"

Guiles shook his head. "If only it were ever that easy." He gestured at the fountain. "It's not like the outside world. Parties resurrected by scrolls are brought to the fountains and must traverse the paths back to their party. It is often quite inconvenient, as some instances are like mazes and mapping dungeons is reserved for those Level 30 and higher. If I had a silver for every time we waited for hours for someone to rejoin our group, I'd be the one living in Millbury Peaks!"

The reminder of the governor's home base was unwelcome, but I stifled thoughts of that little problem and faked a chuckle. "Why do you think there are instances at all? Why doesn't Solara just bring down her wrath on these places?"

"Those resurrected by spells rise where they fell. In both cases, there is no resurrection sickness. I am unfamiliar with attribute penalties. What are those?"

Hm, none of that, then.

"Never mind."

Guiles's eyes flickered and, after a moment of blank expression, he gestured. "Let's sit at the edge of the fountain to replenish ourselves, and I will answer any questions you have."

"Is it safe here?" Priya scanned the hallway at the opposite end of the wide room.

"Yes. Wards protect all entry areas from demon and beast incursions. This is where adventurers prepare." He gestured to the fountain again. "Come, sit awhile, and listen."

Hadn't Cain, from *Diablo Universe* said something like that?

8

W e sat and I unleashed the flashing icons in my field of view. Beautiful words filled my interface as an undulating pulse of victory soared through me.

You have reached Level 17!
+1 Constitution
+1 Dexterity
You have three attribute points to spend.
Your companion Priya has reached Level 14!
Priya has four attribute points to spend.
Since Priya's disposition toward you is Beloved, you may spend four attribute points.
Your companion Desini has reached Level 19.
Desini has four attribute points to spend.
Since Desini's disposition toward you is Beloved, you may spend four attribute points.
You have reached Level 18!
+1 Constitution

+1 Dexterity
You have six attribute points to spend.
Your companion Priya has reached level 15!
Priya has four new attribute points to spend.
Since Priya's disposition to you is Beloved, you may spend
eight attribute points.

Sharing the quest to save Roshan with my tank had been a smart move!

All the work to get Roshan back had been worth it. I felt the same calming power of her presence like I had before I lost her. But two levels made for a thick pile of icing on what was quite the tasty cake!

With the extra attribute point I received each level, the icing turned German Chocolate. Desini and Priya still only received four points per level. I flipped open the Player's Manual in my HUD and searched with a simple thought.

Bound NPC Attributes:
Unlike players, who receive an additional elective attribute
point per level beginning at Level 15, all soul bound NPC
companions receive four points per level until they reach
Level 20.

Good to know.

I assigned our attribute points, following my standard method where I received Dexterity and Constitution, and Priya received Intellect and Wisdom. I might have given her a little more Constitution, but she was a ranged caster, and we now had a healer to bail her out if she took damage.

I was still pissed about what she'd done, but I needed to grow up.

All of Desini's points went to Constitution. She was a

meat shield. If she started losing aggro, I'd up her strength next time.

Once I'd ticked off the attributes and given a cursory scan to the results in our mana and HP pools, we sat for an hour as Guiles laid out some lore. For once, we had some time to spare.

The races of Enora had attributed the ways of their world entirely to their goddess, Solara, and her evil opposite, Hokrahm. All things were as deemed by Solara, and generations of mythology explained things they couldn't otherwise understand.

This sounded vaguely familiar.

Solara created wards that kept the evil presences of the instanced dungeons inside. Demons served the bosses who ruled over these instances.

The more Guiles explained, the more questions I had. I tried to remember we were there to kick some ass and asked only the ones that distracted me most.

"Maybe you can explain why Solara doesn't just destroy these places. If she's all-powerful—"

"If?" Roshan blurted. "Gemini Fowler!"

"Sorry! Fine. *Since* she's all-powerful!" I awaited an expression of acceptance before carrying on. "Since she's all-powerful, why doesn't she just wipe them out?"

All of them.

"An admittedly grand question, Gemini, worthy of an answer. The recurring theme of my studies of Enoran history is balance. In nature, there is balance. In magic, there is balance. For prosperity, there is poverty."

For bullshit, there is religion.

"Most of all, in the struggle between good and evil, there is balance. Where there is Solara, there is Hokrahm."

"Speak not the name of he who you would not invite to

your hearth!" Roshan barked. She made some symbol with her hands that involved tapping her forehead, then her stomach, and pulling an earlobe. It was such a blur I couldn't have repeated it.

"Roshan, Clan Fortwan," he softened his tone and leaned toward her, "my people have a saying. 'To deny evil is to give it quarter.' Your sentiments prove futile when we sit in the belly of the very thing you fear."

"I fear nothing" Roshan raised her chin. "I am guided by the Light."

"You bleed it. I beg your pardon, priestess, I seek only to ensure a special group of adventurers is armed in the best way possible for a treacherous journey ahead. We have to focus on the threats before us at every turn, and you need not worry about conjuring evil with your words when you are promised its physical presence ahead." He paused to give her an opportunity to respond.

She parted her lips briefly, pushed them back together, then nodded.

"Today, you write a history I think will be adopted in the annals of many races. It is imperative you maintain mental soundness and are physically prepared, for there are grander battles to fight than against sentiment, and your destiny is tied to two great creatures in the child of the Guardian of the Tree of Solara" —he pointed at Priya— "and the Shénhuà, reborn." He thrust a thumb at me.

"Shénhuà?" Roshan threw her hands up to her cheeks and slid off edge of the fountain. "Sh... sh..." she couldn't seem to repeat the word.

Oh, yeah, she missed all that. Pregnancy, Zhara being Priya's mother... oh, and I'm a mystic creature, the second coming of the all-mighty-and-powerful beta tester of yore.

Damn, I should've covered it last night. What else did we need to cover?

It seemed her continent had beta testers as well, and the lore surrounding them had been much the same. It made sense, really. I had to fan her for five minutes before the wide-eyed expression painted across her face dissipated. As I held her head in my lap and waved one of my gloves, I peered at Guiles. "You were saying something about balance and how it kept Solara from destroying the instances?"

"Yes. Cultural beliefs vary, but mine favors the idea that, if Solara were to destroy this place in which we sit, and the beings we seek were removed from the dark pools of life, it would free dark energy for Hokrahm to create new, more dangerous creatures. Such evils might be set loose on the world instead of being confined to these instances. Long has he labored in ways we can't comprehend to get a foothold and spread his influence across Enora.

"A timeless battle between Hokrahm and Solara has raged for the prize that is this world, and should Solara allow his minions to take domain above-ground, well, we've seen the results in the east and the rotten landscape above us. The Plague Barrens resulted from one of Hokrahm's own creations—the grootslang. So powerful in magic are these vile beings, they broke the wards Solara put in place to harness the spread of the demon influence after the spread of the blight.

"To free up the dark pools of energy for more evil souls to enter the world would be to unleash a shadow on the people of Light like the world has never seen. This is why we believe Solara built her tree in the Dark Wood to ensure the Light's energy flourishes on high, so darkness may only flourish below."

Wow. This dude has words.

"When I met Roshan, we entered an underground place through a tree in the Dark Wood—which is an ironic name, now that I think about it. A minion of an underlord called Caym held her captive as he commanded minions to burrow into the ground, building tunnels. That place wasn't instanced. So, what keeps those minions underground?"

Guiles laughter was devoid of humor. "A patient demon underlord. Caym seeks to gather more power unto himself. As he sits imprisoned by the wards, his demonic abilities must allow him to communicate with those on the outside. I would dare say this minion was once an adventurer who failed in his quest to overthrow Caym. He likely groveled for his life and pledged fealty to his new, dark lord in exchange for his survival."

"I doubt it," I shook my head. "Crohl was low-level."

"Which might have been Hokrahm's own doing, but I have no answers for that. However, that you say they burrow deep in the ground makes sense. Powerful artifacts lie deep in the soils of Enora. Fed by the magical essences of the world above, they come in many forms. Indeed, if Caym could locate and excavate such an item that has flourished over the ages feeding from the energy of the Tree of Solara, that would draw much power to him."

"Man, this world is deep." As soon as the words left my lips, I worried they violated the rules for communicating with non-players.

But then Guiles nodded. "Deep and dangerous."

I peered down to find Roshan's focus affixed to me. "Forgive me, lord."

I smiled at her and rubbed a thumb across her full cheek. "There's nothing to forgive. Just a little fainting spell, is all."

Roshan struggled for a moment, then finally sat up and turned. She kneeled, bending low and setting her arms on the stone floor beneath, touching her forehead to the ground. She muttered something indecipherable.

I tilted my head to one side as a glow surrounded her. "Babe?"

Guiles gripped my arm, hard, and shook his head. "Silence."

I quieted. Her mutterings formed no coherent words, despite the fact I should understand any neutral or lawful languages. A wave of light extended from her fingers splayed on the floor, and golden tendrils escaped their tips to wrap around my ankles and up my legs. The light surrounded me, my temples thumped, and the sound of my blood running through my veins was static in my ears.

At long last, Roshan raised her head. She reached out with a thumb and touched it to the center of my forehead.

"Long have my people awaited your return. I bless you, Shénhuà, in the name of our great goddess and giver of life, Solara, that you may be guided by the Light she gives. I shall henceforth call you master and serve your every need by your command. My reward is to serve as I bathe in Solara's Light in my lowly human form. Blessed be thee, my beloved." Then she lowered her head again and muttered some more.

You have received a blessing!

The Blessing of the Shénhuà

Blessed art thou! It is proven! You are the mystical traveler, the rebirth of a race of magical beings who graced the world of Enora two millennia ago! You will prepare the way for the second coming of the Shénhuà! Though your trials will not be easy, you will forever be known as the one who led the way to receive millions of players to the new world of Enora Online!

Congratulations, Gemini Fowler! Your destiny has been revealed!

+5 Permanent boosts to Strength and Intelligence
+3 permanent boost to Wisdom
New Title Available: **Prophet**

"What the hell?" I yelled.

But no one cared. I threw a glance at Desini as she sat on the edge of the fountain, staring down at the priestess with a wide-eyed gaze. Guiles sat silently next to me, his head bowed in reverence.

A chill erupted in my bones despite the warmth cast by Roshan's blessing. The contradiction of physical sensations confused me and for whatever reason, my mind shot to Priya. Distress washed through my brain as she became my focus.

My heart dropped when at first I saw the empty space where she'd been sitting, and I jumped off the fountain as cold crept through my spine. My half-elf huddled in the corner of the room farthest from the fountain, her arms embracing herself as she shivered violently. A furious scowl wrinkled her features, her white teeth grinding so the lumps of her jowls worked.

My initial thought that she'd been hiding resurrection sickness vanished when her eyelids fluttered open, revealing black balls of obsidian glass beneath. I was punched by the awareness that the outer edge of Roshan's glow ended near the tips of Priya's boots. She struggled to fold herself into the corner and pull her feet clear of the halo.

"Roshan. Stop." Seeing as she'd already buffed me with her blessing, I didn't think interrupting would be so horrible, and Priya's unbridled fear tore at me so hard, my knees quivered. Although a part of me expected Guiles to chastise me a second time for interrupting, he surprised me with his harsh response.

"Roshan!" he barked from his perch on the fountain.

The priestess stopped muttering and glanced up at the angry elf.

"Cease your incantations and rise at once!"

Roshan jumped to her feet as all eyes turned to the corner where our companion huddled in a dark shadow of suffering.

I stepped closer, but Guiles grasped my sleeve and pulled.

Desini launched from the fountain, but Guiles's boot shot out and tripped her, sending the mishon sprawling.

"No!" Guiles cried. "No one approaches without my leave!"

Silence filled the room like a thick scent. Desini clutched my hand, and it wasn't long before Roshan grasped the other. Where I might otherwise have taken comfort from their physical gestures, the mixture of fear, sadness, and utter hatred mixing in a concoction of emotional soup crossed the airwaves and commanded my focus.

What seemed a lifetime later, Priya's blue irises reappeared. With a final shudder, the shivering ceased. She glared at each of us.

My heart's rhythm pounded at my Adam's apple and I released a breath I hadn't realized I'd been holding. "Babe?"

"How did I..." Fear rattled her words before they could escape her throat so she sounded like she smoked a pack a day. "I don't know what happened. One moment, Roshan was praying..." Her lips pouted. "Must you all stare at me, so? Must you be so far away?"

I stepped past Guiles, scurried over to Priya, then knelt next to her.

The elf stood aside as Desini and I dropped to our knees.

"I don't know what happened," Priya said.

Desini slid in front of me and embraced her. I took a step back.

"It's her shadow affinity," Guiles said.

We all turned to find him sitting on the edge of the fountain again, one foot on the floor, the other crossed over his knee. It struck me as out of character.

"The blessing Roshan cast upon the traveler was... well, beyond her level. The Light surged through me in a way I haven't experienced, except when viewing Priya's ward."

A hand squeezed my shoulder, and I glanced back to find Roshan standing behind me, frowning in thought. I shared her disposition. We were the anchor and the leader, and we were both helpless.

"Am I dangerous?" Priya asked.

Guiles nodded. "Wonderfully so. As you gain experience, you will become a force against those who stand in your way."

"And to my allies?"

"No, Priya. They are your bound companions. While your magic might conflict with Roshan's, it is no direct danger to her any more than hers is to you. Your reaction was instinctual, but..." He peered at Roshan. "I would recommend you give such blessings at a distance. Just to be safe."

"I will," Roshan said. "I am sorry, Priya. I didn't know."

"I know you didn't."

I saw it as a testament to Roshan's grit that she stepped forward and embraced her friend.

"If it was as you say, *above her level*," I said, "the question is how Roshan blessed me that way."

"I'm baffled, as well," Guiles said. "I cannot even see the name of the blessing in my interface. Are your stats boosted?"

I nodded. "Permanently. Thirteen total points."

"Thirteen?" Gules stared at Roshan, his mouth gaping. "Thirteen? Do you think you could share these blessings?" He burst into laughter and paced back and forth, reminding me of how he had in a back alley in Brumhill when he'd discovered I was a mythic, straight from his peoples' lore.

Roshan shook her head as she leaned against the wall next to Priya. "No, I..." Her eyes flared for an instant.

Desini clicked one of her claws between her teeth.

I dismissed it as a nervous habit then turned my attention back to Roshan. "What?"

"Zhara. Near her tree. When you and Priya... at the cave... She laid hands on me. She had me channel the Light without the aids of weapons or the statistical boosts granted by my robe. I glowed blue, and she offered me a gift. When I asked what gift, she said it would avail itself. Now I understand."

Guiles clapped his hands one loud time, causing us all to jump. "It is amazing! You people! If only I'd received such boons so early in my adventures! Well! That makes sense. Zhara channeled the spell through you. You say you were standing by the Tree of Solara when she gave you this lesson?"

Roshan nodded.

"Right! To bank such a blessing in a low level would be a difficult endeavor, with your limited mana pool. Such concentrated energy could only come from a source of great power, like the roots of Solara's Tree. You have channeled a spell through ley lines deep in the ground. Amazing!" Guiles shook his head. "That you contained the blessing while you were captive only to channel it now is a tribute to your devotion to the goddess. Your teacher must have been a great man."

Roshan gripped my shoulder again, "He was what you say."

Desini grasped Priya's hands and pulled her to her feet.

"Everyone feel better?" Guiles asked. "We have a long day ahead!"

"We're still going in?" Priya asked.

"Really?" Desini asked.

Roshan floated across the room to the fountain, picked up her staff, and raised it high. "Revel in the power of the Light, my friends! The work of the pious is never done, and there is evil to conquer." She paced toward the gleaming surface of light that separated the preparation room from the dungeon-proper.

Roshan was kick-ass.

"Someone's ready," I said.

"Roshan?" Guiles beckoned. "We should prepare before we break the plane and enter the dungeon."

Roshan turned, lowered her staff, and blushed. She met our curious glances. She was single-minded when it came to this shit.

"Come friends, gather around," Guiles said. "First, eat your best stat-boosting foods. While we nourish ourselves, we'll talk tactics."

Thump! The floor shook.

Vibrations tingled in my feet.

Guiles's head whipped around toward the dungeon entrance.

Thump!

We all followed his gaze as my heart mimicked the bass-rich sound out there in my ears.

Thump! Thump! Thump!

A shadow fell across the floor outside the transparent magical barrier. The lower half of what my mind equated to a lizard appeared in the doorway and turned in our direction. A massive head craned from the top of the doorway, and the thumping in my ears grew louder, though no longer caused by heavy footfalls.

Shit is about to get very real.

I ground my teeth, but not out of fear nor foreboding. While the others probably saw the wide gaping mouth of innumerable sharp teeth that could easily snap me in half as they eyed two thick tusks that could impale the breadth of me four times over, I saw something else—

My first victim in an instance in Enora.

Then the beast bellowed, inviting our challenge.

9

The massive tail swept around then slammed into Desini's plate armor. She careened backward and slammed into the stony wall. Frozen pellets fell from the sky, coloring the beast's scaly hide in blue glimmers of frost as Priya's hands glowed icy blue. The illuminated yellow arrow released from my bow zoomed across the ivy-covered hallway, impaling the side of the beast's jaw just as Guiles re-materialized behind the monster and jammed both his daggers into its hulking tail.

Your bow skill has reached Level 80.
You have learned a new skill:
Exploding Arrow
Infused by the power of mana, a missile of flame explodes
upon impact, inflicting 36-45 fire damage
Minimum Level: 15
Cost: 25 Mana
Cooldown: 10 seconds
Additional Effect: Burn

+2 fire damage every five seconds.
Requires no ammunition
Bleed effects are negated when using this skill.

Guiles ripped two long tears into the beast's flesh as I nocked another arrow. Blood spurted streaks across the elf's face as the Ice Storm spell dissipated. The beast's tail swung and slammed into the elf, but after a ten-foot slide, he threw his arms out and gained his balance.

The creature gave an ear-shattering roar.

Guiles charged forward in a blur then plunged a dagger into the monster's hide. With the blood painting his face and the crazy smile painted across his mouth, the elf reminded me of some crazy highlander at war.

Critical Hit!

Priya's hands swirled around each other with smooth grace forming an orange tracer, then a flash of fire exploded between the creature's tusks. The blast reflected in the monster's irises, but its rapt attention remained on Desini, who cursed the beast in her unique vernacular.

"Overgrown lizard-like scum! We shall smite thine smelliness to the burning underworld!"

Roshan raised her free hand then cast a flash heal on Desini. The priestess's face was the calmest of all, her focus intent, and drive unhindered as she timed her casts.

As the green numbers floated above Desini's head, I focused on her health bar. Roshan's low level meant weaker heals. No matter how much damage she mended, Desini netted a loss with each incoming strike.

I stepped toward Roshan as I loosed an uncharged

arrow. "Take a second off your count between heals. It doesn't look like you'll grab aggro, and we don't know what abilities this monster might pull out. He could blow away a significant chunk of Desini's health all at once."

"Understood, master. I will keep her topped off."

"Great. And don't start calling me master. One of you is bad enough."

Her health wavering at around fifty percent, my feline-like tank rose then charged across the space, slamming her shoulder into the leg of the beast. Despite its mass the MOB stumbled backward. Guiles dodged to avoid the retreating hind claw it planted to regain its balance.

I released another arrow in a blur that lodged into the beast's neck.

Critical Hit!

Tusked Demon Gila
-78 HP
(Bleed Effect)

Bonus effect: Arrow replenished
Your bows skill has reached 81.
Your ranged attack skill has reached 38.

Nice. The ability replenishing 20% of my arrows had executed—or proc'ed, as gamer nerds liked to say—and the critical damage meant my Penetrating Arrow ability had gained power with the extra points in dexterity and weapon skill-ups, which were happening about every fourth arrow fired!

Priya flashed a wall of fire in the Gila's face and it turned. I feared it would stomp after her, but it parted its lips and bellowed instead, another ear-shattering sound that filled the hallways and left me disoriented. The half-elf's golden curls blew backward in a high wind then settled. Above her head, yellow text floated and jiggled.

Silenced!

Well, that kind of sucked, but it just meant I would have to hit harder.

I grinned like I'd just unwrapped a new bicycle at my birthday party as I withdrew another arrow. The wrinkles on Priya's forehead deepened with confusion at my expression.

She threw her hands out. "Why are you smiling, dude? I can't cast!"

"Guiles!" I barked. "Priya is silenced!"

"Understood!" the elf yelled as he thrust his blades into the demon gila's leg, gripped it with both hands, and let his weight drag him down to the floor as the long dagger ripped a ferocious gash.

I wondered if there was a leather worker in Enora who could make him a BAD MOTHER FUCKER wallet.

No sooner had I chuckled than the gila whipped around, its bloody tail toppling the elf to the floor. It spun in a full circle, swiping Guiles toward me as if sweeping up a mess on its backswing. I jumped over him as he slid under.

With a quick glance over my shoulder, I grinned. "What, you can't handle a level nineteen elite anymore?"

Guiles shoved his hands over his shoulders, rolled into a ball, and shoved himself up and onto his feet with deft agility. He reversed his grip on the daggers. "I'm not used to being Level 20 anymore, silver lips." He activated stealth.

"How about this? Whoever gets the killing blow receives the first ale courtesy of the loser who doesn't?"

"You're on!" I yelled and nocked an arrow.

"It's a wager. Get your coins ready, *Shénhuà!*"

I drew back on my bowstring then released it, but the arrow flew wide of my target.

Then Priya charged.

I ran a quick inspection.

Priya is silenced.

"Arrrr!" Priya screamed as she wielded her staff high overhead.

"Dirty droppings of worm filth!" Desini yelled as she swung her sword in a wide arc. "Motherless son of a demon whore!" She twisted and sliced up the gila's belly, opening a gash. Green liquid splashed her, but she spat as if it meant nothing then bent her back at an impossible angle to dodge the incoming claws of the beast's response swing. "Stinking pile of reptilian scales!"

Priya slipped in the green fluid then fell hard on her ass.

I laughed so hard, my next shot missed by a mile.

Priya slid in the gross body fluid, struggling until she reached her feet. After throwing me a quick scowl, she turned and swung the staff at the beast's knee, about two feet higher than her head.

Priya hits Tusked Demon Gila, if you want to call that a hit.
Tusked Demon Gila
-1 HP

"One health?" Priya yelled as she swung again. She eyed her staff too casually for someone who stood at the foot of a giant gila. "I thought this thing did ten to fifteen damage!"

Priya nicks the Tusked Demon Gila.
Giant Gila
-1 HP

Blood streaming from a gash in her forehead, Desini's health had dropped to about thirty-five percent. Roshan's mana pool was getting a tad low. But it was the former's pain tolerance that impressed me most. If the realism of Enora extended to non-players, getting slammed around and sliced open sucked donkey balls for her as much as it did me.

Priya taps the Tusked Demon Gila.
Critical Hit!
Tusked Demon Gila
-3 HP

Priya's mana looked good, her wisdom score for her level sped her replenishment, even in combat mode, but it was even faster while she wasn't able to cast. Unfortunately, her melee could use some work, and if I didn't control my laughing, I'd never hit the beast with my bow.

"Damage is relevant to who or what you're fighting and their level!" I barked.

She continued to bat away with her staff. Gods she could be hardheaded.

"Priya!" I yelled, meaning to warn her away.

Guiles threw me a warding glance, and I stopped. He grinned, and his meaning came to me. He wanted me to let her learn the hard way while things were under control. I returned the smile and turned my attention to the rest of my party. "Roshan! Desini! Potions! Now!"

They each raised their hands and winked their eyes. Potions appeared in their grasps, then they drank. Desini's health jumped about twenty percent! Guiles's potions didn't screw around, and my tank was buffed! Roshan's Mana jumped to half-full.

Priya's hands glowed again as she tested her spells at close range. Just as she halted her cast and turned to return to her original position near me, the gila swung its tail in another full rotation. This time, it got beneath her, and whereas Guiles slid across the floor, Priya flew.

Watching her sail through the air, I cringed. Then she hit the ground, thumping hard and rolling until she came to a halt on her back.

Guiles ripped his dagger from the beast's tail and yelled without turning his head. "Casters stand in the rear... especially when silenced!"

When Priya got her wind back, she pushed to her feet then sneered at the beast. Tendrils of lightning radiated between her fingertips as her blue casting bar filled.

A thick bolt of lightning shot from her palms then impacted the creature's head, causing it to slam against the wall.

Priya casts Lightning Pulse On Tusked Demon Gila.
Critical Hit!
Tusked Demon Gila
-72 HP

The Gila's HP dropped below ten percent. It shimmied off the wall, righted itself, then tried its silencing bellow again. But this time, the text above Priya's head was green.

Tusked Demon Gila uses **Stifling Roar**
(*Resisted*)

"Nice try, you fucker of mothers!" Priya screamed.

Close enough.

I released a Drilling Arrow and pegged the Gila right in the eye. Its health dropped below five percent. It reared up, wound back one of its short, burly, scaly arms, then punched Desini hard in the chest, sending her flying backward into the corner of the wall. Text above her head reported:

Stunned

I stared at her, open-mouthed.

Spinning stars over her head? Really, Enora? That's just precious. You're a cheese ball.

Gods, I needed to find her a shield, but the damned cost was beyond prohibitive, more than anything else I sought in Trowlsby. I guessed there wasn't a high demand. It wasn't like the hills were teaming with adventurers... yet.

With my tank temporarily incapacitated, the beast turned its one good eye on me. Although Priya had slammed the gila into the wall with her lightning spell, it chose me to focus on. Probably because of my arrow, lodged in its ruined eye, streaming white fluid dripping from the wound. My ass muscles clinched as a low growl rumbled in its chest.

Rut-row-Raggy!

An infuriated roar filled the room, then the gila stomped in my direction.

Desini shook her head to clear the cobwebs as she stumbled to her feet.

"Incoming!" I nocked another arrow as the massive beast bore down on me.

Guiles flashed into view. He stood high on the demon lizard's back, the elongated blades of his curved dagger raised high. When he slammed them into the demon's neck, the bastard elf grinned at me.

I eyed the monster's health and saw why.

He'd been waiting for just the right moment, and then he'd activated Spine Snap, to finish it.

Cheating mother...

I dove to one side as the demon gave its final cry and slammed into the floor where I'd stood.

You have vanquished:
Tusked Demon Gila
Level 19 Demon Reptile
(Elite)
1750 XP

Guiles leapt from the beast's back then rolled across the floor. He sprung up next to me and sheathed his daggers with a flourish.

Dude was a freaking super hero.

We gazed upon the bloody result of our first battle together. Green and red splatters I likened to a Pollock replica painted by a teen on LSD covered the walls. Was it morose that I found myself missing the camera on my cell phone? I'd have loved to send M3y3r and Katelyn from my old guild that shot with a caption of 'killing room floor.'

Without bothering to look at Guiles, I chuckled. "You waited until we got him low enough for your Spine Snap to finish him, then you sprang it."

The elf turned and patted my back a few times. "Try

not to take it too hard. You're not the first fool to wager against an elf hundreds of years his senior with one-hundred times your combat experience." He paced toward Desini and muttered, "Imbecile."

"Hey, screw you too, buddy." I laughed.

"While gratified by your offer, you're too scrawny for my taste."

Not only was Guiles a man of words, he was a man of *last* words.

When he offered a hand to help Desini from the floor, I performed a cursory check of my combat logs, focusing on my tank. My suspicions were confirmed. She was a natural. Although Priya would sometimes over cast and draw her enemy's ire, Desini was like a bird of prey, perched and waiting for her target to make the wrong move.

Roshan was a lower level, and accommodating her shortcoming required more frequent spell casting and cost us a health potion. So, there were two sides to that little handicap—one, she had to over-heal to keep up with Desini's loss of HP, and two, she drew less aggro because the heals replenished less damage. In turn, Priya and Guiles drew some aggro.

A glance at Roshan's XP bar revealed she'd jumped over a third of a level in the single encounter. If this first fight was any indicator, she would gain ground on the rest of us.

Guiles made me sick. The man's every strike was measured. His level had dropped the second we stepped through the magic barrier and into the dungeon, and even though he complained abilities he learned after Level 20 were unavailable to him, he out damaged all of us more than a simple level advantage should have.

And then some.

Priya approached. Her eyes glimmered with excitement. "I never imagined I would be in such a precarious situation as this, yet I surge with excitement." She clasped my hand and rose on her toes to kiss my cheek.

I turned my head and bent, giving her quarter.

She held her lips close to my ear and whispered, "I defied you, Gemini. I allowed my emotions to get the better of me. I will endeavor to do better. I have dishonored you with my rogue actions and set a poor example."

I gave her a few short nods and kept my tone low as I carefully voiced my reply.

"We're a team. I watched you bleed out in Brumhill because of that man. Sparing him took all the restraint I could muster and that was just so he could deliver a message. You chose to send a different one, but as I've said to all of you from the beginning, you act of your own free will. I won't judge you for doing it just because it contradicted my plans."

Whether it's my life or not, it's still a game.

I pulled her close to embrace her sideways. "In a sense, you were right. If we go through life letting people walk on us, we'll just be covered in footprints. But I'm not angry because of what you did. The way you went about it was a shifty violation of our trust. My disappointment stems from how you lured us into complacency only to take advantage of us. The deceit."

Priya peered up at me for a few long breaths, then she nodded.

Though I was still acclimating to her emotions, the one I sensed seemed to linger somewhere in the area of guilt.

"I'm sorry. I will do better."

"You're used to doing things your way, Priya. I understand that. Life in the woods, primarily on your own, would make anyone independent. But you're part of a family now, and we all love you." I beckoned with my fingers to draw Desini and Roshan over. "I propose that from now on, we discuss major decisions and act with the majority. I'm willing to accept when you all vote against me, but trust is everything."

Roshan rubbed a circle on my back. "Then my first vote is against this proposal."

"What?" My eyebrows shot up. "Do you see the contradiction there?"

"Solara has blessed you, Gemini. You know our strengths and weaknesses as if they're second nature to you. Even when you've—how do you say it—screwed up, you have shown the humility of a leader." She turned her gaze on Priya. "Gemini seeks to let you off easy for your betrayal. But it is no small thing, this action you took, and though I forgive you as Solara would require, you must earn the trust of your family again."

Priya chewed her lip. After an uncomfortable silence, she nodded.

"I pledge to earn back your trust." She leaned forward and kissed Roshan's cheek.

"I still think we should vote on our situations," I said. "I respect your ideas."

Desini gave a curt nod. "I vote that Gemini leads us."

"You're missing the point."

Roshan mimicked the Mishon's nod. "Seconded."

"No, you—"

Priya smiled, albeit sideways and lacking teeth. "I vote yes."

Roshan clapped her hands as if slapping dust away. "It is settled."

They used the democratic system I'd postulated to over-rule me and leave me solely in command.

Before I could argue against it, Guiles summoned us. "Party, to me!" He stood at the opposite end of the hallway, near the dungeon entrance, and gestured before stepping inside. After we crossed through the magic barrier, he pointed at the fountain. "Since we have it, set your hands in its waters, replenish your energy, and then we'll proceed to the real fighting."

"You didn't consider that *real* fighting?" Priya asked.

"What, battering an elite MOB's knee with your crooked little staff?"

She faked a scowl.

Guiles chuckled. "It was real enough, my Elven sister, but experience tells me it was but a prelude to what's coming. We might spend days in this Solara-forsaken place." He turned his gaze on Desini. "And I have little doubt when we come out the other side, your party will be changed forever. But we should get on with it."

I stepped to the fountain and dipped my hands into its cool waters. A chilly sensation spread up my arms and throughout my body, my head cleared, and the soreness in my bow fingers washed away. When Desini reached into the pool, the green goo and blood vanished from her face and gear.

"Call me crazy, but you're prettier without all that muck."

"Silence, master." Her cheek twitched like she'd smile, but she beat it.

Guiles's crimson war paint also vanished. I eyed the water to see if it absorbed the filth, but it remained transparent and blue. Another little detail to remind me I was in a game world.

The elf sat on the edge of the fountain running the tips of his fingers across the crystal tubes. "It's been years since

I've seen one of these. So much time has passed since Brugh and I adventured, I'd forgotten the serenity these things give off. Depending on the size of this place, we could find one or two others."

I'd forgotten about Brugh. The giant warrior with the massive, jewel-encrusted great sword had acted as Guiles's firewall back in Brumhill, when we sought out our Elven trainer. It felt like ages ago.

"Where is Brugh, anyway?" I asked.

"Around. Brugh wanders. Restless type."

"I see. Tell me something, Guiles. If you hadn't seen the mage outside, how long would you have followed us without our knowing? And why go to the trouble?"

Guiles raised one shoulder and dropped it. "You left Brumhill with low skills, low levels, and a quest to retrieve an entropy crystal. Our mutual shop keeping friends Breeder and Leira preferred a little insurance. After all, even mystical beings require help from time-to-time. Wouldn't you agree?"

An image of two men lying in the road between Brumhill and Warrington with their throats slit from ear-to-ear as Desini and Priya slept inside the cart was evidence enough of that.

"I wholeheartedly concede the point. But don't you have anything better to do?"

Guiles chuckled. "Funny. Brugh had the same query. The expedient answer is 'no.' I have nothing better to do. Truth be told, I don't get summoned for much weapons training in Brumhill."

"I always want the truth to be told."

"Good. From me, you'll have it, no matter how hard it might be to hear." He slapped his hands on his legs.

"Then why don't you start with why you were in a shit hole like Brumhill."

"Do we have to do this now? You don't trust me?"

"It's not a question of trust," Priya interjected. "You've saved us twice. I think Gemini has reservations about my mother and thinks you might be tangled up with her somehow."

I tapped my nose and pointed at her. I got three sets of confused gazes for my trouble, but Priya was ready for those, too.

"That silly expression means that I'm right."

"Your mother?"

"Zhara," Priya answered with derision.

I cleared my throat. "He wasn't around for that part."

"She's your mother?" Guiles asked. He shook his head. "Your pairing takes on even deeper meaning." He stood then clasped his hands behind his back. He reminded me of a history professor at my community college who would pace in front of the class like that, his gaze glued to the floor as he pontificated about the significance of events surrounding Octavius in Ancient Rome.

"I will compromise. You get the abbreviated version." He didn't wait for any objections. "When the king absorbed the University and its satellites into the monarchical government many decades ago, the faithful of Brumhill—of whom there were few, believe me—sensed Enora's energy flowing from the Dark Wood. Something changed.

"I'm an elf. Where magic and religion are concerned, they're as ingrained into my consciousness as the daggers sheathed in the back of my belt."

"I see. Your curiosity would naturally be piqued." I nodded.

"You do not yet see, but that's none of your own fault.

Word traveled to my people of a magical being living in the forest. You see, Zhara never showed herself until the magicians of this continent were under duress. Due to a set of inconvenient circumstances I required a place to lie low, and since Brumhill is exactly what you called it, I thought it as good a place as any."

"You're not going to tell us why you were on the run?" I asked.

"As I said, short version now, longer story later. We all have our secrets, Gemini, and they are ours to keep or share when we see fit. But I make no secret of the fact that I would lay down my life in the service of Zhara, Guardian of the Tree of Solara. I believe she sheltered me from prying eyes in Brumhill. In return, I pledged my service through prayer. I might never have stepped into the Dark Wood, because it wasn't my place to enter her domain, but the energy in Brumhill fed my soul, and I knew it was a power worth protecting from the darkness. You don't begin to grasp your blessings." His gaze turned to Priya. "None of you does."

He paused while we all exchanged looks.

"In short, my time came. You needed a mentor. And I am just the elf for that job." He raised a finger. "But! If you ever deem we should part ways, you need only say so and I will leave you to your destiny. Until then, I will serve your party for as long as you will have me because it is both my debt to Zhara and Solara as well as my desire to return the Light to this world."

You have been offered companionship.

Guiles, *a fierce rogue of some renown has offered to become your companion and mentor. If you accept, Guiles will follow you until you decide it is time for him to depart.*

Would you like to accept Guiles's offer?
Okay, I hadn't expected that. This bad ass Elven rogue and weapons trainer is offering to accompany my party wherever we go!

Still, I pushed my luck. It was a pitfall of my inquisitive mind. "What about Brugh?" I asked.

The elf tilted his head to one side for a moment, his white hair barely moving with the gesture. "What if we leave discussions of Brugh for when we're with Brugh?"

I wondered from his tone if the two had a falling out. If that was true, then the warrior's loss was my gain.

"I'm honored you would adventure with us and join my party, Guiles. I accept your offer of companionship and welcome you as a mentor."

Guiles *is now your companion. Increase disposition with this NPC for an opportunity to bind him to you.*

Guiles gave a curt nod. "Formality sounds suspect on your silver lips, mystic, but I thank you. The honor is mine. One day you'll see that." He stepped closer and extended his hand.

I rose long enough to grasp it and match his smile with a genuine one of my own. "Welcome to the party, Guiles. May we adventure long and successfully together."

But not just adventure, right? Coexist! How could I have forgotten?

In the excitement over recent level gains when we completed the *Rescue Roshan quest*, I'd forgotten the reward about which I'd been most curious. "Shit."

"What?" Guiles released my hand.

The answer waited in my Bag of Holding. I focused on

my interface and scanned the filled slots for the item I'd been promised by Lucera.

And it's there!

I withdrew my hand from the bag and clutched the object in a firm grip. Then I unfolded my fingers to reveal a blue crystal stone with a shining red rune shaped in a box with two lines forming an angular roof. Cheesy, but effective.

The women slid closer on the edge of the fountain to eye the crystal as a light bloomed from inside.

"Ancient City of Ninn!" Guiles snapped, taking a step back. "Is that a…"

Priya shuffled over and leaned against me. "Hmm? What's that? It's pretty."

Desini tilted her head to one side.

Roshan wore a confused look. She ran the tip of her soft finger over the carving. "A rune. But I've never seen such a stone in all my days of mining. I wonder at its value."

Foundation Stone

An exceptional and scarce item, this magical stone can be buried in the place of your choosing to create a township's foundation.

A township is an adventurer's settlement where you can grow a military presence, establish residences, build crafting halls, establish trade routes, and expand your claim of Enora's lands.

Type: Immortal Stone of Power
Quality: Legendary
Durability: Unbreakable
Recoupable item
Soulbound to G3m1n1 Fowler

Guiles shook his head in disbelief. "Every time I think I have a grasp on *how* touched you are, I find myself humbled."

I was fucking giddy. "Pretty cool, right?"

Guiles cocked his head back. "Shit."

10

Guiles muttered to himself as he moved ahead of us down the wide hallway of rough, chiseled stone walls strung with thick strands of ivy. Although his movements were naturally fluid, I took his heavy footfalls for his version of stomping. I hurried past randomly mounted torches with a passing curiosity as to who hung them and after a quick jog, caught up to the elf. His brisk pace left me thankful for his shorter strides.

"... how many raids I'd joined in the hunt for one of those things, you'd be less—"

"I get an inkling you're a little bugged-out that I have a foundation stone."

The elf spoke without slowing his gait. "A *little bugged out*? If you mean *miffed*, yes, I'm finding Solara's will to be a whimsical thing." He lowered his voice to a mutter again. "Level 17 with a foundation stone. Ninn-be-damned. Unbelievable."

"Guiles." I tugged one sleeve to slow his pace. "If you're my companion and I have a foundation stone, that means you have a foundation stone."

Guiles came to an abrupt stop, and I ended up a few paces ahead. Down the hallway the women halted at a distance, their expressions hesitant as they whispered to each other.

He stepped closer and punched my bag with one finger. "You possess a soul bound item for which men would kill a million demons. The fact you didn't faint upon touching it tells me you have no inkling what a legendary item is."

"You still don't get it. With all sincerity, what's mine is yours." I gestured behind him and down the hall. "Those people are my family, now. You've become my companion, too. Your offer to be my mentor is a gift I don't take for granted. I might not always agree or go the way you want me to, but you'll be heard." I aimed my best mood-lightening grin. "I mean, what kind of asshole would I be to ignore the advice of a hundred-year-old elf who just conned me out of a pint?"

"Gah. A pint." Guiles shook his head.

"Fine, fine. Be that way. But let me be direct. If I build a foundation, you'll have a new place to lie low from whatever threats sent you to Brumhill. Your skills and wisdom are much more valuable to me than any place, but they could be useful to many if we built the foundation together."

As if I knew what a foundation township was. Player housing? A guild hall?

"You would need a weapons trainer?"

His tone reminded me of my eighth grade English teacher. The old bat had adopted that same tenor when testing my logic. Thoughts rocketed through my mind as I sought the answer the elf wanted to hear, but when it came down to it, I was swayed by the discussion at the fountain minutes earlier. Only the truth would serve us.

"No, I mean you're much more than a weapons trainer.

I would rely on you to teach us your peoples' history about magic, weapons, and dark underlords. I'd like to learn more about the Governor of Knall and other obstacles we face, now that I realize his interest in us isn't going to wane anytime soon. Not to mention, you probably have crafting skills."

"Many," he confirmed.

"Hell, without you, we might as well be wearing diapers around here!" I threw up a hand. "I've been so focused on rescuing Roshan, the stone slipped my mind. It was a quest reward for saving her. Can you believe that?"

Guiles stood stony eyed for a few seconds before swiveling his head to the women. "Tell me, Gemini, what does this woman mean to you? How is it you've impregnated the daughter of an immortal—who is quite possibly an immortal, herself—and yet the two of you and this woman you met on the road risk yourselves and your destinies to bring her back? It can't just be that she's a Light priestess, so, tell me."

I matched his hard gaze. "She's one of mine. By that, I don't mean I own her. I mean I adore her. She appeared at a time I otherwise might have died. She saved my life." I pointed down the hallway. "Those women are my family. I would pry open the chests and shred the lungs of anyone who tried to take them from me again. Hence, I plan to one day pay the Governor of Knall a visit, before he pays us one, because Roshan wants to be with me and although it might make me sound simple, my loyalty is that easily earned. She *wants* to be here. That means she has a say in what we do, where we go, and what's the best way forward for our family."

"It sounded earlier as if she had different ideas about who was the decision maker in your *family*."

"I didn't know you'd been listening, but it doesn't really matter. Whether she desires a vote in our decisions or not, Roshan will enjoy the fruits of this foundation stone and any other spoils like everyone else."

"Just because she wants to be with you?" he asked. "There must be more."

"There's plenty more. The fact Solara herself offered me a quest to get her back has a little something to do with it." I was stretching the truth, but I couldn't very well talk to the elf about Lucera, the A.I.'s extension.

"You spoke to the goddess?"

I shook my head. "The quest appeared in my log. But these are details for another time."

My response was a rewarding bit of payback.

"I guess it just comes down to this, Guiles. Do you want to be here? Tell me now, because regardless of what this artifact in my bag means to you on an egotistical level, your attitude about my having one screams of one emotion foreign to my team... jealousy."

"Jealous!"

"I'm not finished. Resentment after a century spent hunting an artifact only to find it in a noob's bag is understandable, but after all I've told you, I have to know if you're the kind who must be master and commander over his own fortress, or if it's as you say and you're willing to be a respected teacher and defender of something larger than yourself." I leaned in. "Because believe me, sir, my foundation will be a place where you will not regret setting down stakes. I don't screw around."

Now that I've completed the used car sales pitch, I'll just have to live up to it.

Guiles uncrossed his arms and let them dangle by his side as he contemplated my onslaught of words. By my best accounting, I'd probably insulted him. After all, he was a much older, more capable, and a wiser man than I. But if it came down to it, and if my new family and I had to do everything on our own, we would. So, I mentally prepared myself for whatever was to come.

"Your words show wisdom beyond your years, *Shénhuà*. Now I see why Solara has forged you from her energy and brought you to this world." He bowed his head, showing me the neat part running down the center. "Forgive my petulance. So overcome was I by the sight of this legendary artifact that it was I who acted like the student. I'm honored you'd share such a wonderful gift after knowing so little of me. Will you grant me your forgiveness?"

Well, that was a nice turn of events. I thrust my hand out. "You're a part of the team now, Guiles. No need for apologies. But I accept it."

The bones in my hand protested as he gripped it and bowed again. "Excellent. Now, shall we rip open some enemies? I grow restless standing in this dank place." He turned and set off without waiting for an answer.

Watching his confident gait as he approached the end of the long hallway, the hint of a smile crept to my lips. I was a lucky bastard, but I wondered how much of that luck was actually the design of Nokuro Takemoto and Enora in preparation for other players to enter the world.

That predestined shit bugged the hell out of me, but it wasn't exactly a concept foreign to games. It just seemed out of place in Enora.

"Are you well, my love?" Roshan asked.

I turned to find Desini and Priya standing on either side of her, each wearing similar inquisitive expressions. I scanned each facial feature, from Desini's round high cheekbones, to Priya's sharper Elven features, to Roshan's coppery, perfect complexion and slightly down-turned eyes. They were all here, just as I'd dreamed for the last week. I thought my heart would explode.

The games were over. Life had begun.

Peering over my shoulder at the ancient elf who'd stopped and turned to face all of us, I nodded. "I've never been better, Roshan. Not ever."

"Then why do you stand there like moss growing on the sunless side of a tree?" She raised her staff and marched past me. "There's evil to vanquish, and I need levels! You all passed me. This will not do. Forward!"

As she marched past, Priya raised her palm to her mouth and her shoulders jostled in her new robe. Desini smiled, gave a derisive eye roll, and set off after Roshan, but she gave my butt a good, hard slap as she passed, causing me to jump.

Priya glanced down at the spot she'd spanked. "Guess you better move that ass, group leader. The priestess is on the warpath."

At the end of the hallway, we came to a door. Well, it wasn't exactly a door, it was a sheet of blueish metal with swells running top-to-bottom on either side. There was no handle. Guiles had already been there for a minute, and he stood there with his arms crossed and his head tilted to one side.

"What do you think?" I asked.

I mimicked his stance and scanned the corners of the obstruction, looking for any crack or crevice that might give us a clue how to open it.

"It's a Bluesteel door, in a place carved out of hard stone, with no handles or levers to open it. It didn't budge when I pushed."

I searched the earthen floor and jagged stone walls but

found nothing of interest. In other VMMOs, I'd often found traps and secret entrances to loot stashes, but here I saw nothing. Then again, this wasn't other VMMOs. An idea occurred.

I stepped forward, balled up my fist, and banged on the door. "Hey! Anybody home?"

"Effective." Guiles chuckled.

Then a muted metal-on-metal grinding sound from the other side of the door caused us both to dispense with our grins and step backward.

"Why do I feel like Indiana Jones right now?" I muttered. A system warning popped up and I dismissed it immediately.

It seemed no one heard me.

The door thumped again, and we took another step backward.

"Hey, shouldn't Desini be at the front?" Priya asked from behind us.

Desini passed on my left as she marched toward the door, clutching her sword.

Guiles leaned toward me. "She needs a shield. While I'm impressed with her ability to dodge, properly arming someone with her wingspan would turn her into a veritable wall of protection."

"Gee, I hadn't considered that."

"You wield sarcasm almost as aptly as she would a shield."

"You rank high on my ledger of smart asses, Guiles. Right up there with the other elf. I wonder if it's a racial trait." The elf threw me a squint, just like Priya's. I clicked my tongue. "Do you know how much shields cost?"

"If I'd known my destiny would bring me here with

more than half a day's notice and that you'd have picked up a cat-tank—"

"I am not a cat, elf."

I peered at Desini's rock-hard ass.

She certainly isn't. Tail or not.

He continued as if he hadn't been interrupted. "I might have brought one of Brugh's spares along. I have good news, though."

"What's that?"

The door banged again, but this time none of us reacted except for some cursory glances.

"Shields are common drop in boss fights... that is, if you survive the boss fight without a shield to protect you."

"That's fucking comforting."

"Agreed," Desini growled. "The elf is of much assurance."

"If you wanted guarantees, then perhaps adventuring—"

The door jerked with a grind. Something clanged from the other side and sent an echo up the hallway. The slab of metal slid into a slit behind the doorjamb. Sparkles of orange light reflected on the floor from the other side.

"I guess knocking worked."

"I suppose so." Guiles ripped his daggers from his sheath, activated stealth mode, faded like the Ghost of Christmas past, then slipped past Desini, disappearing through the slit in the doorway.

From behind me, Roshan whispered, "You are out of position, noob."

Priya stood with her staff clutched in one hand with its end on the floor. Roshan held hers high, and I noted the wiry muscles of her forearms. At the door, Desini held her sword at the ready.

Here we were in a dungeon beneath a place called the Plague Barrens, with a door sliding open in front of us, and I was the only one who hadn't drawn his weapon. But having Roshan around to call me a noob was music to my ears.

Scooting back a few steps, I shimmied my bow off my shoulder and nocked an arrow.

Then the demons bum-rushed us.

11

Mishon grunts filled the air as Desini jammed her sword into the narrow doorway and shifted a foot behind her. I thought she'd give way to the incoming creatures, but then I realized she was anchoring herself for the force to come. Blood gushed from the throat of the first demon as her blade sliced through its hardened, purplish flesh.

"No, Desini!" Guiles barked. "Push forward, and fill the doorway to create a bottleneck or they'll surround you all!"

The mishon lowered her shoulder and activated her Charge ability. The result was fucking glorious!

The short, brawny demon leading the crowd sailed backward, slamming into the crowd filtering through the door and sending them flailing back into the unseen area beyond. One green-skinned foe slipped around the demon dominoes and skittered forward. I raised my foot and kicked it in the groin. It reeled just long enough for Desini to fill the space inside the stone door frame.

A blinding flash filled the room from behind. The demons raised their arms to shield themselves, but it was too late. Roshan's scepter had appeared and fulfilled its purpose as text bounced above our enemies' heads.

Blinded

"Where were you hiding that?" I yelled, setting the sole of my boot into the next demon's chest and straining my muscles to drive it back.

Desini sliced at its neck with a brutal swing, then hot blood splashed onto its shoulder and poured down its chest.

"A woman must have her secrets!" Roshan yelled, raising the scepter again. Although the scepter was low in level and a majority of the small regiment flooding toward us resisted its blinding effect, a few threw up their arms to block the light from their eyes, which helped to maintain the bottleneck. The inherent problem was that her staff would've better boosted her casting power. Her low level was enough of a handicap.

"Switch to the staff! You've got to trust me!"

With a growl to gain demon enmity, Desini spewed her variant of expletives. "Die, you filthy, slimy beast! Back to the underworld with you, ferret-faced bag of rat meat!"

Fire exploded a foot in front of the mishon, then one of the minions contorted and blistered.

Wrath Fiend
Level 18 Demon
Servants of higher demons, wrath fiends are known for their muscular upper bodies and short, poisonous claws.
Strength: 16
Dexterity: 9
Intelligence: 2
Wisdom: 1

Constitution: 14
Charisma: 1

For the first time in my Enoran tenure, my interface displayed enemy attributes, and I didn't understand why. Because I was in a dungeon? But that question was less important than what was missing from the line indicating race and level. "Non-elites, Desini!"

Priya was only three steps away, but I had to shout for her to hear me over the growls, shrieks, and Desini's professions of love for demon kind. "Priya!"

The half-elf wonder turned toward me between spells, a sneer on her face.

"Help keep them blocked off until we can burn them down. Use Ice Storm to slow them while our tank keeps them at bay!"

Priya's faced morphed into an expression of angry pleasure. She nodded. "I like this very much!" Her hands glowed blue as she raised them over her head like a cat about to claw yarn just out of reach, her casting bar grew, then pellets of ice filled the area in front of Desini.

The effect was instantaneous as the Wrath Fiends slowed to a crawl, as if they floundered through molasses. The reduction didn't slow their attack speed through, and the fiend closest to Desini clawed three jagged wounds across her neck in a blur. She faltered and screamed, stepping backward and swiping the wound with the back of one hand.

"You vile, squalid demon shit!" She stunned the demon by punching her pommel into its face, then she spun the weapon, swung it overhead, then swept down and sliced the creature's arm off below the elbow. In a sickening display of efficiency, she brought the weapon through on her backswing and ripped the beast's head from its shoulders. The skin surrounding the blade on either side of its neck stretched into long strands before it snapped apart, resembling strands of cheese stretching from a slice from a slice of pizza being raised from a pan.

Gross. I turned back to the crowd and nocked an arrow. "Fucking nice, Desini!"

Above her head, red text appeared at two-second intervals.

Skin Rot
-40 XP
Skin Rot
-37 XP
Skin Rot
-41 XP

Ew. Not so nice.

I angled myself to one side between arrows to get a better look at the wound and found festering, greenish skin forming around the gashes. Blue veins budged and snaked across her neck. Desini gasped for air as she swung the sword, but her expletives came strained.

Roshan casts **Minor Heal**.
(Healing Over Time)
+12 HP
+15 HP
+11 HP
Roshan Casts **Flash Heal**.
+45 HP

Extending the draw on my new Exploding Shot, I

waited for energy to flow through my arm and, when my hand glowed bright, I unleashed the energized arrow.

Critical Hit!

The rest of the combat log message went ignored while I watched the up-and-down ticks of Desini's health as the more powerful degradation of the skin rot slowly dominated the lower-level healing spell.

We needed to wrap this up.

Another wrath fiend slashed the side of Desini's neck just as she thrust her sword into the chest of its neighbor. The two demons' shoulders slammed into each other, pinning them in the doorway. Desini pressed her foot into the chest of the beast she'd run through and used the leverage to pry her sword loose, then she turned her attention to the one who'd just ripped at her.

"Putrid minion! The Light comes for you!"

She stabbed out at the demon, but it dodged and struck her again with its short claws, this time in her cheek.

Roshan casts **Flash Heal**.
Critical Heal!
+72 HP
*Healing Over Time (**Minor Heal**)*
+11 HP
+9 HP
Minor Heal *expires.*
Roshan casts **Flash Heal**.
+42 HP

I loosed an arrow, tagging the offending demon near his lobe-less ear as Desini sliced at its arm in a wild swing, but more demons poured forward and forced her back into the hallway as they struggled to get through.

A purple cloud whooshed into existence just outside the doorway. Guiles appeared, his daggers punching holes in a demon's chest. He vanished again then appeared behind another, slamming both blades into its back then thrusting upward so he ripped the flesh from waist to shoulder blade.

*Guiles activates **Spine Snap.***
Critical Hit!

Wrath Fiend
-97 HP
(Bleed)
-21 HP
-17 HP
-2 HP

*Guiles has vanquished a **Wrath Fiend**.*
237 XP

Behind him, in the exterior hallway, a line of corpses told me what he'd been up to while we blocked the door.

Suppressing my combat log with a thought, I focused on the battle, firing arrows in an autonomous motion and, as one of my arrowheads lodged into the shoulder of a demon, I found myself awed by the rapid movements of our rogue as he slid from enemy to enemy, dropping them at Desini's feet as if they were little more than minor nuisances, creating a pile of demon scum that increased the difficulty for the others to advance to the doorway. But the welts building up on Desini's face and neck worried me.

I peered at the bodies stacked atop each other and checked my combat log again.

*Desini attacks with **Sword of the Defender**.*

Wrath Fiend
-40 HP

*Desini attacks with **Sword of the Defender**.*

Wrath Fiend
-37 HP

The attacks my tank was unloading were equivalent to auto-attacks in other games, but I couldn't figure out why. Her Stamina bar was still three-quarters full—plenty of room to sneak in some abilities. If we hadn't been in the middle of a battle, I might have perused the logs of our earlier combat to see if this was becoming a habit, but since this wasn't the time, I just yelled a command. "Desini! Use Swipe!"

When activated, Swipe would swing in a wide arc and strike up to three enemies. She hadn't used it once during the battle, so engaged had she been with her vocal diatribe and wild strikes at the beasts.

When my tank thumped her forehead with the heel of her free hand, I dismissed the idea of reviewing the log. I shook my head in disdain at her lapse, but she was still new at this and it was easy to forget that when watching her. It wasn't like she'd been running around her whole life swinging swords at an onslaught of crazy, snarling enemies. To the contrary, she'd traveled on a cart and kept her head down in the presences of others.

Mental note—Earn the title of 'master' she bestows on you instead of thinking like a judgmental douche bag.

Desini activates **Swipe.**

Wrath Fiend
-31 HP
Wrath Fiend
-27 HP
Critical Hit!
Wrath Fiend
-67 HP

Desini vanquished **Wrath Fiend.**
237 XP

A punch shoved Desini backward and three fiends stuffed into the doorway. The middle one lunged forward as the swipe swung wide. He stretched out his crooked arm, claws extended and ready to swipe at her face again.

But this time, Desini was ready.

She shoved out with her boot heel, kicked the demon square in its knee cap, and snapped it like a twig. When the bastard dropped to one knee with a squeal, she flipped the sword over and plunged it from high to low, right into the space between his shoulder and neck.

To buy her time, I fired an arrow in the nose of the creature on her right using Drilling Arrow, which dropped the non-elite like a bad habit.

Guiles slid his dagger into the back of the demon snarling on Desini's left and, just like that, we were back in business. My tank stepped back into the doorway, reasserting her control. A flash of golden light and a tympani of triumphant music filled the world from somewhere behind us. I smiled, but otherwise ignored it.

A tiny black dot appeared just in front of Desini, off to Guiles's left. While he opened the jugular on one of the few remaining demon fiend bastards, I blinked furiously, trying to clear the strange apparition from my eye. My next arrow sailed wide. Then the dot spread outward to form a black oval with purple swirling smoke in its center. As it expanded to about six feet in diameter, the wrath fiend closest to Desini glared in horror and flailed its arms as the black void sucked it into oblivion.

"Nice!" I yelled at Priya as a second Demon was pulled into the black nether.

I readied another arrow and nocked it, but the battle was over.

Desini stepped back from the door, sheathed her sword and doubled over to grip her knees. Though her stamina gauge was still more than half-full, her chest huffed wildly. She projectile vomited to complete the effect. To my surprise, Guiles cringed and stepped away from the stomach eruption, as if it was acid that could burn his boots.

"You okay?" I set my hand on Desini's back.

She stood straight and nodded, but a glance on my party pane revealed her health bar was only 30% full. I ticked off a few seconds, eyeing it with interest. It wasn't recovering. Though Roshan had closed up the wounds, the surrounding flesh was cracked and colored a sickly gray-green.

Roshan cast another heal. Desini's HP shot up, but as I counted off seconds, I realized she was losing health every three.

I focused on the wounds.

Flesh Rot

Desini
-21 *HP*

With an HP pool of 710 when buffed by her armor, I knew Roshan could keep her on her feet, but it woke me to the realization I had no countermeasures for poison or curses.

"Flesh rot," Guiles said. His thoughts mirrored my own. "I coat my daggers with poison, but I have no cure for it with me. Had I known we'd be entering a dungeon, I'd have stocked up on healing potions and antidotes." He stepped closer to our beautiful meat shield and though he spoke consoling words, his hand remained dangling at his hips. "Worry not, child, the rot holds only because you were struck multiple times. It will pass with time as long as Roshan keeps you topped off." He eyed our healer. "Using your HOT to keep her steady will reduce the need for stronger heals and preserve your mana."

Roshan eyed him suspiciously. "HOT?"

"Every Light Mage's first healing spell heals over time."

"Oh. Yes. Of course. I've been using it, I just haven't refreshed it since it last wore off."

Minor Heal had been the lone spell at her disposal when first we'd met a long week earlier. I assumed she'd become enamored with the power of her Flash Heal like a child who'd discovered Rocky Road and left vanilla behind.

Been there. Done that. Guiles was already teaching valuable lessons, and I liked the way he went about it. Void of judgment.

Roshan raised one hand and cast the spell with little effort.

Guiles blinked each eye in succession and bowed. "And

congratulations on Level 12, priestess. If I remember correctly, you should have learned a new spell."

I turned, expecting to find Roshan wearing the joyous expression I'd seen the first time she'd leveled with me, back in the subterranean shit hole beneath the Dark Wood. But her brown eyes gleamed with focus on Desini as she waited for the right moment to top her off. She paced over to our tank and raised Desini's chin to inspect the wounds.

Her glowing fingers touched the mishon's skin. "I'm sorry I cannot cure this, my friend, but I pledge to become more sophisticated in the ways of healing so I can better serve you."

"Your heals make me feel much better, Roshan," Desini said. "I'm humbled by your kindness." Desini bowed her head. Then she turned to one side and painted the wall with her remaining stomach contents. The greenish tint surrounding her wounds was gone after she wiped her sleeve across her mouth. Only the gray tinge remained.

Flesh Rot
Desini
-7 HP

Flesh Rot
Desini
-3 HP
(*Flesh rot expires*)

"You got it all," I said. "Give her a few Flash Heals to fix her up, then let's wait for your mana to recoup. We can talk strategy in the meantime."

"Should she eat instead?" Priya asked. "Then Roshan can replenish her mana faster."

"I like that you're thinking strategically, but Desini's food buffs are still active and I don't want to waste food. Roshan's Wisdom is solid for her level, so she'll recover quickly enough."

Roshan cast the heals, and Desini breathed a cleansing sigh. Then my healer leaned against the wall and crossed her arms beneath her bosom.

"She needs a shield," Guiles muttered next to me.

I jumped. "Gods, how did you get there? I didn't even see you move. I wish you wouldn't do that."

He ignored my commentary and cocked his chin toward our healer. "Why do you stand, priestess?"

"Why wouldn't I?" Roshan asked.

He glanced at each member of the party, in turn. "All of you should sit, or at least kneel."

"Why?" Priya asked. "I'm not tired. I'm ready to go!" She pumped a fist in the air. "Let us—"

Guiles shook his head and thrust a finger at the ground. "Sit, fools."

Priya's words caught in her throat as her jaw dropped, but she didn't respond.

"Sit and watch."

We all sat, and I glanced at my party interface as Guiles spoke.

"Quiet your minds. Let the Light flow through you. Focus on cleansing your body with warm thoughts of Solara's grace." He studied me. "Or visions of sex with Elven women—whatever sets your mind at ease."

"I grow fond of this elf," Roshan said. "His piety is a..."

Her words trailed off as I focused on my HUD against the back of my shuttered eyelids. I was acquainted with the way our resource bars ticked fuller every two seconds, but after a few long breaths, everyone's health and mana reserves gained significantly more replenishment per tick. "Fuck me."

"Again, you are too scrawny for my taste." Guiles chuckled, but I was too embarrassed to join in.

When she made the same realization, Desini's response did nothing to allay my humiliation. "And I call *you* 'master.' Perhaps it is to Guiles I should have 'hitched my wagon,' as you like to say."

I shook my head in derision at myself. *RTFM— Read the fucking manual.*

Guiles stepped to the center of our circle to stand over us, his hands behind his back. "Try not to be too hard on Gemini. If anyone is to blame, it's me. The effect only occurs in these instanced prisons. We draw from our mana, energy, stamina, and later, our spirit pools to do Solara's bidding and advance ourselves through the vanquishing of her enemies. In return, she provides us this natural buff to increase our recovery rate when we let her Light flow through us in meditation. Simply sitting or kneeling will increase our recovery, but meditating in the glow of the Light intensifies the effect. The quieter your minds, the better. But understand, during combat you recover your resources at a much slower rate. Even if you managed to enter a meditative state while in combat, you would not increase your regeneration speed. I've seen enough monks try. Next time we fight together, we'll fill our stocks with potions to supplement the shortcomings of being in combat."

"Thank you, Master Guiles," I said.

Desini's jaw dropped open and her eyes flared at me for a moment, then she stared up in awe of Guiles.

She repeated my sentiment. "Thank you, master."

"Oh. Um, yes." Guiles bowed. "I live only to serve,

ladies... and sir." His tone changed as he presented a new subject. "Now, Gemini, I believe your companion's attributes need attention."

A smile crept across Roshan's face. The flesh of her rounded cheeks turned pink.

"Why aren't you sitting?" I asked Guiles.

"I took little damage. As you will see at level twenty, if you choose to be a rogue, hunter, or ranger, your energy pool—unlike mana, health, and spirit—recycles quickly. I kneel in the wake of combat only when my health gets low."

"Ah."

I brought Roshan's attributes up, opting for the abbreviated version.

Roshan has reached Level 12!
Roshan has four unspent attribute points!
Since Roshan's disposition to you is beloved, you may spend four attribute points.
Roshan has learned a new spell!

Smite

Smite your enemies with an arc of Light magic causing 12-15 damage.
Damage scales with level.

"Nice, Roshan. Looks like you finally got an offensive spell."

She nodded enthusiastically. "I will smite my enemies with abandon."

"No," I said, "you will manage your casting like Priya and resist the temptations that draw aggro from your tank."

"Yes! Of course!" She threw an apologetic glance at the tank.

Desini waved a dismissive hand. "Worry not, priestess. I will keep them angry with my hatred of them."

Priya held out a clawed hand and lightning tendrils crackled between the fingers. She halted her cast, and the light winked out. She was flipping it like a switch.

"Your people wield no shortage of confidence," Guiles said.

"They're *our* people now," I corrected. "And why wouldn't they be positive with an accomplished dagger-wielding, centuries-old elf like you backing them up?"

"Both points are well-received. But come, now that everyone is back to form, there's work ahead, and I fear you've seen only the weakest this wretched place has to offer."

"Are you always this encouraging?" I asked as the elf paced away from us.

"Yes!" he yelled over his shoulder.

12

And boy, did the elf have it right! Whatever ideas I'd held about trash mobs was wiped clean by what we faced on that first day in the Plague Barrens instance. We struggled through two more waves of wrath fiends and had to rest after each occurrence so Desini —and once, Priya—could rest until their flesh rot had healed.

It seemed Priya's wand came with a load of aggro. The first time she cast the stone effect on one of the wrath fiends, it screamed a shoulder-shivering howl and dragged a stony leg behind it as it lumbered toward her like some B-Movie horror monster, snarling and drooling. Though we picked that one up, another she stoned during the conflict had shown a strange intelligence, battering away at Desini until the stone spell dissipated and then charging Priya.

I'd had to scrounge deep in my combat log to validate the demon had delayed its response intentionally. That it would climb the aggro chart, hold its ground until the effect passed, then charge the caster was so tactical in nature it kind of blew my mind. I'd never seen that kind of intelligence in a mob.

Hence, Priya shared in the flesh rot, but unlike when Desini first encountered the disease, Priya didn't vomit. Instead, she huffed and huffed, insisting no one talk to her as she peered at the ceiling with her hands on her hips instead of allowing herself to double over and let it go.

My Elven baby is tough like that.

A scan of my combat logs and a little math showed Roshan's low-level healing-over-time spell was operating at the cap-per-tick, which meant she was out-leveling the spell. While a higher-level spell would create more powerful heals, the capped status of the lesser spell meant heal-over-time ticks were generating more critical heals. Flash Heal was also ticking up, and judging by its description, she still had room to work before she reached the maximum with any consistency. Maybe a couple levels.

At the end of the third wave of wrath fiends, my experience bar was mere inches from filling. Priya was only a tick behind me.

While the halls kept straight despite their roughly excavated stone walls, they also grew shorter as the ceiling bore down on us. Sharp turns made for bad sight lines. A veteran of more tactical games than I could name, I taught everyone who wasn't named Guiles how to "slice the pie"—to take the forks at a wide, rounded angle with weapons at the ready.

During one of those turns, I spied a faint movement and analyzed the area.

Corrupted Corpse
Level 21 Undead
(*elite*)

This inky stretch of hallway was void of the torches lining the walls at intervals behind us. I sliced the pie, bow at the ready, and two tiny glowing orbs blinked to life in the distance. At first, I thought they might be gems or glass set in a far door. Then they blinked. My mind flashed with memory of the first time I met Priya when she'd been in a dim underground tunnel under the control of a dark caster.

A banging sound reminded me of a screen door at my grandparents' place in Iowa when they'd failed to thread the hook through the metal eye to secure it before retiring for the night. I focused on those urine-colored glowing orbs.

Corrupted Corpse
Level 21 Undead
(elite)

These guardians are the undead remnants of adventurers who braved the depths of the Plague Barrens and failed in their quest. Their souls imprisoned by an evil presence upon falling, their bodies are left to wander the halls in defense of their dark lord's territory.
Strength: 17
Dexterity: 9
Intelligence: 4
Wisdom: 2
Constitution: 19
Charisma: 3

"Inner Illumination, Gemini," Roshan whispered.

I nodded and cast the spell, lighting up the hallway before me. The corrupted corpse sauntered in our direction. An open wound that would never close streaked across its forehead to reveal dried purple flesh beneath. The surrounding facial skin was white with cracked black wrinkles. A single tuft of hair streamed down from the crown of its skull and swept against the back of its hunched shoulders. It sneered as it banged the pommel of a one-handed sword against a buckler.

"I think it's trying to intimidate us," I whispered.

My group's expressions didn't signify intimidation. To the contrary, they looked poised, ready to pounce.

As the zombie banged the shield again, I nudged Desini with my elbow. "Well, I guess we found you a shield. All you have to do is pry it from his cold, dead fingers."

Desini's attention shifted to the buckler. One side of her lips perked up, revealing two sharp cuspids. Her green irises shone with resolve as she marched forward, sword clutched in a white-knuckled grip.

"Come, stinking undead wretch. Let us release your soul to the nethers."

"Yes!" Roshan barked in her warm, low voice. "Let us cast this prisoner's soul into the light of Solara's bosom!"

If they'd checked our adversary in their inspection panes and missed where it said this minion's soul was captive elsewhere, I could take that as another example of how their interfaces lacked when compared to mine.

I raised my bow as Desini's silver plate clanked down the hallway and leveled the tip of my arrow on the undead's nose. I wouldn't fire until it rose after Desini used her Charge ability and slammed it to the ground, but it never hurt to gauge the distance early.

The undead threw a wrench into the machinery when it charged and slammed Desini to the ground, instead. Then it stepped back and pounded its buckler, taunting her from above while blocking our way forward.

"Oh, shit!" The part of me that had been a long-time

gamer rose to the surface as I laughed. "Damn, girl! You gonna let that punk lay you out like that?"

Desini shot me one of those incisor-revealing snarls usually reserved for our enemies before turning her attention back to the corrupted corpse. "Make light if it makes you feel superior, master, but be sure to stand well away from the conflict so as not to get your soft body bruised." The mishon cast me a final glance revealing every ivory tooth in a wide, gaping smile.

We were having fun now.

The undead's sneer vanished as it peered at me, then back at Desini. The way it stepped forward, I didn't think it appreciated the lack of seriousness in our demeanor. Its weapon swung down in a high arc.

Desini raised her sword and parried the strike, then swept her legs to one side and clipped the ankles of the white-skinned undead warrior. It thumped hard on one shoulder and dust puffed into the air.

I was duly impressed.

My tank rolled backward then sprang to her feet. She slammed her sword down into the buckler over and over as her victim struggled to reach its feet, her screams of fury matching the rhythm of her blade as it clanked on the shield.

Guiles slid up the hallway and took up the position on the other side of the elite monster, but he couldn't engage until Desini stopped banging on the beast long enough for it to rise and give the rogue a target. Guiles smiled and nodded. I returned it.

Yeah, I like her, too.

Taking a tactic from her playbook, the corrupted corpse kicked Desini's ankle and caused her to stumble backward. The distraction allowed it to struggle to its feet. It raised the buckler and banged it with its sword pommel again, urging Desini forward.

The cat-like tank shook her head.

She banged her chest piece with one fist. "Come to me, you stench-filled hunchback of rot!"

"Aaaarrrrr!" the undead bellowed.

Over Desini's head, jostling red text appeared.

Provoked!

Uh-oh.

Now we had mobs who provoked us! Gods, I loved this game.

Life.

Whatever.

As she closed the short distance, sword raised high, the undead's lips spread into a sneer. It crouched and drew back its blade to strike. The zombie had drawn Desini easily with the ire-inducing ability she'd used on countless mobs. And the way she charged forward with her weapon overhead, I worried the creature would run her through.

Guiles exploded into action, slamming his dagger into the corrupted corpse's back. Its plan foiled, the undead soldier jolted out of its hunched position. But then it lurched forward and thrust its weapon out so the sword disappeared behind Desini's charging form for a split second, then my tank's back ripped open and the blade reemerged covered in syrupy crimson.

Her tail shot up in the air and went stiff as she tumbled. Blood splattered onto the floor beneath.

Critical Hit!
Desini

-320 HP

The massive damage cut Desini's health in half. As the sword slid from her gut and the corrupted corpse drew it back, a wide smile crossed its face as it glared down at her.

"Dah!" it growled. "Dah! Dah! Dah!" It banged the shield with each utterance.

The mishon's hands clutched her wound, and her sword rattled to the floor.

(Bleed)
-37 HP

She struggled, sitting half way up then dropping back down. A second try proved equally fruitless. I'd never seen the likes of this in a game, either. The undead had severed her abdominals.

Roshan casts Flash Heal on Desini.
+47 HP

Nice, but not nearly enough. If I didn't do something, Desini was a sitting duck.

"Ah!" I bellowed as I loosed a half-charged arrow. It slammed into the creature's shoulder and exploded, driving it two steps back.

You use Exploding Arrow.

Corrupted Corpse
-36 HP
- 4 HP (fire)
-4 HP (fire)

Guiles seized the opportunity. He vanished, reappeared in front of the undead, then unloaded a barrage of dagger strikes.

Guiles activates Combat Flurry.

The blades ripped across the creature's chest and solar plexus in a blur of furious punches. The corrupted corpse jerked and convulsed with each motion as the elf pounded its torso like a middleweight boxer punching the breath out of his opponent—except with blades.

He's blocking the undead's access to her.

A white glow surrounded Desini, and the blood flowing from her midsection slowed from a pour to a dribble. Roshan's hands glowed gold as she prepared a follow-up heal.

I nocked an arrow as Desini crossed an arm over her wound and struggled to her feet, grunting pain with each motion, her breath catching in her throat. Then she was bathed in a second white light as I loosed another arrow. It sailed wide as the undead dodged one of Guiles's attacks and removed itself from my arrow's line of flight.

The guardian swept its sword wide and caught Guiles on the hip. Blood splattered and streaked the far wall. He stumbled sideways despite his capped dexterity, but he threw up his forearm to catch himself on the stony bulkhead.

So, he's not perfect. Shocker!

The corrupted corpse's sword was already coming around for the next strike.

"Ahhhh!" Desini bellowed and text appeared over the undead's head.

Provoke!

"Payback's a bitch, mother fucker!" I yelled, sending yellow energy into my hand for a Drilling Arrow.

Critical Hit!

Corrupted Corpse
-39 HP

I felt like such a wimp. I nocked another arrow, prepared a Perforating Arrow, and fired. Again, I missed. My lack of accuracy was pissing me off. Where I'd effortlessly picked off fiends earlier, I was hitting at a rate of one-out-of-three on this elite bastard.

Mechanics! Since the mob was a higher-level elite, my accuracy suffered like it would in any other game. No matter how I practiced my archery, there would be penalties in my ability to hit. I'd just gotten to where I thought of Enora as a real place, where my muscle memory instead of my mind controlled the outcomes. But this wasn't Earth! If I wanted more accuracy, I needed to reach higher levels and to increase my ranged weapon and bow skills. It was all a question of figuring out what was treated like reality, and what mechanics would function like a game.

I refocused and nocked another arrow just as an explosion slammed into the elite bastard.

Priya casts Flash Fire.

Corrupted Corpse
-31 HP

That was in tune with what I was doing for damage but her strike wasn't even a critical hit. In fact, I knew that was the max damage that spell could do without a critical, so the fact she'd burned the elite for that much damage was fantastic, especially since she was the lower level. But as the realization struck that I was surrounded by NPCs who were more efficient than the player in the equation, I felt like an inadequate wuss. It was time to focus.

The monster's health was just above fifty percent. I loosed another arrow and connected with its neck, but it paid me no mind as Desini had reengaged, gathered its ire, and shoved at its buckler, her face burning red. The lower half of her back under the midriff-revealing armor was smooth again, but when I checked my party window, I found Roshan's mana pool at less than half.

She'd done a good portion of the work needed to get Desini to her feet, but it had cost her. The blue bar ticked infinitesimally as I counted off a few seconds. I made a mental note to focus points on her wisdom to speed that up.

All this detail you focus on is why you aren't doing enough damage! Focus!

Guiles's ghostly form pushed away from the wall, sliding behind the creature. I allowed myself a quick glance at Roshan. A sheen of sweat covered her forehead while she readied another heal for Desini. The strain of her constant outpouring of magic showed in the taut skin of her forehead and the jutting knobs on either side of her jaw.

I loosed another arrow, stepped toward her and leaned in. "Breathe deeply, Roshan. Remember what Zhara showed you in the Dark Wood. Be calm."

"Away from me, noob. I am trying to keep our defender on her feet, and you stand limp like an old man!"

Damn!

"Right." I held my position next to her and readied another strike.

A flash of fire exploded in front of the corrupted corpse's white face, and this time the dried flesh on its cheeks wrinkled and blistered. A sneer rose on its lips as its eyed Priya before returning its focus to Desini.

"Hold, Priya!" I ordered.

Priya lowered her hands and waited without a word, but her curled lips and the emotions pouring onto me from her showed she wanted to burn that motherfucker to the ground for what he'd done to Desini.

I charged and loosed a Perforating Arrow. It slammed into the monster's temple with a green flash, and I knew I'd landed a critical before I even glanced to the bottom center of my translucent interface.

Critical Hit!

Corrupted Corpse
-56 HP

Hey, that was a little more like it. The corrupted corpse had dropped to about forty percent of its total health.

Its gaze twitched toward me, back to Desini, then at me again.

"Don't try it, you blistering boil of death's stink!" Desini growled.

The corrupted corpse slammed its buckler up and into Desini's face, causing her to falter backward as it turned and charged toward the back line of attackers. Toward me, in particular.

Guess I did enough damage to piss it off!

Text appeared above Desini's head.

Stunned!

She wouldn't be able to rend the bastard and slow it down until she could growl at it again. It was coming, and it was coming fast.

"Priya! Ice Storm!"

My dark caster readied the spell as I jogged backward to create some distance. A blue meter appeared above her head and emptied as she channeled the spell. It would take a second for the frost effect to take hold—assuming the elite didn't resist.

Ten feet.

I took another lunging step backward.

Five feet.

Pellets of ice tattered dead white skin, and pops of blue frost glimmered in its rotted flesh as its movement speed declined.

"Spread out!" I barked to Roshan and Priya. Reaching my free hand behind my back, I gripped one of my daggers but left it sheathed so I wouldn't change classes unless I had to. The last thing I wanted was to kick off a global cool down and end up with just a blade and no abilities. But then, as if a voice spoke inside my head, I remembered a gift given to me by Zhara, Matron of the Wood and protector of the Tree of Solara.

Nature magic!

I relaxed my grip on the dagger and raised my hand as a glow bloomed around my fingers. Just as the undead warrior raised his sword to strike at me, three things happened.

First, my Vine Entrapment spell sprung up from the floor, sending shards of stone flying into the air as the green tendrils wrapped around its legs.

Second, a bellowing howl echoed down the hallway as

Desini growled, forcing the undead to turn and peer over its shoulder at her.

Third, Guiles exploded into action, stabbing with both of his long, curved daggers.

The guardian howled in anger as the elf dropped to his knees and ripped the daggers down either side of its decrepit spine. Desini zoomed across the space and swung from high overhead, lodging her blade into the corrupted corpse's forehead. It creaked as she struggled to wrench it free from the dead bone, then fire exploded in front of the monster's face and melted the flesh to the skull underneath.

My tank's sword came free, and she raised it for a final blow. With an effort, the beast raised its buckler to block, and in the poorest timing ever, Desini activated Swipe to finish the bastard off.

The buckler cracked and rattled to the ground in multiple, shattered pieces. So much for getting Desini a shield.

"Dammit!" I yelled.

The undead wavered in a circle on its feet.

Guiles stood straight again, leveled his daggers on either side of its neck and raised his lips to its ears. "Return to Solara now, brave adventurer, and find comfort in the bosom of the giver of life." With a wide back-handed swipe, Guiles crossed his blades through the center of the monster's neck and separated its head from its body, which crumbled to the ground like a sack of stones.

Weapons were sheathed and long breaths expelled. We all dropped to our asses to recover, except for Priya, who nudged my hip with her boot and thrust her hands onto her hips.

"You didn't think entangling some of these monsters might have proven useful?"

"I'm not a spell caster. It didn't occur."

"Some *Shénhuà*, you are." She rapped on my forehead with her knuckles, and I couldn't help but smile.

"What do you people think the Shénhuà are? I'm just a dude."

Roshan leaned back on her hands. "*Shénhuà* are a race wiped from the face of Enora eons ago. The scriptures of my people claimed they would return to bring light back into the world and fight for the meek."

"I believe your people derive their scriptures from a more ancient race, Roshan." Guiles smiled. "Namely, Elven Kind."

"Bah!" Roshan said with a dismissive wave. "I see the reputed egos of the 'Elven Kind' are well-reported. Believe what you will, pointy ears." She winked at him.

"But Gemini is not just *Shénhuà*," *Guiles continued, unabated.* "He is what my lore calls the *traveler*. The legend of the traveler is that he or she would come and clear the way for the coming of more *Shénhuà*. If the prophecy is true, this separates him from the rest of the mystics. You are the forebear of a bright future filled with mystics, Gemini."

This aligned with my earlier quest text. My destiny, revealed. It would've been nice if I had any say in it. I could slap Nokuro for that grand omission. The longer I spent in this world, the more I learned things weren't what they seemed.

Enora has built my custom storyline so that I come and prepare the way for the other players because Infinity Designs screwed the pooch with another player.

"I see," was all I said.

Roshan shook her head. "You cannot see. None of us can know Solara's will until it is upon us. We might only serve."

Trust me, I see. I see just fine. Clear as day. All the talk of non-interference in the world, as-built, was a crock, as proven by the existence of my preset narrative. I might have free will to do what I want, but Zhara, Roshan, Priya... it was all convenient, at the least. All preparation for me to clean up someone's mess.

"Right. Solara. Gotcha."

"Your faith will grow as you expand your understanding of the Light." The eastern priestess squeezed my leg. "In the meantime, I'm refreshed and feel ready to go forth and smite the next demon scum you place before me."

She rose. Guiles smiled at me.

"You attract the most interesting companions, but something told me Solara had a hand in it."

"Your intuition is no joke, elf dude. I'd say she had a huge hand in it."

"Now my love speaks with faith!" Roshan raised her staff high. "Come, there are enemies to vanquish, and I wish to bathe my skin in the sunlight again in this lifetime."

After a nice long gander at her femininely muscular legs, I rose to find Guiles staring at me in what I thought expressed derision.

"What?"

The elf shook his head and turned to follow Roshan and Desini down the hall.

13

Lava Beetle? What the hell is a—

A scent akin to sulfur burned my nostrils as the low beast scampered across the dim side room we'd wandered into. Its feet clicked the stone floors in a speedy rattle, and I could barely make out its black form as it closed.

Desini raised her sword to brace for an attack. Then its jowls parted, and the ridges in the roof of its mouth glowed to light the space in front of it. An orange ember the size of a basketball lobbed from its throat and painted a tracer across the black background. Our tank spun away, but the lava ball splashed onto her pommel hand and droplets rained to the floor, burning holes in the stone.

"Ah!" Desini screamed in agony. The mishon clutched her wrist with her uninjured hand while embers ate through the flesh and burned the bones beneath to black ash. Her sword clattered to her feet as her powdered fingers broke up and drifted to the floor like she'd tapped burning cigarettes.

Desini shrieked another high-pitched wail and, after an initial cringe, the horrifying sound urged me forward.

Screw aggro!

I notched an arrow and fired. The arrow bounced harmlessly off silver stripes crossing the creature's carapace.

"Go! Go! Go!" I ordered. "Light it up!"

Guiles vanished in a cloud of purple-and-black smoke and reappeared behind the eight-foot-long beetle. As he readied his daggers for attack, my lips parted to share my intel about the exoskeleton-covering shell. But when he reappeared, he crouched and shoved his dagger beneath the posterior side of the natural armor, right in the beetle's soft backside. The shells unfolded as if the beast would fly away, and if not for Desini's howling, I might have laughed at the idea I would advise an elf who so outclassed me.

When the shell spilt up the middle and the halves fluttered into the air like wings, it served only to open access to the meaty flesh beneath. Pus bubbled around two new slits as the elf took advantage of the opening. Scurrying in a circle quicker than I'd thought possible, the beetle lunged at the rogue. Guiles flashed purple and his body swiveled at the waist in a blur, dodging the incoming melee attacks of the creature's hard, jointed front legs.

Guiles employs Spirt Dance
Evasion +15%

White light surrounded Desini as she glared at her cauterized stump. Porous bone threaded outward from the wrist to reform her hands and fingers. Blood vessels crept across it like serpents. Then skin weaved across the tendrils like liquid that solidified behind the wave.

That shit was gross.

Though tears streamed from down her cheeks, Desini wasted no time in snatching her weapon and lunging forward with a growl.

The beetle swung around, but the nerves Guiles severed in its back caused it to tilt to one side. A glow emanated from its throat as its jowls opened for another lava attack.

This time, Desini bent over backward and balanced herself with a touch of her free hand to the stone behind her, and the fiery ball splashed harmlessly to the floor beyond.

Since MOBs with fire attacks often enjoyed resistances against the element, I set aside thoughts of my Exploding Arrow and opted for a Drilling Arrow. The projectile split the beast's pus-filled flesh just before the shells slammed back down. The lodged arrow snapped in half, but its damage was done.

Lightning flashed from above as a deafening crackle filled the air. Three arcs of hot electricity zipped down. The beast's right eye sizzled, then melted sclera oozed from the wound. My party loved popping eyeballs.

Priya started a new cast right on the heels of the Thunder spell.

Yeah, burn this bitch down!

Desini swept up from her backbend, her forward momentum swinging her like a catapult. She sliced the silvery edge of her blade down and across the beast's jowls.

The beetle shook its head furiously. Clicking sounds emanated from its throat.

With a short step backward, our tank drew the pommel across her chest as she twisted, showing the beetle her profile, then lunged, ramming the full length of the sword down its throat.

Her cheeks burned rosy with hatred just inches from the beast's. She twisted the sword, shoving her arms into its jowls to plunge her blade good and deep.

In a well-timed show of her new offensive skills, Roshan sent an arc of curving white light slamming into the beast's temple.

Roshan casts Smite!

Lava Beetle
-17 HP

The beetle's shells rose and fell again as its health dropped to thirty percent.

I clinched my teeth, squinted, then loosed an arrow that slammed into the creature's neck just beneath the tip of the hard shell above.

"Nice shot!" Priya exclaimed as she curled her fingers into claws.

Lighting tagged the beetle, rippling across its shell as Priya's Pulse spell made contact. Though I'd expected it to have little effect, electrical fingers of light strobed across the carapace and caused the beast to convulse. Its health dropped to fifteen percent.

"Nice shot, yourself!"

"Thank you!" She dropped her hands to her sides, then her lips moved silently. I realized she was counting off her cast times so as not to draw aggro. My throat swelled with pride.

I readied another arrow, but then the rogue drew my attention. In a flurry of motion, his daggers ripped and sliced across the beetle's face.

The heavy beast thumped to the floor. A streak of lumpy, black blood ejected from its bowels.

Ugh. Nice touch, Enora.

A golden flash surrounded Roshan, and she clapped her hands in front of her like an excited child being told they were going to Disney.

As we sheathed our weapons, I circled the beast.

Lava Beetle
Level 21 Bug Corpse
(Elite)
These subterranean beasts of the Coleopteran family are known for fiery orange lava that ejects from ducts in their throats.
Strength: o
Dexterity: o
Intelligence: o
Wisdom: o
Constitution: o
Charisma: o

Desini grasped her wrist and flexed the finger joints of her replenished hand.

"That must have hurt." That was easily the worst understatement I'd uttered since coming to Enora.

The mishon squinted. "Do you think, master? Perhaps you should reach down its throat and see if you can replicate the sensation. You should really experience the full effect."

I lurched forward and clutched her breastplate. "Are you okay?"

Her eyelids relaxed at half-mast. "Yes, master. I am a mishon. A tough woman. Allow me a few minutes to recover my mental bearing."

"Life at the front can suck." I spun on my heels, then paused and turned back to peer down at the hard carapace. "Wait a second. Priya, can you come over here?"

The half-elf, who'd already settled herself on the floor next to Roshan to recuperate, raised her gaze. "Why? I'm refilling my mana."

"It will refill. Please get up."

Guiles appeared at my side and followed my gaze. I pointed at the line where the beetle's shell split and traced it in the air with my fingertip. "Do you see what I see?"

Though I'd been addressing Guiles, Priya answered. "I see beetle droppings. I claim no fondness for the odor, either. Perhaps we should rest in the hall."

Guiles smirked at her.

I shook my head and reached into my bag, withdrawing the two skinning knives I'd purchased in Warrington. I wiggled them between my thumbs and fingers.

"I'm not going near that thing," Priya said. "If you want to try to get skin from a shell, you go right ahead."

"Genius," Guiles added. He nodded approval with his arms folded across his chest. "Truly inspired, Gemini."

I offered a knife by the handle. "I assume someone of your renown has high skinning skills?"

"Considering the extensive detail of your interface, you should already know this, *Shénhuà*. Perhaps you should pull your head from whatever dark cloud hinders your sense and become familiar."

"I'm a genius. I'm a distracted idiot. You're making me dizzy, Master Guiles."

Accepting the knife, he worked with me to pry shell away from the underlying, brainy flesh. Holding it vertical with each of us grasping one side, we nodded in unison and squatted to scan the place where shell attached to muscle. His blade sliced away at the sinew, and I mimicked the motion as best I could, but my clumsy hands reflected my low skill level, requiring much more trimming. But to my utter satisfaction, my skinning skill advanced twice.

Occupational Skills:

Not to be confused with combat professions, occupational skills allow people to earn a wage, run a business, or create weapons, armor, and potions to supplement adventuring.

Skinning: 19

Rank: Apprentice

Tool tip: Skinners strip hides from vanquished animal beings —and sometimes humanoid ones—to be used as raw materials by leather workers, clothiers, blacksmiths and other professions. Tanning is often selected by skinners as a secondary occupation to create leathers.

To remind myself, I checked the rankings.

Occupation Levels

Beginner: Levels 1-10
Apprentice: Levels 11-20
Adept: Levels 21-30
Journeyman: Levels 31-40
Expert: Level 41-50
Master: 51-60
Grand Master: 61+

Two more ranks and I'd be a journeyman! Though it was my lone occupational skill thus far, the rewarded skill points spawned brief fantasies of sweating over a forge, pounding metal with a hammer to shape it, and working a loom. Crafting had been my jam in Light of Babylon, but here it would take on a different meaning and require more realistic effort.

When we finished the job, I tested the shell's weight and smiled. Then I held it out as Guiles stepped next to me. He nodded and scanned the oblong carapace from top to bottom.

"I spied the reflection of a fountain's waters around the corner at the end of the hall." He peered over his shoulder. "Sister Priya, when did you last slumber?"

Priya shrugged. "Last night. Why?"

Instead of answering her, he spoke to me. "Perhaps we will rest near the fountain for a while. Priya and I can work while the rest of you sleep, and perhaps I can serve another purpose."

"What purpose is that?"

"My kind take the study of history seriously. I assume Priya would enjoy learning how the City of Ninn above us came to be a desert of black sand, and I'd hoped a discussion about our shared heritage might be to her liking."

Tiny dimples dipped in her angular cheeks as her lips ticked up on either side. She pushed a wave of excitement my way.

Though I suspected she was coming to terms with Zhara's reasoning for taking her back into the wood to protect her during the mage purge of almost fifty years earlier, her mother's decision to keep Priya at arm's length to ensure she didn't remember her past left a hole I often sensed across our Elven bond. It wasn't until Guiles's offer spurned the exhilaration she sent across the airwaves that I realized the source of that emotional gap. Priya wanted to know herself and her people.

Since she'd learned her true identity and the impact

she'd once had on the world at the university in Warrington, a new hunger had risen. Where Zhara kept her distance, Guiles offered an opportunity to learn and, by proxy, kinship.

"That sounds amazing." I clapped him on the shoulder. "Maybe I'll listen in."

To this, Guiles shook his head. "Humans and the mishon need sleep. Elves can go days without, even more when we age. Let us stand watch and, with your leave, I will bond with my new sister. The two of us can work on this idea of your yours." He tapped the shell.

"I fucking love it."

"How you rejoice while using modifiers showing discontent confuses me." He shook his head.

Roshan, Desini, and I snuggled together on the furs withdrawn from my bag. I enjoyed the warmth from either side as I slept in the middle. The mishon spooned me. Though I was utterly surprised, I enjoyed her warmth without a word.

Before we hit the furs, I withdrew the undead warrior's leather armor scraps from my bag and tossed them to Guiles and Priya, who sat on either side of the beetle shell across the fountain from us. The crystal blue waters reflected off the jagged stone ceiling and, when coupled with the low sound of Guiles's voice, alleviated my tension.

We'd seen a crazy amount of battle that day and, other than a few flaws, we'd kept the party in decent shape. We'd faced trials with skin rot and the lava beetle melting Desini's hand with a direct hit, but we'd come through otherwise unscathed.

After what had happened to Desini, I suspected NPCs

experienced suppressed pain. There was no way she could otherwise have experienced the disintegration of her hand and recovered so quickly, unscathed. I'd have passed out. It was also possible there was pain mitigation when inside the dungeon.

We'd looted no coin thus far, and that was disappointing. The sword dropped by the Corrupted Soul had been of common quality, but Roshan had drooled over the ruby in the hilt. That was a good sign. She assured me she could separate it without damage and insisted I not inspect it, so she could surprise me with the results. Her giddy demeanor was so uncommon, I readily agreed.

Before I drifted off, I recalled fantasies about learning new skills moments earlier. Then impatience crept through my brain as I considered all the lessons I'd yet to learn in this world. Roshan knew gems. They all knew how to cook. They all had experience with forestry. There were several professions split between them. I knew jack shit outside of game mechanics and combat strategy—and I didn't always prove proficient at either.

But in unshared skills, I also sensed an opportunity. I felt like a kid at a candy counter with the foundation stone burning a hole in my pocket like a silver dollar. The prospect that they could teach each other skills—and eventually educate me—cast light upon my dark thoughts and delivered me to the warm grasp of sleep, despite being in a dungeon beneath one of the most dangerous places on the continent.

14

Every sharp tooth showed as our statuesque tank ran two fingers along a line dividing black and silver areas of the beetle shell. A silvery reflection gleamed in one eye. It was the first time I'd ever seen someone cry with joy over a piece of equipment, yet it was understandable. I almost joined in upon reading the new message in my HUD.

Congratulations, G3m1n1 Fowler!
You have invented a shield!
Shield of the Lava Beetle
Level 18
Fashioned from the shell of a lava beetle, this shield is known for its very high fire resistance.
Type: Shield
Slot: Off-hand
Quality: Very Rare
Can be crafted
Durability: 100 of 100
+80% fire resist

Crafted by Guiles Renard
Invented by G3m1n1 Fowler
As the inventor of this creation, you own exclusive rights over the blueprints. To develop blueprints for sale to other players, NPCs, or at a trading facility, visit an architect's table or build one.
What other inventions might you develop?

I almost jumped out of my boots. Invention? Exclusive rights? Holy shit! Although Guiles had constructed the armored shell, Enora granted me credit for its concept. Fantasies about wealth and the economic impacts on Enora flooded my brain. When I considered the prices and rarity of shields, I could make some serious coin when players someday flooded Enora. Then again, how many people would fight these things just to get the shell and forge the shield?

Shit.

I was drawn back to the present when Guiles tapped the grooves in the front of the shield.

"Priya and I cut two slits near the tip and two near the bottom, here."

"Yes, your hammering racket woke me," Roshan said.

"Funny," I interjected. "I slept right through it. I guess being wedged warm and cozy between beautiful women will do that."

Desini nudged me with her elbow and blushed. Roshan smirked.

Guiles continued. "After stripping and smoothing the leather straps we fashioned from the undead warrior's armor, we fed them through the slits and crossed them. I sewed an arm grip where they intersect in the center. Desini can slide her forearm in and pull here to tighten it."

Desini clapped her hands. "My enemies will fall beneath the fury of my Charge skill for sure, now!"

I chuckled. "They certainly will. And look, it's tall, so it gives you plenty of protection, while not obstructing your view over the top."

Desini threw her arms around Priya and kissed her.

"I don't know why you're kissing me." She cocked her head toward Guiles. "He's the one who did most of the work."

The mishon stepped toward Guiles. "Now that we are companions, might I thank you in the way of my people, master?"

"If it involves kissing me—"

Too late. Desini slammed her lips to Guiles's and sucked so the kiss made a smacking sound when she let go.

Guiles ran his sleeve across his lips and nodded. "Well, then. You're welcome, Desini."

When I sat on the edge of the fountain to check my arrow count and tighten the cord on my bow, cool sensations crossed my flesh and drew my focus toward the blue waters siphoning up the crystal tubes where it recycled into tiny water falls. "Is it me, or does this thing boost the spirit?"

"It recharges Spirit, though at a much slower rate," Guiles informed me.

"Slower what? No, I meant it makes me feel better, gives me energy." My head swiveled in a classic double take. "Wait! Is Spirit actually a thing?"

His smile suggested I was but a babe in the woods. The pause grated on my nerves because I was impatient to hear whatever he was about to wax on about.

"Spirit is another resource pool received at level twenty, just like energy for rogues and fury for some tanks."

"Fury. I like the sound of this," Desini said, though her

gaze continued its endeared trek up, down, and across the breadth of her new plaything.

Guiles raised a single finger. "But it is a very different pool. All adventurers received it and Spirit affects each individual differently. My kind believe it to be the truest representation of Solara's energy. Abilities discovered through it can be cast once per day. But they empty the pool and spirit is slow to recover."

"So, they have a twenty-four-hour cooldown? What kinds of abilities?"

Guiles drew out his words as if I was dense. "Again, it depends on the person. You cannot buy scrolls or learn spirit abilities by leveling as an adventurer. Instead, you must meditate and learn to clear your mind so you might receive Solara's gifts. You will receive one unique ability and can learn other lesser skills as you level." His head cocked back. "I wager your gifts will be great."

That bore promise.

"Anyway, you receive twenty Spirit at Level 20 and gain one Spirit per level. The higher you level, the more Spirit you receive."

"More meditation, huh?" I hated the idea already, but I liked the potential for more abilities.

"You say that as if you swing a scythe from your tongue. Trust me, your gains will be well worth quieting your busy mind, mystic."

"I'll take your word for it. And you can bet your Elven ass that I'll take you up on it when I hit Level 20."

"Wager accepted."

I ignored his strange humor. "So, is everyone ready to go kick more ass?" I eyed my XP bar. "I'm itching to finish off this level, and I have about a cunt hair left."

"Wretched!" Roshan barked.

"Foul!" Priya agreed.

"Master!" Desini chided.

Guess that word holds equal weight in Enora.

"I apologize for my vulgarity." I bowed my head, but when I looked up, the three women had already strode off toward the next magic barrier.

"Truly," Roshan was muttering. "That such a blessed creature would use such…"

Her voice trailed off. Guiles shook his head. "Much to learn, indeed."

On the other side of the barrier, the dungeon changed. Gone were the stone walls, replaced by narrower, circular tunnels carved into the earth. The scent of mud filled the air. It reminded me of the place where Roshan and I had rescued Priya from the dark caster Crohl—and his master, the demon underlord, Caym. I wondered what demon lord might have carved out this little piece of Hades, but my wonderment was soon replaced by a slithering sound as we came to a recessed area on the right.

I couldn't tell if it was a room or a hallway. If the latter, it was a wide one. So wide, I dismissed the idea almost out-of-hand, though it was impossible to tell for the gray mist filling the area.

When I heard slithering, I thought, *snake.*

I did *not* like snakes.

The four of us stood staring at the mist in a row, Guiles and Roshan with their hands on their hips, Priya and Desini with their fingers interlocked between them.

"That sounds promising," Guiles said.

"What? You know what it is?" I asked.

"No idea. But it moves, which means it can be killed, which means at least two and likely three of you will level when we're finished mutilating it."

Someone's paying attention.

"Sound logic," I said, hopefully without a discernible lack of confidence.

"Agreed," Desini said. "Now, how do I see it so that I might run it through?"

Guiles peered up at her and stretched his lips into a toothless grin. "Another benefit of having an accomplished rogue in your party is reconnaissance. I'll have a look first, lady mishon"

"I am no lady," my sexy cat-like beast-of-a-woman replied.

"Oh, yes," I muttered low as I watched her tail wag above her rock-hard bottom. "You most certainly are."

Desini's ears perked up atop her head. I'd forgotten her magnified hearing. I cringed at my carelessness. Peering over her shoulder at me, she slid the tip of her tongue past her teeth.

"Contain your urges, beast." She shimmied her backside and slapped my nose with the soft tuft of hair at the end of her tail.

Umm...

"Please proceed, Master Guiles." Priya released the mishon's hand and threw me a look over her shoulder. "For-ever, your mind in your pants."

So, she'd heard it, too. I made a mental note to relegate my base urges to the silent voice inside my head.

Guiles glanced back and forth between us, shook his head in derision for what had to have been the thousandth time since we entered the place, then activated stealth. His ghostly form crossed the threshold and disappeared into the mist.

The hallway's dead silence reminded me of the high overlooks on the Blue Ridge Parkway in the Appalachian

Mountains, where my parents took me as a kid. But this was eerie. The thick, prominent slithers in that fog were the lone sound against the quiet void.

The slithering stopped. Silence dominated. The women crowded together, and Desini unsheathed her sword. I threw a hand gesture at Roshan and Priya to draw them back from our tank then shrugged my bow off my shoulder. I whispered, "Maybe we should take a step—"

"Ahhhh!" A tentacle flew out of the mist and uncoiled, tossing our rogue over our heads and into the wall behind us as his arms flailed.

We all stepped back, but then a tentacle slipped around my ankle and yanked me to the ground.

"Oh shiiiiiiiiit!" I yelled, reaching back to grasp for anything I could grab ahold of in the hall. Just before I passed into the cloudy blindness of the mist, the three women slid their feet away from my clawing hands, each diverting their gazes toward the ceiling as they stepped away.

I'll be a son of a bitch!

"I believe our rogue is unconscious," Desini said from somewhere on the other side of the foggy threshold as the beast pulled me in.

"Mm, seems so," Priya said. "Ideas?"

As I was dragged across the packed earth, my knuckles scraped the earthen floor beneath. That made it hell to unsheathe my daggers, but I eventually yanked them free.

*You have changed your class to **Assassin**.*
Global Cool-down: 30 Seconds

Global cool-down be damned, I would not let this thing do—well, whatever it did—to me. As I slid against my will, the cold surface scratching the lower part of my exposed back where my armor and shirt rode up, I conjured the scariest image I could imagine, involving something slimy with a gaping mouth of many teeth.

I didn't want to feel teeth. Re-spawning too many times could drive a motherfucker crazy with undesired memories. Forget the resurrection sickness that would grow longer in duration each time. So, I strained my abs to sit up and slid on my ass instead of my back. Then I began to stab at the tentacle wrapped around my ankle.

Mist Lurker
Level 19 Cephalopod
(Elite)
Known for numerous strong tentacles, mist lurkers possess a gland that secretes a fog to shroud them from enemies.
Strength: 27
Dexterity: 21
Intelligence: 15
Wisdom: 2
Constitution: 20
Charisma: 1

At least its constitution wasn't outrageous, although so far, it seemed I'd be fighting it alone! Black blood splattered my arms as I took wild stabs and opened the slimy thing's veins beneath the thick amphibious skin. Though shivering consumed my body with disgust at the wretched thing, I stabbed and stabbed.

The bleeding tentacle raised my leg in the air. The back of my head banged into the packed earth, then my chest hollowed out as my body lifted off the ground. The mist cleared just enough for me to see a large white ball with a tiny purple area in its center. Gazing at it, wondering what it might be, I raised my blades.

Then it blinked.

"Ah!" I screamed and slammed my dagger into the massive eye. If anything, I was consistent.

An implosive roar sucked the air out of my ears. My skull shivered inside my head. Before I knew it, I careened through the cavern, blind to my flight path. I exploded out of the mist and over the heads of my party then slammed shoulder-first into the jagged wall before tumbling hard to the ground. The wind exploded out of my lungs, and I heaved for breath. My spine erupted in protest.

Roshan stepped close and pointed a clawed hand at me. It glowed white, and the warmth of her light spell infused me with healing magic. The women had their backs pressed to the wall, staring at the mist, weapons at the ready. Roshan rejoined them.

Guiles grunted as he got to his feet. Then he thought better of it, slid back to his duff, and leaned against the wall.

"Okay, so that just happened," I croaked.

"To both of us." Guiles peered at the women standing nearby. "Though it appears our companions would not meet the same fate."

"Yeah," I said. "Thanks for all your help."

"I healed you, noob," Roshan said. "What do you want of me?" She turned her nose up and looked away.

"I cast the icy spell," Priya said, "but then it occurred that I had nowhere to aim."

"Ha! Trust me, babe. Anywhere would've been fine. Anywhere would definitely have been better than nowhere."

"But you're always telling me to conserve my mana."

"That's a shitty excuse, and you know it."

She smiled. Roshan chuckled. Desini covered her mouth and turned away as her shoulders bounced.

"Insufferable bitches."

They roared laughter. Even Guiles joined in. "Credit them for their senses of self-preservation, my lord."

I chuckled a little, though I didn't want to. "So, who's going in next? Hmm? How about my brave mishon woman? You ready to put that shield to use?"

She shook her head. "I cannot block what I cannot see, master. Do you think me a fool?"

Priya nodded agreement. "Men. They flail blindly into the depths and think they can do whatever they want, with no thoughts as to the consequences."

"Hey! I flailed nowhere! It dragged me! And when I reached for help, where were you three?"

"Are we still discussing this?" Roshan asked. "You are the leader, no?" She eyed the other women and awaited agreement. Each nodded to provide it. To my surprise, Guiles shrugged and nodded with them. "So, devise a plan, leader. Shall we smite this beast, or will you sit on your backside complaining?"

"Grrrrr." I winked in succession and checked my abilities. If I'd been stupid enough to forget my Vine Entrapment spell earlier, maybe there was something else I overlooked. I opened the main page of my interface and eyed tabs, but it came to me before I found the one I'd end up using.

Pushing my back to the wall and rising, I raised my hand and focused my energy in front of me. My fingers glowed azure. The women stepped further away, and I sneered at them. I wasn't sure, but I thought I saw Guiles leaning in the opposite direction, as well.

Then my wolf faded into sight.

Guiles's jaw dropped. His head swiveled toward me, and he pushed himself up the wall. I got to my feet and held out my hand. The wolf came, and I scratched its head.

"Time to earn your keep, big man," I said.

The wolf yawned, sniffed the air, then turned to face the mist. A low growl emitted from its jowls.

"How is it you summon this beast when you have not even reached Level 20?" Guiles begged. "How does but a hunter, beast master, or a warlock summon companions?"

I smiled from one side of my mouth and threw him an exaggerated shrug. "Shit, fool. I learned that one at Level 2."

The taut flesh of his narrow cheeks glowed white as he pressed his lips together. His forehead turned pink. He growled his words through clinched teeth. "By Solara's grace and all that is holy in Enora!" Guiles turned and kicked the wall. Then he stomped further away and folded his arms. He kicked the wall again.

I watched in confusion for a few heartbeats. Even my wolf turned in wonderment with its head cocked to one side.

The elf wheeled and stomped back. "As your teacher, I will share the common tool of instruction. Are you ready to receive this wisdom, Lord Traveler?"

"Um, I guess s—"

He cuffed me on the side of my head.

I rubbed furiously at the offended spot near my temple and pressed my back into the wall. "Hey, what the shit?"

"You had a wolf this whole time, but you let me walk in there blind? Did Solara forget to add common sense when she constructed you from a dung beetle and dropped you in the forest?"

Roshan's chin ticked up. "Solara does not forget any—"

Her words ceased in her throat when Guiles shot a laser glare in her direction.

"Well, she didn't exactly drop me in the forest. I mean, I had to walk there but—"

He cuffed me again. A prompt popped up on my HUD.

Guiles has challenged you to a duel.
Do you accept?
Yes/No

"I get it." I held up an acquiescing hand.

"Accept." He wasn't asking.

"Guiles, seriously, you made your point. Thrashing me isn't going—"

"I am not trying to duel with you, cretin. I am showing you something important."

With a sigh, I accepted the duel. Guiles's eyes flashed red and a circle of light appeared beneath his feet, painted orange.

"Now that I have your attention, sass me once more so I might properly smite you."

Note to self, learn how to forfeit a duel.

I held little doubt the elf meant it. He gripped one dagger behind his back but made no effort to hide when he unsheathed it. This dude was a bad motherfucker. Which meant I'd better withdraw my head from my dark orifice.

"I'm taking over your group. You will promote me to leader. Additionally, I'm about to instruct you about how we will proceed from this moment forward and, until you are breathing fresh air again, you will obey. Nod your head."

I nodded, in awe. After all, this guy was an NPC. It was pretty incredible to think a non-player had such a robust personality, but even more so that I hadn't even thought about that facet of Enoran life in days.

"I will scan every inch of your interface and determine what skills you have and which I might not have noticed. We'll compare what I see to what you have. Then you will read aloud any tabs to which I have no access. While I admit this is partially my fault for not being as thorough as I should, it is time I recognize this situation for what it is. Roshan!"

Roshan shuffled over in a damn hurry. I hadn't seen her scurry like that since she rushed after the demons underground in the Dark Wood after receiving her first combat-based level. She bowed her head. "Yes, my lord elf."

"What is the word you used earlier to describe this fool traveler."

"Word, my lord?"

"The word used for new adventurer's and tradesmen by your culture."

"Ah!" she held up a finger. "Noob, my lord." She shot me a glance which I met with a head-lowering glare.

"Thank you," Guiles said. "Until we leave this place, I will call you noob."

"Wait just a—"

Guiles stabbed me in the temple.

Guiles attacks!
Mortal wound!
G3m1n1 Fowler
-350 HP
Guiles has defeated you in a duel.

The world erupted in white light as my body levitated, then I settled on my feet. My party encircled me. Each of the women held their heads low in reverence as the elf wiped my blood off his blade.

On my sleeve.

"That time, I made it quick. Next time, I will let you bleed a little while we continue our conversation. Now. Let us try again, Master Gemini."

Now I was mad, but as I stared into the eye slits of the Elven rogue, I realized I had no way out of this situation. Future players were in for a rude awakening when they encountered these non-players. But one thing they'd have that I didn't was the ability to log out.

Welcome to your life, son.

"Have you something to say?" Guiles asked, daring with his glare. "Your eyes shift in constant thought, as if you're distracted. Are you focused?"

My chin bobbed.

"Perhaps a drop of wisdom resides within, after all. Here's the plan. I will call out commands to our party. We will follow the strategies discussed throughout our conquest —*if* you can call a rag-tag bunch of amateurs stumbling over yourselves a conquest—and we will only vary from said strategies when I call for it. Priya!"

The half-elf jerked. "Yes, my lord?"

"What is your primary offensive spell?"

"It is Flash Fire, my lord."

"Good." He peered at me. "Priya knows her staple. Roshan!"

"Yes, my lord elf. My primary role is to heal. I will lead with my heal-over-time spell to prop up our lovely tank, then use Flash Heal as my primary tool to keep her pain at bay, that she might focus on vanquishing our foes. When a monster is at low health, I will use smite to... smite it, my lord."

"Good. Roshan knows her role." He cocked his chin toward Desini. "You have shown competence, so I will not insult you."

"Thank you, master."

His expression softened. "Solara saw fit to bring you before me in Brumhill. Long I waited for some sign from her. So, I had little doubt it was my duty to follow you and assist until you could stand on your own. But I know how a man's pride works. Especially a human man. Hence, I concealed myself from you. I saved you from your mistakes.

"Now, I will teach you how to stop making them. If you accept this tutelage, you will be made better for it. If you do not, you may dissolve our companionship, and I will be on my way. Answer."

Well, when he put it like that...

"I accept."

"Good. Call your blasted wolf."

15

The furry beast charged into the mist with a purpose, barking as it tried to gain the ire of the creature inside. Through the fog, the barking cycled around the room and grew in intensity. I could almost see the wolf dodging tentacles as they reached for him.

Guiles nudged my elbow. "Now. Call your animal."

"Yo, Wolfie!"

The barks grew louder, and the mass of hairy muscle charged out of the mist. We stood up the hallway, off to one side as the tentacles slid out of the fog. I readied my bow, and the party formed a semi-circle. Once the wolf had returned to me, it pivoted and growled low.

Tentacles filled the hallway. My beast lowered its head, eager to attack.

"Just wait, boy," I said. The beast didn't spare me a glance, but I was pretty sure he was listening.

Then we got our first look at the mist creature. Guiles plan had worked. Once we were out of reach of its tentacles, it had advanced into the hallway.

Covered in the same slimy, spotted skin as the tentacle that had grabbed my leg, one of the beast's giant eyes bled mucus down its front.

"Did you do that?" Guiles asked.

I nodded.

"Hmm. I underestimated you. I didn't even land a strike."

I didn't know if he was trying to reduce my animosity toward him or what, but I nodded again as I raised my bow, nocked an arrow, and held. The fact was, I'd been disappointing myself since I entered this world. It was a miracle I'd only died once. But it was in this moment that I realized my failures weren't because of my lack of capacity as a gamer. I failed because survival in Enora meant you couldn't treat it like a game.

"Yes, wait for it. Your target will be the other eye. I want to see... yes! Right there. Priya!?"

"Yes, brother?"

"Look beneath its foul head to where its neck would be if it weren't just one big ball of slime. Do you see the trickle?"

Priya leaned forward. "Yes! The mist seems to be spouting from tiny holes."

"Right. Desini will engage. Priya, when she angers our new enemy, aim your fire spell for those holes. Focus your energy on your targets to concentrate your power."

Desini's new shield slammed into the beast as she activated Charge. To my utter surprise, the mist creature fell back, but it recovered in a strangely agile twist of its slimy body then balanced on the bends in its tentacles again. One reached wide around Desini's shield, but she swung the edge of the modified beetle shell to that side to halt its progress then drove the shield into the animal's ugly mug again.

Fire exploded on the beast's right side. The slimy flesh bubbled and sizzled, and the slow stream of mist halted. Guiles grinned at me. Then he flashed into ghost form and slid down the hallway, jumping over tentacles to position himself behind the beast.

As ordered by Guiles before the fight, Desini swept her shield to one side to share her glare with the beast. She growled to stay at the top of its aggro table. I had to admit, it worked—the creature hadn't looked away from her. Another flash of fire melted the slit in the monster's left side, then the mist streaming from its glands ceased.

The elf's a genius.

When Guiles exploded into action, I loosed my arrow. It sailed true and, though I missed the eye, it opened a deep wound above that caused orangish blood to pour into it, for the same effect.

Roshan Flash Healed Desini at regular intervals while her healing-over-time spell helped to prop her up. Now that the creature was blind, I focused my fire on tentacles while Priya burned and Guiles stabbed the body.

The battle was tactical. Desini held the beast's ire. Guiles ripped at its back. Priya burned its head and used no other spells. My role was to weaken the tentacles it used as legs.

Before I knew it, we'd dropped the bastard on its slimy ass. Golden light flashed around Priya then funneled into the air as we advanced in level.

Priya has reached level 16!
Priya has five attribute points available.

Since your disposition with Priya is beloved, you may spend five attribute points.

"Congratulations, sister," Guiles said, "We will need to acquire some training for new skills as you won't receive any more automatic ones until you reach twenty. But don't worry, I'll see to it. For now, distribute your points."

I ran an abbreviated check on Guiles since he now showed up on my companion tab.

Guiles
Level 20 Rogue
(Level synched. Actual level, 50).
Attributes (Actual):
*Strength: 24**
*Dexterity: 48**
*Intelligence: 37**
*Wisdom: 34**
Constitution: 42
Charisma: 21
Guiles has nineteen attribute points available.
You may spend all of Guiles's available attribute points.
Since Guiles has a disposition of friendly toward you, you may spend one attribute point per level gained. Increase disposition to spend more points per level.

Guiles gathered us into a circle.

"You will not always have time to prepare. For instance, when we encountered the wrath demons, they came quickly and in numbers. We had to think on our feet and follow some well-known guidelines. But when I have cycles to strategize, I always find it to be time well-spent."

There were several nods and words of affirmation.

I remained silent.

Guiles continued. "We should move forward. I'm on my fifth day without sleep and will have to take rest tonight. But since the fountain is close, let's replenish ourselves a final time."

We sat on the edge of the glassy structure with our legs crossed.

I peered at the elf's XP bar and noted what I'd missed before... it was a quarter full.

"Guiles?"

One white eyebrow ticked up.

"So, you know how I can spend attribute points on behalf of my companions?"

"Yes. I just instructed you to do so."

I squinted at him. "Yeah, *boss man*. You did. What you didn't do was tell me if you'd like me to spend yours."

The elf jerked.

"His?" Priya asked.

"His?" Desini asked.

Roshan sat on the lip of the crystal fountain with her legs crossed, her eyes closed, and her full lips relaxed, as if she hadn't heard a word we said. A subtle lilac light embraced her in a glowing shell similar to one I'd seen as she practiced meditation with Zhara in the Dark Wood over a week before. I guessed such concerns as our Elven companion's spare attribute points held little interest, or that she'd so quickly dropped into a meditative state she didn't hear us. I thought about what Guiles had said about Spirit abilities earlier and thought I might be served by some meditation with my priestess.

"Are you going to lust after Roshan, or are you going to explain?" Priya asked.

To this, one of Roshan's eyes opened, answering my query about whether she'd heard us.

"I wasn't lusting."

"Right," Priya said.

Desini eyed Guiles. "Our leader has appetites."

Guiles showed a distant gaze. He was off, somewhere else. To cast off their misconception about my ganders at Roshan, I pressed on. "Yes, it seems our Elven companion hasn't spent all his points. Mister Always-Be-Prepared has nineteen available. Why is that, Guiles?"

Guiles peered at the floor. "I had no idea you could spend the points on my behalf. It hadn't occurred that simple companionship..." His voice trailed off, and he took on a contemplative gaze. "But now that we've realized it, your question is fair."

"Yeah, maybe it's time for the longer version of your story. Why would an adventurer retire to Brumhill, hide behind his former tank in a back alley, and give weapon training on the down low when he hasn't maxed his attributes?"

"Brumhill is where I hide out," Guiles said.

"Tell me something new."

"You see, I'm somewhat of a wanted man."

16

"You didn't think this was useful information?" I asked.

Guiles pointed a long finger at me. "You, too, are a wanted man."

"I wasn't accusing you of anything, Guiles. I just wanted to know why you thought it wasn't worth mentioning."

The elf shrugged. "You'll forgive me, Gemini, if it didn't exactly come first-to-mind as we fought demons in a dungeon beneath the most wretched place in Rubal."

"Rubal?"

Sighs burst all around me.

Roshan answered. "I am from the east and yet know the name of the continent on which you sit, Gemini Fowler. My goodness. You came into this world with an empty kettle behind thine forehead, waiting to be filled."

I wasn't sure I liked the tones with which my companions were using my last name. Peering into those pretty faces and hearing words my mother would have used to chastise me made my nose twitch. Since I couldn't say what I wanted out loud, I changed my approach. "Maybe I'm the reason you all are turning so snarky, so I'll set that aside, thank you for the geography lesson, and ask that we return to the question of *why* our new companion is a wanted man."

The elf peered into the crystal blue waters of the fountain and nodded. When he spoke, he adopted a more casual tone. "*Shénhuà,* you're not the only one at odds with the king's esteemed regent of our lands. As my tale is long and we are standing in the depths of this evil place, I'll offer the abbreviated version and answer your remaining questions, later. Agreed?"

"I thought you already gave the abbreviated version," I said.

"I couldn't possibly tell you everything in the time we have. So, I can tell you enough to satiate your curiosity or we can move on. Choose."

I nodded.

"Good. Now. Are you aware the Governor of Knall is a feudal lord of a sprawling area surrounding Gynas Peaks?"

"Yeah, I learned that from a guy in a tavern."

"A tavern." He shook his head. "I'm not going to ask. The governor is the primary provider of grains through the northeastern half of the kingdom. His lands were bequeathed to him by our former king."

"How much land is it?" I asked.

"All of it. If it is green and lies north of the Plague Barrens, it is his until it reaches the king's lands to the north and west, or the sea to the east. Endless acres. It would take weeks on Desini's cart to cross from the southern end of the governor's lands from the northern edge of the Plague Barrens to the Wildlands far to the north."

"Wildlands?"

I was pleased when my lack of geographical knowledge earned no sneers from my party.

"A lawless desert filled with barbarian tribes. But we digress if brevity is our concern."

I conceded the point with a curt nod.

"As with any feudal system, there are serfs who work swaths of land for a share of the sustenance. Most farm their lands for generations only to find they're left with diminishing fruits for which they labor. The governor calls it inflation. Since they maintain no ownership of their lands, any who display a spine could see their land divided among the surrounding families and be cast off into poverty in the cities, or life in the wilds.

"I learned the governor's lawmen and regiment leaders added to the hardships by coming for crops before they were ready and blaming the farmers for planting too late, or mismanaging crops when the weather was uncooperative, or myriad other excuses. In exchange for keeping their lands, the families gave up what few heirlooms they had, and, if they couldn't pay in that way, their sons were conscripted and their daughters taken."

"Daughters?" Desini growled. "For their betrothals?"

Guiles shook his head. "The betrothal of a farm girl to the governor's lords would be an insult. They marry the highborn kin of royal blood. No, these farm girls were lent as little more than playthings to the Governor's noble friends, many of whom were so steeped in privilege and entitlement, they'd established the most vulgar appetites.

"I would not dishonor such esteemed company as yourselves by describing the atrocities visited on a young woman who escaped and fled home to tell her tale, but suffice it to say, the violations of her purity were so vile that when she returned but a shell of the woman she'd been before to recount the tale, it spurned outrage.

"When the governor's troops came to tamp down the ensuing revolt, where farmers burned their own farmlands to send their message to the feudal lord, slaughter ensued."

"Why am I not surprised?" I growled.

Guiles raised a shoulder in a half-shrug. "My party and I found such a ruined girl on the road to Trowlsby after clearing the wilderness around a camp we maintained in the northeast, closer to the Elven Coast. Lizandra's family had been one of those slaughtered, and she was left pregnant and alone, having only survived by a timely flight. Her father had the foresight to stock her with what little food he had before sending her off to seek refuge among the elves.

"As many times as I've seen pain visited on beings of this region over the last century alone, I admit to having become numb at the sight of peoples' sufferings. In the time I spent with Lizandra, I glimpsed a potentially mighty spirit, but her true nature had been tempered by haunting recollections of the travesties visited on her.

"To this day, I clearly recall the dullness in her eyes as she recounted her tale. Lizandra was little more than skin and bones by the time we found her, yet she harbored no interested in food. Besides what one of the governor's harsher lords visited on her, she'd been beaten on the road and robbed of what little dignity remained.

"When she impressed upon us the fates of the serfs who burned their fields and refused to relinquish their daughters, I found myself in a state I'd not visited since I was a younger elf. I found new meaning in the first tenant of Elven society."

"Which is?" I asked.

Desini answered in his stead. "Protect those weaker than yourself."

Guiles bowed appreciatively and peered at the cat-like fighter with fresh appreciation. "Yes, Desini. You honor me."

Desini bowed her head. "Considering the loss I have both witnessed in others and experienced myself, I find this tenant to be especially memorable." She looked up and met his gaze. "But please, Master Guiles, forgive my interruption."

"There's nothing to forgive." He gave a conciliatory nod. "When I learned what was happening in the governor's lands, I found myself spurned to action, but my party wanted no part in it—except for Brugh. Priya and Gemini have met my long-time companion and, though he is a large man of much brawn and a quick tongue, his heart is soft regarding mistreatment of the slight of stature.

"With the approval of my Elven Queen Mitral, I trespassed onto the lands of the governor and led families with daughters who wanted to escape out of the king's regent's lands. Hundreds came and found shelter among my kind in the concealment of the forests of the Elven Isles."

Priya nodded. "Many places to hide in dense forests."

"Indeed. And since the land channel leading to them is the lone access aside from taking to the sea, my people have held the Isles since the City of Ninn fell, so long ago. Many refugees remain there today, and I am proud to call Mitral my queen for her adherence to our traditions."

"She sounds like a conscientious leader," I said.

"In her wisdom, she has proven many races living in harmony have much to offer each other." He shifted his weight. "After we led a second exodus, we were discovered by a regiment of the governor's men patrolling the roads in search of the traitors who would defy the king's own regent. Though my elven volunteers held our own, the governor's numbers were too great. Many were lost that day, though Brugh and I fought to the last."

"Did the governor go to your forest? Seek out the elves for the return of his serfs?"

"No, Gemini. The governor might be a wretched man, but he has not held power for these decades under two kings by being an idiot. One does not simply enter the Isles uninvited. Instead, the governor built up his forces and surrounded his lands. Patrols circled the outside perimeter of the eastern border with the Elven lands, and anyone caught trying to escape was skinned and hung on poles for the wildlife to finish."

Desini nodded. "The sight of such an atrocity is the reason I stopped traveling that far north."

"The governor put a price on Brugh's head and on mine. The dark mages were called out to cast their scrying spells to search for us while his men scoured the countryside and southern towns for us on foot."

I peered at Priya. "The Währsagers Prantu mentioned. The scryers."

"You met Prantu?" Guiles asked. He thrust his hands onto his narrow hips. "The blessings she puts in your path, my mystic friend."

In other times, I might have asked how he knew of Prantu, but now, I wasn't surprised. Prantu had been Priya's right hand at the University in Warrington. Guiles was old as hell. It wasn't strange he'd know about the wizard. "So, if the governor sought you out, did you lie low in the Forest Isles?"

"Though my people would've protected me, I didn't long to cause a new war on the continent, and the governor would've demanded my extradition from Queen Mitral. She wouldn't have given me up, but I didn't want to put her in that position.

"Mine was a name the governor could attach to the resistance. I knew the regent's pride would keep him from calling for the king's help in the quelling of the defiant serfs and the elves who'd harbored them, so my people would be safe as long as I disappeared.

"I planted clues that Brugh and I traveled across the sea to the eastern continent—our companion Roshan's home."

"You pulled a feint," Gemini said.

"A feint?" Guiles considered the words for a moment and then smiled. "A fine metaphor." He chuckled. "A feint, indeed. The plan was for my elder brother, Kelrin, to book passage to the east on a ship, call himself Guiles, and leave a trail the governor could follow without being obvious. If anyone high enough level to check his status would've bothered, they'd have found my name, courtesy of a shadow spell cast by one of our Elven mages and right hand of the queen."

"The right hand of your queen is a shadow mage?" Priya asked, wide-eyed.

Guiles nodded and allowed a smile to slip out. "Yes, Priya. You must let go of your struggle about whether your shadow affinity ensures you a destiny of evil. Only the affinity created by your actions can do that. Live as a creature of Light, and you will be a creature of Light."

"Thank you, master elf."

"You're welcome. Now, where was I? Ah! After Kelrin left his trail to the east, I assume he stayed there long enough to spread some lore before returning home. Meanwhile, I traveled south to Brumhill."

"Why Brumhill?" Desini asked.

"Ah!" Guiles held up a finger. He turned his attention to Priya. "Tell me, young brethren, why do you think Brugh and I might have chosen Brumhill?"

Priya raised her eyebrows and poked her chest like a kid in a classroom who wanted to be sure the teacher was calling on her.

"Zhara."

Guiles shook his head. "No. Try again."

Priya's head cocked back as if physically struck by his response. "No?"

"Be more specific."

Priya nodded. "Right. The Tree of Solara."

Guiles nodded.

I shook my head. "What about it?"

"Ugh. Much to learn."

"I would appreciate if people around here would stop treating the mystic as if he were stupid. I woke in the forest with amnesia! Stop being jerks."

"Oh," Guiles grumbled. "That's a fair point." He peered at our companions. "We'll stop assuming Gemini has any knowledge of our world beyond what he expresses and be more open to answering his questions with less judgmental tones. Solara made him the way he is, so we will honor her plan, regardless of whether we understand it. Agreed?"

Nods all around.

Priya gripped my hand. "I'm sorry, Gemini."

Desini looked down at her boots again. "I, too, have treated you with undue disregard."

Roshan slapped my shoulder. "I will comply. Noob."

I gave my head a derisive shake. "So, the Tree of Solara?"

"Right. The tree is the center of Light on this continent and perhaps throughout the world. Enora is too vast for us to have any inkling of where it ends or what other sources there might be. We know it isn't the only source, but I have not heard of one so powerful. And since scrying is shadow magic..." He waited for one of us to finish his thought.

I opted in. "The mages couldn't see you in Brumhill because it is mere miles from the tree. It shrouded you from their magic. Like an umbrella."

Faces screwed up in confusion.

Note to self, invent the umbrella.

Guiles pressed on. "I worked out a little deal with the current mayor's father—it often works that way in these small towns—and changed my identity. As I had not returned to the Elven Isles to visit with my queen's right hand to change my name, I made a new ally in the proprietress of the Crescent Moon."

"Leira?" Desini and I asked at the same time.

"Yes. Leira. She has no love for the crown or its regents, and there is something to be said for having experienced allies. Also, she has gazed upon the Matron of the Wood—a rare thing, indeed. I believe she serves as devoutly as any of us despite her sometimes-gruff demeanor. I also found a trustworthy confidant in Mister Breeder. You've all had the pleasure."

"Yeah, Breeder wouldn't tell anyone shit," I said. "I like that guy. And I got the impression Leira was at the university when the king's proclamation pissed off a lot of magic wielders."

"Breeder is a shrewd businessman, he is a decent human being. Did you know he owns three armory shops in the region?"

I nodded. "Run by his sons."

"Right. Right."

A thought occurred. "So, are you the real reason he works the small one in the middle of nowhere?"

Priya huffed. "I reject your assertion that a place so near my home is the middle of nowhere."

"You used to be the head of the university in Warrington," I retorted. "The Dark Wood is not your home."

Her head cocked back, much like it had earlier, as she contemplated my words. "Shit. I don't know why I'm so defensive."

"You're adopting your companion's linguistic flairs," Guiles said.

Priya's nose wrinkled up. "*Shit* is a fine word. Very expressive. But *fuck* is even better."

"If you say, sister. Now. It's time to continue our push forward. Would you all agree?"

"One final question?" Priya asked.

"Make it fast."

"Might I ever visit the Isles? It would warm my soul to meet so many like me and learn of my heritage."

"You only have your entire, immortal lifetime to make it happen," Guiles said. "I'm certain the daughter of Solara and one who shares our blood would be well-received there. But you must focus on your duty to Solara and serve righteously. Now, shall we press forward?"

I certainly thought so. Roshan raised her eyelids and nodded enthusiastically as the other two women stood and adjusted their gear.

The Light priestess raised her staff and was off without a word.

But Guiles called her back. "Roshan?"

She turned and bowed her head slightly. "Yes, master elf."

"While I admire your fervor to do Solara's will, you are inexperienced. Let me make clear the recipe for success." He didn't wait for her approval. "The tank leads at all times unless Gemini is called upon to pull a single beast out of a crowd to keep us from becoming overwhelmed. This is why he carries the bow. You are the healer. You have no shrouding ability, and your place will almost always be at the back of the group so that you might be protected. Have I been clear?"

Her cheeks colored as Roshan's gaze sought each of us in turn. Watching as her jaws worked and her color leveled out, I sensed a paradigm shift in that expression, as if she'd just had a come-to-Jesus moment. An epiphany had been forced upon her.

She wasn't in charge.

From the first time I met her, Roshan's drive was unquestionable. Though I didn't know the roots of this trait, I'd come to admire it. But in the larger group, where the party's success depended on a level of consistency to counterbalance the unpredictable mechanics of each encounter, I couldn't have agreed with Guiles more.

The two of us weren't exploring underground tunnels anymore, taking on what faced us as it came, unprepared. That experience beneath the Dark Wood taught me important lessons about the world I'd entered, where my unseen enemy strategized, drawing me into a trap, and brought up minions from my rear while sealing me in at the front— using Priya, ironically.

That first experience with Roshan made me understand why the A.I. prevented Takemoto from telling me about what to expect. My recent interface message, which stated my destiny was to clear the way for other players, took it further. It made me aware of a most crucial element to my existence in a new world—Enora wanted me to succeed because something was fucked.

As to Roshan, she was an adventurer now. A healer upon whose survival we all relied. One piece of our bond was that neither of us had been prepared. She'd spent her life hiding her abilities, like a caged tiger who escaped to unleash its potential on the prey of the world. If my healer and companion fell against the foes we faced, the rest would fall after her. Maybe she'd find a certain hope in how important she was to all of us. Maybe Guiles's instruction would redefine her, so that she saw she wasn't just serving her goddess by charging forth to vanquish evil, but rather had been called upon to provide service to others. I thought that was a concept she could appreciate.

Her gaze fell on me. "When we were in the Dark Wood, you had me stand at the back, and I was taken by Priya." It was like she read my mind.

"I was not in control of my faculties," Priya explained.

I shook my head and sent her a quelling emotion.

Roshan continued her thought. "But now I see the logic. I have less protection and health and, since my role is not direct engagement with our enemies, I should operate at a safe distance. Yes, master elf. I will adhere to your tactics."

She stepped to one side and gestured everyone forward. I flashed her a quick smile, and she kissed the air in front of her. I found the gesture out of character. While Priya was the more playful and affectionate type, Roshan was all business when it came to burning down the bad guys. I didn't quite know what to make of it, but, then again, I hadn't known her for more than a few days, cumulatively. It just *felt* like I'd known her forever.

When we reached the remnants of the mist creature, I noted that it still lay in the hallway outside its room. Guiles confirmed my suspicion that, since we were inside an instance, the corpse would remain until we cleared the dungeon. Unlike other scenarios I'd encountered, he had no theory as to why this was so. That was better than calling it Solara's will, I supposed. But if I pressed he'd probably say just that. So, I didn't probe.

The mist had cleared from the room where the beast had lurked. Apparently, the fog held a second property of which we'd been unaware—it masked scents. The place was a horror movie. A slaughterhouse floor. If the walls had been built of stone like the earlier parts of the instance, they'd have been painted in blood. Skeletons littered the place, but all the armor we found was rusted and eaten through. Metal weapons, the same.

We found no bags and no coin, which seemed like a dirty trick, but if I was being honest, the less we found meant the less time my olfactory sense was in that constant state of panic bringing bile into my throat at the horrid, putrid scent assaulting it.

The earthen hallway turned to the right after the mist room and then began a steady rise uphill. Crevices formed on either side of us, sinking deeper and deeper into the dirt. My quads burned, and sweat beaded on my forehead as we climbed. Then the walls widened until they were so far from us, the torches lining them became specs of light in the distance.

Standing in a massive cavern near the top of the incline, we stared out at a wide, circular plateau seen only by the courtesy of glowing green crystals set into the soil around the perimeter. I likened the sight to a massive helicopter pad viewed from the sky at night. A shimmering rectangle of purple light glowed beyond the sprawling platform. It was like the doorways we'd seen beyond the two fountains we'd encountered, except it had the stone framing of the one at the entrance.

I eyed one of the green crystals.

Soul Cell

These crystals imprison the souls of fallen adventurers.

I recalled text I'd seen in my HUD when facing the Corrupted Corpse earlier and scanned my logs to read it again.

These guardians are the undead remnants of adventurers who braved the depths of the Plague Barrens and failed in their quest. Their souls imprisoned elsewhere by an evil presence upon falling, their bodies are left to wander the halls defending their dark lord's territory.

So, one of those crystals held the soul of the undead warrior. More importantly, the being who imprisoned it there and sent the warrior out to guard his domain was likely nearby. I shivered. Then, embarrassed, I scanned my party to ensure no one had seen. All clear.

"To the right," Guiles whispered as he leaned toward us.

I refreshed my Inner Illumination spell. A glow washed over the plateau illuminating the scene. What I'd mistaken for a crevasse surrounding the platform was a perimeter of deep water reflecting the green crystals' light.

Just as our rogue had said, a shadowy figure was huddled into a thick ball on the back-right side of the plateau. I might have mistaken it for a rock if the form hadn't expanded and shrunk as it breathed. A low rattle emitted from it as it exhaled. I focused.

Bordock

Level 20 Lower Grootslang
(Grand Boss)
*The demon minions who brought blight and destruction to
the ancient Elven City of Ninn, the grootslang, are vicious
creatures with myriad dark abilities who are rumored to have
been the first sentient beings born into the world of Enora.
Known for their love of precious gems, grootslang often
surround themselves with magical stones and draw from
their power to live for centuries and possibly thousands of
years.*
Strength: 34
Dexterity: 27
Intelligence: 21
Wisdom: 17
Constitution: 41
Charisma: 19

I eyed the stones surrounding the platform with renewed interest.

Apparently having followed my gaze, Guiles leaned in once again. "Legend has it the greener they glow, the more souls bound within."

"Legend?" I whispered. "You mean you've never seen one of these before?"

The elf shook his head and lowered his tone to a whisper. "No, and if lore holds true, we might wish we hadn't. With such an inexperienced group, this could prove... challenging." He stared at the green crystals surrounding the platform. "Very challenging."

"Are you saying one of these things could capture our souls?"

Guiles shrugged. "Do you want to find out? Perhaps we should shuffle across the platform to that entrance, beyond."

Now I knew the elf was tripping. I didn't battle all those minions, fight lava spewing beetles, and get thrown around by a mist monster just to turn back now. This was a game world, regardless of the fact it was the most realistic game world ever created. This place was built so that people like me could come in and kick its ass.

Yes, there was pain to be had. I'd certainly experienced my share. But the sight of glowing purple lines tracing a chest as high as my waist on the opposite side of the platform numbed my sense of self-preservation. I was a loot whore. There would just have to be pain.

My team needed levels and upgrades. We were making enemies in the outside world. No loot was dropping. Most of all, my gut told me the contents of that bitch would finally give me a sign of whether Enora paid up when one earned it or if I'd be better served by plowing a field somewhere and taking up farming.

A rumbling voice of such depth it made my lungs rattle came low on the still air. "It is too late for such trifling thoughts of retreat, ancient one."

"The grootslang who predated us all calls me ancient," Guiles said.

A sudden energy numbed my feet and lent the sensation I was sinking into the ground. The edge of the platform closest to us glowed the same shade of green as the crystals surrounding it. One of my boots rose from the packed earth against my will and lurched forward.

"I can't stop," I muttered.

"Nor I," Guiles strained as his foot raised against his will and stomped.

All my companions lumbered forward. My foot pounded to the earth with such force, the shock reached my kneecap. Then the other boot dislodged and rose. All five of us crossed the glowing line, stepping onto the platform. As I struggled to bring my foot back under my control, the narrow line glowed brighter. A sheet of light climbed to form a high barrier behind us, reaching thirty feet above our heads. Then my boots tore free of the unseen power's grip, and I tumbled to my knees.

We were sealed in, and the bastard hadn't even waited for us to step voluntarily into the combat arena.

The huddling monstrosity unfolded and rose into the air. Wide, smooth wings spread out to its sides. Its serpentine body hovered inches off the ground, floating up and down as if a pulsing mattress of air supported it from beneath. Its massive, slanted eyes glowed green as the wings spread, revealing its wide, round body. The demon beast stood at least a story tall, and I suddenly wondered at my sheer stupidity for having wanted to fight it over the contents of a chest.

"Long has it been since adventurers have entered my domain. I've sensed your souls since first you encroached." The rumbling, throaty voice crept through me like a thousand slithering earthworms, and my flesh broke out in goose pimples.

Guiles turned his head so all of us could hear. "Spread out. Roshan, keep your back to the barrier. Priya and Gemini, fan out to the left and right to avoid a wipe from single AOE attacks. Desini, prepare yourself."

"Wipe?" Priya asked.

"It means all of us die," I answered in Guiles's stead.

The rest of us moved without question, but Priya and I shared a final glance before pacing away from each other toward opposite ends of the platform. One side of her upper lip turned up in a sneer, and a wave of aggression crashed over me.

That half-elf didn't give a damn. She just wanted to burn shit down.

Black circles appeared in the center of its vivid green sclera as the grootslang ventured to the back-center of the platform. They fell on Roshan, who'd stepped off to my left and raised her staff into the air.

"Welcome, priestess. Long has it been since I suckled at the flesh of a morsel of the Light. I shall save you for last when you might rinse the taste of these foul interlopers from my tongue."

"We know you don't eat people," I said. "We just beat down one of your slaves. So, how about you drop the theatrics and let's roll?"

The green glow brightened around the black irises as they passed over Guiles and stopped on Priya. It was as if I hadn't spoken. The grootslang jerked forward.

"Fascinating!" The creature's bellow shook the platform. "Come forth, creature, and let me see you better."

Priya's sea-blue irises glowed green as her head swiveled toward our enemy and she took a few short steps forward. The grootslang's eyes brightened, and it rose a few feet higher.

"A creature warmed by the Light, but awash in shadow." The monster shuddered and hovered left and right, its wings rippling first, its long, thick tail following suit. "Such power I sense in you, short one."

Ooooh, you don't want to call her that!

Priya scowled.

"Tell me, what is this energy?" the grootslang said. "What is your line?" I stepped forward a few paces, but the grootslang lowered its head and growled fury at me. "Hold your place, peasant, or—" It jerked back. "Another puzzle! You wear not the scent of Enora! What are you?"

"I'm Gemini." I peered around at my party, trying to come up with significant words to mark this memorable occasion. When stories were told of our encounter with this mythical beast, I wanted our names to be revered. But try as I might, I had nothing. So, I went with, "I've come to cut off your head and shit down your rotten neck!"

The eyes glowed so furiously, they illuminated the whole platform for an instant. "A mystic! So that is it! Solara has finally sent her minions to the realm of Bordock! Finally, a challenge!"

"Um... yeah. Sure. That's it!"

The head lowered itself toward the ground then the creature locked its gaze on me. "Yours will be the finest souls ever to grace my cells. Come forth, traveler, that I might send Solara a message she will never forget and shift the balance of power in the name of Hokrahm!"

An orange glow surrounded the massive beast as its tail rose high in the air and slammed to the ground. A burst of energy shook the platform, throwing us all backward into the invisible barrier. The strange light wall flexed and stretched as it absorbed our impact and slung us back into the ring.

Text filled the bottom center of my field of vision.

Bordock executes Tail Slam!
Party-wide effect: Attack down.

Desini launched forward, shield held high, sword clutched in a white-fisted grasp as she screamed and charged the beast. I shivered with anticipation at the first impact of her new shield, thinking it couldn't grace a more suitable target. She covered the last thirty feet in a blurry instant, slamming hard into Bordock.

And falling hard on her ass.

Desini executes Charge.
Bordock resists.

The grootslang hovered as an orange disc appeared overhead and began to fill clockwise.

"Stand at the barrier!" Guiles barked. "Cast from as far as possible!" He faded into stealth, but two beams emitted from Bordock's eyes and penetrated Guiles's as if the two glared at each other through tubes of light. The stealth effect was broken as Guiles jerked to a halt. A matching lemon glow surrounded the elf as his chin tilted upward and his eyes turned obsidian.

Bordock casts Charm.
Guiles (Minion) is charmed.

Bordock's mouth spread into a gaping, toothless grin. "Kill the shadow caster first."

"Yes, master." Guiles turned and marched toward Priya.

nd just like that, I was in charge again. "Priya, kite Guiles, but stay away from Bordock!"

"What? Did you say 'kite?'"

Gah!

I caught her attention. "Run!" I made a running gesture with two downturned fingers. "Around the circle!"

Priya sprang past me and off to the right side of the platform as I turned and raised an arrow to my bow. I nocked it and aimed for Bordock's left eye. Just as I prepared the launch, Guiles broke my line of sight as he stepped past me like I wasn't there, his singular interest in the mother of my child.

Mother of my child? What are you thinking about?

I swung my foot out and tripped him, sending him sprawling face-first into the packed dirt platform. A few steps toward the rear pressed my back to the barrier, but my Elven mentor simply recovered and continued to stomp after Priya as she ran in a wide circle around the grootslang. If she'd been kiting, per se, she would have stopped a safe distance from Guiles so as not to approach our enemy's rear until she had to. But we'd save classes on game theory for later.

Bordock slammed his forehead down into Desini's shield. A blue swirl appeared above my tank's head as she shifted lazily from foot-to-foot.

Bordock uses Head Butt!
Desini is stunned.
-121 HP

Time seemed to creep as I watched the battle log stack at the bottom of my screen, three lines at a time, and readied the arrow again.

Roshan casts Flash Heal.
Desini
+41 HP
Roshan casts Minor Heal.
+13 HP
(HOT)

Priya stopped once she'd safely passed behind the groot-slang and turned.

"The fuck are you—?"

She raised both her hands high overhead and formed claws. They glowed blue as a full casting bar appeared beneath her avatar on my party interface. It emptied as she cast.

A blue circle appeared beneath Guiles's feet as his foot-steps dragged.

Priya casts Ice Storm.

Guiles (Minion) is slowed
Guiles
-21 HP
-14 HP
-17 HP

You fire a Drilling Arrow.

Bordock
-17 HP
(Attack decreased)

Ugg. Shitty damage! Damned attack down effect!

I eyed the new icon of a sword with a line through it on the right. A timer counting down beneath it showed ten more seconds' duration. Where the rest of my party members were framed in green, Guiles's outline was cast in red and a small icon depicting a hunched over beast blinked.

"Priya! Keep Moving while he's slowed! We don't want to damage Guiles! Get out of range and focus on Bordock! Cast Flash Fire! Then run again!"

Priya moved, disabling her cast, which required her to stand stationary. She crossed the platform behind Desini, who'd regained her composure and now cursed the beast. "Oversized winged worm of stink!" Her sword sliced the air in a wide arc and viscous, glowing green fluid dribbled from a shallow wound in Bordock's lower belly.

An orange dial appeared above the grootslang's head, and a cone of light covered the ground in an arc in front of him. It formed an oblong triangle beneath Desini's feet so the tip was beneath Bordock, representing the area an effect would impact.

"Desini! Move out of the cone!"

Though I was convinced she'd take a massive blow, the agile mishon dove into a forward roll then sprang to her feet on our enemy's flank. Two quick swipes of her sword opened wounds in the demon's hip.

Desini attacks Bordock.

Bordock
-34 HP
-36 HP
(Attack Down)

I fired arrow after arrow, finding my towering target with some frequency, but each time I aimed to blind him, Bordock evaded.

An explosion slammed into Bordock's face. A couple seconds later, just as I unleashed a Drilling Arrow, another exploded high on his chest.

I turned to check on Priya. She finished casting another spell just in time to escape Guiles's grasp as he lumbered after her in a trance.

"Now that's how a mother humper kites! Good job!"

She ran passed me and, to my utter disbelief, grinned from ear-to-ear. She laughed maniacally as a surge of airy emotions washed over me.

Priya was stone cold. Crazy!

Just as I nocked an arrow, Guiles's icon on my party interface flashed red-to-green a few times, then stayed green. The elf turned and charged toward the grootslang as the surrounding glow dissipated.

Green means go, bitch.

Attack down expires.

Awesome, now maybe we can do some damage!

Guiles vanished in a cloud of smoke then reappeared an instant later standing atop the thick tail of the hovering beast. The elf would be good and pissed at what had just happened, and I wanted to witness the results mathematically, so I activated my combat log's high-detail function with a quick thought as I nocked another arrow.

Guiles activates Spine Snap.
Critical Hit!
(Base critical hit chance 10% + surprise attack 5% + Spine Snap multiplier 15%)

Bordock
-137 HP
(Base Weapon Damage: 18 x 500%=90 HP Ambush x critical multiplier 2=180 - dodge check (failed) x defense rating)

The defense rating was hidden, so I couldn't work out the math in my head. But there was little doubt Bordock's rating was high, and Guiles was our biggest damage-dealer, by far.

Light spun in a disc over Bordock's head.

Bordock readies Tail Slash.

"Desini!" I yelled, but the disc filled quickly with the short case and I was already too late. The hovering monster's body lowered to the earthen platform and swung in a violent circle, slamming his tail into Desini and batting her to the far-left wall.

Guiles flew off the beast's tail in the other direction and sailed through the air with his arms out to his sides like someone being crucified and, just as he neared the ground, he whipped his arms to his chest, raised his knees to his abdomen, tucked his head and rolled. Though he still slammed into the invisible barrier at the end of the maneuver, I knew his agility had saved him from much more damage.

Luckily, my two casters and I had been out of the melee attack's range.

The boss turned its back to us then sped quickly to the rear of the platform before reeling around to face us again. Another casting disc appeared above its head. We were all standing at the outer perimeter of the platform, so as long as he wasn't readying an all-encompassing AOE, I wasn't too worried about the direct damage.

I tallied.

Desini

47% health

Roshan

95% health

Priya

76% health

Guiles

42% health

Gemini

94% health

"Roshan, throw Guiles a heal!"

Guiles was cast in a subtle white glow as Roshan cast her heal-over-time spell, then he was washed in a brighter glow as she brought his health to eighty percent with a Flash Heal critical.

Bordock readies Soul Ejection.

What the hell is...

Two crystals slotted into the dirt on either side of the platform shot green arcs of light into the center of the platform. Boots formed atop the dark earth at the impact points, followed by shins and knees adorned in leather, next waists, then leather clad chests, and arms wielding spiked maces. Their heads were transparent. Spreading out, the ghostly minions engaged.

"Adds!" I yelled.

Harvested Soul
Level 17 Demon Minion
Strength: 19
Dexterity: 17
Intelligence: 13
Wisdom: 11
Constitution: 21
Charisma: 1

I gauged their trajectories as Bordock reengaged Desini. They were after the casters.

Turning, I found myself at the tip of a triangle where Roshan, Priya, and I formed the points. As the MOBs closed, my gaze switched between them, and I froze.

Priya or Roshan?

The sore muscles from the tension of my bow hand caused them to quiver with fatigue as I drew to my fullest tautness and filled my arrow with energy. I swung back and forth between targets.

Then, from another place and time, Katelyn's voice echoed through my head. My former girlfriend and the woman who'd made it possible for me to come to Enora instead of ending up worm food spoke common sense.

Healer first, dumbass!

Whipping around, I loosed my arrow, admonishing myself for my hesitation as it flew across the space and slammed into a minion's back. The summoned spirit faltered, took another lunging step forward, then slammed the spiked mace into Roshan's temple, causing her to plummet to the ground with a thud.

It had taken only a moment's hesitation.

"No!" I nocked another arrow and fired without feeding mana into it. It slammed into the zombie's shoulder.

The minion turned toward me.

That was just fine because by the time it reached me, I'd be well into my work with his little friend. I wheeled and took aim at the minion attacking Priya, but it was already laid out on the ground in flames. Guiles marched away from it and reengaged his stealth ability. Those two had tag-teamed that bastard down with malice.

By the time I returned my attention to the other one, he was on me. I ducked beneath his weakened swing and brought my fist up to connect with its chin.

This had no measurable effect except to bust my knuckles.

As it brought the mace on the backswing, a primal scream filled the air. The creature turned.

I followed its gaze to find Desini facing us, her shoulders dropped low, her chest rising and falling. The minion charged after her as she returned her attention to the boss.

Guiles reappeared behind Bordock and cut slits into his back. Desini lurched a few feet forward in an instant and this time, the boss didn't resist the Charge. Instead, it stepped backward, fell, then bounced back onto its tail.

I didn't care, though. My arrow was leveled on the minion Desini had taunted away from me. With its health bar at just below fifty percent, I didn't think I could take it down with a single shot, but I needed to stop it from a rear shot at Desini because it had an increased chance of critical hit. Her health was already below forty percent. The skeleton wasn't an elite, so maybe I could get lucky.

Lowering my aim and letting out my breath, I fired. The arrow sailed true, ripping into the summoned minion's foot just above the heel and slowing its pace to a limp.

Golden letters exploded in the air in front of me.

NEW SKILL LEARNED!
Achilles Clip
Level 15
Ranged Attack
Cost: 15 Mana
Damage: 9-13
Cooldown: 15 seconds
Slows target by 35% for seven seconds.

I focused on nocking another arrow, aimed for the back of the minion, then brought it down. It slammed to the surface, its mace falling inches short of Desini's boots. Seems were weren't a bad pairing, either. Eat that, Guiles and Priya!

Bordock readies Charm.

The light in the grootslang's eyes glowed brighter and brighter as the casting disc over his head spun. I *recalled the way* the tubes of light had locked the gazes of our enemy and Guiles.

"Turn away! Face the barrier!"

I spun around, facing the light wall as a flash filled the surrounding air. Priya and Roshan faced the same direction as I, away from the boss. When I turned back, my attention shot to Desini. I found no evidence of the yellow aura of the charm effect.

It had worked!

"Don't fail me again," Bordock groaned.

Guiles stepped out from behind the massive grootslang, glowing yellow.

How did he get him again?

Grootslang casts haste on Guiles.
Movement and attack speed increased by 35%

"Yes, Master," Guiles spoke in a monotone. Then he zipped across the platform toward Priya.

"Priya! Kite!"

The half-elf began to cast in an effort to slow the rogue's advance, but I knew by the rate at which Guiles closed, it was too late. By the time the first ice shards struck him, he was on her.

She tried to slip away, and for a moment I thought she'd escape his reach. But then his knives worked into a rapid blur of motion and slices opened in Priya's chest and shoulders.

Guiles activates Combat Flurry

"Roshan! Focus on Priya!" I turned. "Desini, attack Guiles!"

Desini raised her shield to ward off a grootslang attack then threw me a confused glare.

"He's going to drop Priya and then he'll turn on one of us! Do it!"

Desini turned and charged across the platform. Luckily, she was attacking from the rear and his Dexterity didn't seem to counter the bash of her shield. Guiles tumbled face first to the earthen floor. At the elf fell, he swept out with one dagger and sliced one of Priya's achilles. Thick blood flowed like paint to her heel.

Desini threw me another glance.

"Back to Bordock!"

While Guiles was stunned, I scanned the party. Roshan's mana was draining too fast as she tried to get Priya topped up. Desini was huffing and puffing, but holding her own. Priya clutched her upper body with both hands as she limped away from Guiles.

I sprang across the platform in long strides. I eyed Guiles. "Sorry, brother!" My mana bar filled as I leveled my arrow and fired at the back of his neck. The elf jerked and pressed his hands to the earth, as if to do a pushup.

A high stomp with my heel brought him back down, onto his face. I readied another arrow as I pinned him. Blue light flowed from the fletchings down the shaft. When the tip flashed bright, I fired.

You have killed Guiles (minion).
0 XP

I scanned my party list. To their credit, they kept fighting. Priya stopped limping and started casting, despite her wounds. Desini curses the grootslang with renewed vigor. I recalled Guiles's reminiscence about fallen compatriots whose blood had stopped flowing through their veins before they could be resurrected and imagined him relegated to lurch around this place for eternity.

No fucking way.

I unleashed a Drilling Arrow and finally connected with the grootslang's eye. Though I got credit for a critical hit, I'd still only taken about two percent of its health. Priya's mana was low. Roshan's mana was nearly depleted.

My own mana was empty and my low Wisdom score wasn't doing shit to replenish it.

"Roshan! Drink a mana potion!"

Bordock was down to ten percent of his total health. We needed to finish this.

The casting disc appeared again.

Bordock readies Death Fount.

The disc filled, and the grootslang spewed orange slime in front of him. Desini raised her shield and evaded most the grossness, but it dripped over the edges and onto her head.

I cringed, fearing it might melt her flesh. Taking a step forward, I loosed another arrow. Then Desini wiped the mess away with the sleeve of her sword hand as if it was a simple annoyance.

I sighed a breath of relief just as Bordock lowered himself onto the slime.

When I saw the grootslang's health tick up a notch, I

peered down at the slime. Desini's health ticked down. Tendrils of smoke trailed across the slime from her feet to the grootslang's slimy bottom. Bordock's health ticked up. Hers ticked down again.

Shit.

"Desini, get him away from that crap!" I pointed at the slime. "He's leeching your health!"

My tank growled in a sound that had no business uttering from soft lips and dashed sideways. She screamed at the beastly demon. "Come to me, you nasty slime worm of Hokrahm's loins! I curse your master for his weakness and will repel you back to the stinking depths of hell from which you spawned!"

Forced by the magical properties of the provocation, the grootslang followed, but not before he'd regained at least five percent of his health.

Well, that's some cheating shit, right there!

I burned with frustration as all our meters continued to drop. Intuition told me we would not outlast the beast. One more cast of that ability when it reached ten percent would push him over the top, then we'd be left here with our proverbial cocks in our hands.

So, cheat! You'd think you'd have learned by now!

I didn't know how I'd missed it, especially considering the events of the day. I eyed the flesh of the grootslang as a thought crawled through my head.

Which one?

My mind conjured an image of silvery, razor-like teeth, and I smiled. Throwing my hand out, I spent the rest of my mana pool in one cast. I might not get another specialized shot off, but I needed a consistent source of damage, and I knew where I could get that.

Furious clicking noises filled the air as my pet materialized in front of me. She peered up at me, bouncing back and forth on her stubby feet.

My porcupunk.

"Go eat that big son of a bitch!" I yelled.

Click tore off after our enemy.

I cupped my hand around my mouth. "And give him the spikes!" I turned to face the casters. "When he hits ten percent, give him everything you have left. Roshan, stop healing at that point and Smite like crazy! Try to top Desini off in the meantime! She'll have to last until we bring him down!"

Though blood stained one side of her face from the mace she'd taken, Roshan bared her teeth. "This evil beast will fall before Her mighty light!"

Click zipped right past Guiles's corpse and shot up the grootslang's back, stopping where the wings met the serpent-like body. She sank her razor-like teeth into a wing.

Bordock
Health 11%

Do it, I thought in her direction.

When a final check showed Desini's and Priya's health were above fifty percent, I nodded. "Now! Everyone! Hit it hard!" I yelled to the remnants of my team.

The casting disc appeared above the grootslang's head.

Bordock readies Death Fount.

Priya's fire exploded in the grootslang's face, the white light of Roshan's arcing Smite slammed into its temple. The pudgy porcupunk launched into the air, turned a somer sault, then exposed the needles from the retracting flesh tubes on her back. I unloaded another drilling arrow and tagged our enemy in its pudgy side.

My stamina bar blinked red, and I dropped to one knee, huffing for breath. An arrow dangled and dropped from my fingers.

Click wiggled like a dog trying to scratch its back in the grass, and the needles dug deeper into the grootslang's meat while the rest of my group unloaded everything they had.

The bar was almost filled. He'd puke that healing shit and this would all be over.

"Desini!" I cried.

Her head whipped around.

"Charge!"

Although she stood mere feet from the beast, Desini activated the skill and slammed into the grootslang. Its massive body shuddered, and the casting disc stopped with millimeters left.

Desini uses Charge!
Death Fount Interrupted!

The grootslang's tail dropped to the ground, and it teetered.

It worked! We got it. We did it.

Bordock tipped forward. Desini rolled out of the way as it crashed down.

Golden light flowed up and through the cavern in five funnels as golden numbers flashed and an echoing symphony of victorious music filled the air. The magic barrier around us vanished, and the chest on the far side of the platform glowed in a dazzling, sparkling aura.

Congratulations! You have defeated a grand boss!
Bordock
Level 20 Lower Grootslang
(Grand Boss)
17, 869 XP
Congratulations! You are the first adventurer to defeat
Bordock!
You have earned the unique title: **Slayer of the Slang!**

It seemed unfair that I could earn titles without having to compete against other players to get there first. After all, shouldn't they have an equal chance to race to the achievements I was earning?

Meh. Screw 'em.

The green glow surrounding the platform intensified. Streams of light rushed from the crystals, snaking upward to the ceiling of the high cavern, revealing low hanging stalactites I'd missed before. Distant screams filled the air, and the souls of the captives disappeared into the rock formations high above.

"Roshan?"

She raised her eyebrows.

"Raise Guiles. Quickly, please."

Despite her sweating brow and huffing chest, the Light priestess scurried to within range and began to cast.

Roshan casts Raise

My heart's thumping doubled its rhythm as I watched the casting bar.

"C'mon," I muttered. It would be just my luck to score someone like Guiles just to lose him this way... at my own hand. What if he'd been bound? Would've that have counted as killing one of my companions and causing permanent death?

The golden glow surrounded and penetrated the elf as he floated off the ground, his arms and legs spread out, and he was set upright and gently onto his feet.

I doubled over and gripped my knees. "Thank the gods, dude."

"Thank you, Roshan," Guiles said in a monotone. "Apologies Gemini. As I stood behind Bordock, I thought I was safe, but he turned to face me at the last moment."

I chuckled as I grasped my knees. Then laughter boiled up in my chest and I let it go.

"No problem, Guiles! I'm just glad..." I huffed for wind as my Stamina bar slowly replenished. "I'm just glad you're okay. Sorry I had to off you."

"It was quick thinking. Fine leadership, Gemini."

"Thanks. Did you get XP?"

Guiles nodded.

"Awesome. At least Enora rewards your efforts."

Roshan tilted her head to the side. "Enora? It is not the world who blesses us, but Solara."

"My mistake," I muttered.

We converged on the beast at the center of the platform and circled it. Uneasy smiles became easier.

"To think that was just a lower grootslang," Guiles said. "Can you imagine what a great one would be like?"

I glared at him. "Do you think you could let the new adventurers revel in their glory for about five fucking seconds before you rain on our parade with your dark thoughts?"

"Forgive me, mythic." He turned and swept one arm in

a long arc toward the glowing chest in the corner. "Please, revel freely in the spoils of your unlikely achievement."

He cocked his chin to indicate the area over my left shoulder, and I turned to follow his gaze. The edges of the chest shone in a golden sheen.

Does that son of a bitch always have to be right?

18

Guiles was right. I knew it the moment I approached the fancy box with gold trim and maroon fabric circling its sides.

The glow surrounding the chest faded. A loot window appeared in my interface when the lid opened with a squeal of its hinges. Each item appeared on a dedicated page with a description and scrollbar at the bottom. A button on each item provided the option to:

Retrieve Item

Alternatively, bouncing arrows allowed me to:

Move Item to Inventory
*Distribute item to **Desini***
*Distribute Item to **Guiles***
*Distribute item to **Priya***
*Distribute item to **Roshan***

Back when I'd first met Priya and rescued her from the

dark caster Crohl, we'd taken a small chest for our troubles that had proven worth the effort to drag across the forest, but no such window had appeared. The chest into which I stared on the platform was too large to be carried whole. After all, we were inside an instanced dungeon, and loot was to be carried or worn by those who received upgrades.

Folded clothing in neat stacks took up one side of the display. I mused over how a grootslang would've so organized his clothes, considering it'd had no arms of which to speak, but I was too juiced to let that little lack of reality distract me. When eyeing the first item, the corresponding box in the loot pane lit up. The name of the item was printed in purple.

Healer's Robe of Advancement

Level 13
Slot: Body
Quality: Epic Heirloom
Durability: 150 of 150
+8 to Intelligence
+7 to resist magic
+7 to healing spells
+10% experience gains when fighting undead or demons
This robe's stats increase with the wearer to whom is it soul bound. Stat increases cease at Level 25.

"Roshan, I believe you will find that fight was worth the effort." The folded robe materialized in my hand. I raised and lowered my hand to test the weight of the thick cloth before holding it out.

"For me?" Her jaw dropped. "It's beautiful, Gemini."

Grabbing it by the shoulders, she held it in front of her and allowed the bottom hem to dump toward the earthen platform. Inlaid pink lilies lined the lapels of the otherwise pristine white robe and golden clasps jingled quietly as it unfolded.

She set her hand on her chest and peered down. "But..."

Though she hadn't finished the thought aloud, I held little doubt what was going through her mind as she pondered the robe gifted to her by the priest who trained her in the east. The man who'd taken his own life in his hands and made her his protégé was gone now, and the robe and scepter were the last remnants she had to remember him. She'd just seen me go through this exercise with Priya outside the instance, so I didn't belabor the point.

"You can keep the robe he gave you," I said. "When we have a hearth, we can find some way to display yours and Priya's... to remind us where we came from. I'll slot it in my bag, right next to Priya's robe."

When Roshan looked up again, she swiped a tear from her eye.

"This is why I am bound to you, Gemini. You have understood me from the beginning."

"I understand you because you don't hide yourself."

Roshan stepped forward and cupped my face in her hands, but then her gaze jumped around at the captive audience, and her coppery complexion turned pale. She pattered my cheek twice and stepped back. "May I put it on now?"

I chuckled. "Do you want to? I mean, it's yours. You earned it."

Guiles turned his back to Roshan and spoke over his shoulder as he turned his attention on the chest. "I think she was asking for us to turn so she might dress with some privacy."

I shook my head. "You're half-right. I think she wanted

you to turn around." I clapped his back, a semi-permanent smile tattooed on my lips.

I extracted a leather belt with an inlaid pattern of barbs.

Creeper's Belt of Thorns
Level 17
Slot: Waist
Quality: Epic
Durability: 130 of 130
+ 5 to Dexterity
+1% chance to dodge melee attacks
Melee attackers take 5% of inflicted damage.

"This seems perfect for you, Gemini," Guiles said.

"Yeah, it's pretty awesome. It even has a little clip here that'll hold my bag." A thought occurred, and I looked up at him. "I'm not sure we'll find much of use for a Level 50 rogue in here."

"Due to the experience, I am now Level 51, Gemini."

I checked my HUD and found the announcement.

He bowed slightly. "My first advancement in over two decades is plenty reward. Since I now have a companion who can increase my attributes, these rewards are more than satisfying."

Though I'd tested ticking up one of his attribute points, I'd found Guiles's level cap status inside the dungeon kept me from doing so. But when we stepped outside the dungeon, the elf and I would speak at length about how to evolve him.

One restriction was his disposition of friendly. I could spend only one point per level gained, but it didn't mean those points wouldn't be available later, if our friendship grew stronger. I wouldn't know for sure unless I spent all the points I could on him to see if it left a surplus. Then there was the whole binding-him-to-me idea, if I spent over five points. We'd have to deal with that, too.

He wasn't exactly weak out in the real world of Enora, so there was no hurry.

I donned the new belt and returned my attention to the chest.

Half-gloves of the Shadow
Level 16
Type: Hands
Quality: Very Rare
Durability: 75 of 75
+12% slow effect to movement-impairing spells
+15 Intelligence
+5 Constitution

Priya was giddy to receive the gloves. They fit her fingers perfectly—all loot fit as if tailored in Enora—and ran halfway up her forearms.

"They're so fancy." She grinned. "Silky."

The last major item in the chest brought my attention to Desini. Her facial muscles stretched into a mask of excitement—which should have added five charisma points—though she stood away from the chest, as if giving it a respectable birth. She couldn't read the description from there, so I pulled out a small box before retrieving her prize. I handed the box to Guiles, and he pried it open.

It was feeling a lot like Christmas on the platform of evil.

Inside were three major health potions and three major mana potions. We had Desini swap out her less-potent potions to the casters and gifted her the three major health potions. Two of the major mana potions found their ways into Roshan's hands, and Priya received the third. Then, gazing up at Desini a final time, I allowed the smile I'd suppressed to spread across my face. The weapon I revealed glowed in a purple hue.

Violet Mace of the Stone Wall
Level 18
Type: One-handed Mace
Quality: Epic
Durability: 110 of 110
46-60 Melee Damage
+15 Constitution
+2% Chance to parry

"It glows with such energy!" Roshan said as I extended it toward Desini. "Surely this is an item forged by the Light, itself!"

"It's beautiful," Priya said.

A hunger emanated from her and I tilted my head to one side as I eyed the half-elf.

Noticing my gaze, she cleared her throat, and her emotions shifted to neutral. "You know, as implements of destruction go."

"Riiiiight," I drew out the word.

"A fine weapon." Guiles nodded at the mace.

Desini held her hands close to her Godsteel plate chest piece as her eyelids fluttered. She glanced from my face to the weapon and back.

"Take it," I said. "It's your new weapon."

Desini snatched the mace to her chest and grinned at me. "When I met you only a week ago, I never imagined how my life might change. Once a messenger who struggled to get by and slept in a cart, I'm now an adventurer and wield such majestic finery in defense of the Light." She knelt and bowed her head deeply. "I swear to use this weapon to defend you to my dying breath, my lord."

I lay gentle fingers atop the soft hair between her ears. "Let's keep the dying to a minimum, Desini. Maybe tone down the 'lord' stuff, too."

But she continued. "No mist creature shall slither before you and live. Not a grootslang shall survive to tell the tale of encountering you to its evil brethren. No undead zombie shall creep before you, no vampire shall speak your name."

Vampire? Did she say vampire?

"I shall bring many warriors to your hearth, if it is your will." She stood, unsheathed her sword from its scabbard, stepped forward, then kissed me.

I was too taken aback by her proclamation to do anything but accept her affections. Beautiful though she was and attracted to her like I was, I still held doubts about a romantic relationship with someone who called me her teacher. I left the thoughts for later and went with my old reliable response.

Snark.

"I'm getting the faint sense you might appreciate your new weapon."

She glared at me for a long moment. "You are—how do you say it?—fucking with me, right?"

I roared laughter. "I am!"

Desini cackled, leaned in, and pressed her lips to my chin. "There! I fuck with you, too!"

"Quite the harem you're building, here, *Shénhuà*," Guiles said.

I raised a crooked finger. "Let's get something straight

from the beginning. *Harem* implies, well, I don't know what it implies. But I don't like that word. When you see me bringing whores to my hearth, you can use that word again." I lowered my voice to a mutter. "Anyone who would call this a harem is a dick."

"Before I would offend the instrument of Solara's own energy, I pledge to cut my tongue from my mouth if ever again I speak that word." The elf rose and took a step toward me. Then he knelt. "For more than a decade, I hid myself from the wretched and corrupt of this world so that Brugh and I might live. But Solara granted me a second chance to serve her as a beacon for my kind. I never fathomed I would encounter a grootslang. I will serve with you for as long as you will have me, Lord Gemini." He stood. "Your leadership in this difficult battle showed strong intuitions. There is hope for you, yet."

My response died in my throat. Did that son of a bitch always have to be right?

Roshan broke the silence as the elf and I stared at each other. "In the east, harems are composed of wives who share the adorations of their husbands and see each other as sisters, much as we do, noob."

My face warmed under her gentle rebuke. Guiles snickered.

She thrust a finger at him. "Never stab my man again or I shall see you smitten. Smited. Smout. Whatever!"

I bowed to the elf and Roshan, in turn. "Now that I've had my second culture lesson for the day and we all seem to be back on the same page, we have work left." I gestured toward the glowing door beyond the platform.

Guiles shook his head and glared at Roshan. She shrugged at him.

"What?" I barked.

Desini said, "You have yet to loot the corpse, noob."

Grrrr.

Roshan shot her a look of appreciation. "Your pronunci-ation is much better than Priya's. My words roll divinely off your mishon tongue."

I paced over to the grootslang and, surely enough, found a small bag lying next to it. I imagined it had appeared when the beast died because there wasn't anywhere on its tubular, winged body to stash it.

I reached inside and felt the unmistakable cool sensa-tion of coins against my fingertips. They jingled as I let them run through my fingers. Eyeing my inventory panel, I choked on my own saliva. A renewed smile crossed my face as I gazed at Priya over my shoulder.

"Try not to faint, okay?"

19

You have received:
137 Gold
57 Silver
45 Copper

The five of us stood near the magic barrier, adjusting our equipment as we prepared to enter the next fountain room. A prompt appeared as I reached out to touch the barrier.

You do not meet the level requirements for this instance:

Ruins of the Plague Barrens II:
The Labyrinth of Vinh
Minimum Level: 20
Maximum Level: 30

Each party member must meet the minimum level requirement to enter this instance. You may use the Return option to open a portal to the Ruins of the Plague Barrens entrance. When you reach Level 20, you may use the pedestal at the entrance to open a portal directly to this gateway.

"Ah," Guiles said. "I hadn't considered this possibility, *Shénhuà*. Apologies."

I waved a dismissive hand. "It's not your fault." It wasn't the first time inside a game world that I'd bank an opportunity for later. Besides, I was pretty stoked at our successes since entering the day before. There were things we could do better, but we showed a lot of potential.

I'd surrounded myself with the right people. Or Enora had. Now, we had to survive the outside world long enough to reach Level 20, come back, and kick the next floor's ass.

Okay, maybe Level 25.

"Let's talk about what's next," I said. "Exiting will put us back in the governor's crosshairs. If that mage showing up at the entrance taught us anything, it's that the stakes have been raised."

Guiles nodded agreement. "Wise, *Shénhuà*. We should discuss this at the entry fountain as we replenish ourselves."

I selected the Return option, and a tiny circle bloomed into a tall portal with warbling orange light surrounding it. Through the opening, I saw the first fountain and Pickney just beyond. We stepped through in turn and found ourselves back in the first fountain room with the horses and the cart.

Desini's horse nickered, and the others' hooves clopped nervously as we materialized. We each patted them and spoke soothing words until they were calm.

"I have a suggestion," Desini said, lowering her shield and leaning it against the cart.

I scanned her high, round cheeks, green irises, and the

slight dimple in her chin. Though other men had mistaken her for a weak creature, I couldn't ask for a better partner to advance with in combat. I'd spent too many years on earth as a socially challenged IT networking nerd to take anyone for granted. "Of course. Make your suggestion."

"The place where my people made their second home after the humans cast us out is to the northeast. The surrounding lands are rich with forests and hillsides of crystalline caves that would serve as excellent shelters from pursuers."

"That sounds pretty great, actually. Tell me more."

"There is much game to be hunted. We would want for little as we take refuge and let political concerns quiet. While we could return south, cross to the east, and then trek north across the mountainous terrain to these lands, there is a shortcut to the northeast if we brave the Plague Barrens for a short while longer. The road forks that direction one day's travel from here."

I peered at Guiles. "You been to the Plague Barrens before?"

Guiles nodded. "It becomes more treacherous the farther north and west you explore, but one day's travel..." He tapped his chin in contemplation. "Yes. That should work. The higher-level black sand worms and serpents are at least two days' journey, and we will evade them if we take that road. It skirts the outer edge of the barrens. The forests of my people are two weeks' travel in that direction, though I wouldn't return there as long as I'm a fugitive, you understand."

I nodded. "I do. The reason you fled in the first place was to spare them a war for your intrusion in the governor's business."

"I appreciate your concise speech, *Shénhuà*," Guiles

said. "A rare trait, as I find humans to be quite the chatty ones."

Desini cut in. "If I may be so bold."

Our heads swiveled toward her and I realized she hadn't been finished speaking. "Sorry! Please, continue."

"You honor me." Her tone said otherwise. "The valley where my people lived before they were evicted a second time is a place you might consider for your precious artifact." She eyed my bag.

"Artifact?" I peered down. "Oh! The Foundation Stone?"

She nodded. "Not that I should recommend such a thing. I don't pretend to know anything about such a miracle."

I patted her shoulder. "I know less about the continent than all of you. I want to hear opinions."

Guiles gave his. "Desini's plan takes us in the right direction. We could scout the place she's talking about and, if we deem it a strong defensive position, act accordingly."

I raised an eyebrow at Roshan and Priya. They both nodded in agreement. "Well! It seems we have a plan." I kissed both of Desini's cheeks, stepped back so everyone stood in front of me, then held up a finger. "But you all need to understand that adventuring comes with the territory. If we choose a place to make a hearth, it will only be a home base. Something we can grow together. I was brought here by Solara to affect change, you can bet your butts I'll do it. That means we'll be moving around, not resting on our laurels."

"I shall serve next to you until darkness is quelled from this region, if it takes a thousand years," Priya said.

"As will I," Desini added.

"For as long as you will have me," Guiles said.

Roshan nodded. "I serve with you, noob, but soon you will have to render unto me the spoils of my patience. You have a promise to keep."

"*Noob*, huh?" Recalling how Desini had once seduced Priya in Breeder's place in Brumhill, I paced toward Roshan and peered down at her full lips for a long moment. Then I allowed my gaze to wander slowly up and down her body. My finger pressed a dimple in her bottom lip, and our gazes locked as I ran it down to the tip of her smooth, rounded chin, just like Desini had to the half-elf on that day. "That's a promise this noob longs to keep."

The unabated red flush in her cheeks had been exactly what I was going for.

Her answer was not.

"The cart is just there. Take me."

"Whoa, I didn't mean—"

Roshan's determined gaze circled the room. "Avert your embarrassed eyes, fools!" Her lips parted as if she'd say more; but, instead, she averted her own gaze and pushed a quick breath between her lips.

"Are you okay?" I asked.

"I shall have what's mine!" She threw up her hands and shook them as she spoke, the sleeves of her new robe flailed. "No more of this talk! No more empty words of ceremony and forging memories! Long has this fruit remained unsullied by a man! Thou will plunge into me now and seal our bond!" Roshan unclasped her robe. "Turn your head, elf."

I was struck by the recent history of my eastern goddess.

Kidnapped. Taken from her family. Hauled across the lands to the ocean and stuffed on a ship. Dragged along a perilous journey that claimed the lives of many to exposure and disease. Then, I found her bound on the edge of a lake. We came together by the will of what I called artificial intelligence, but she called a goddess. We bonded. Evil fell before us within an hour of the time we met. She leveled. Her purpose, found.

She was taken by Priya and Crohl. I stole her back.

Again, she was kidnapped by the governor's men. And again, I rescued her.

We'd played love games the previous day, but not the one she wanted. The one that would bind us, in her mind.

Roshan wanted me, but I didn't think it had much to do with sex. The sometimes gruff, mentally-charged enemy of darkness lacked the one thing she'd so desired for the longest time.

Security.

Shocked glares surrounded me. Desini gasped. Guiles took a step backward and turned his back to us. Priya barked a single, uncontrollable laugh then slapped a hand over her mouth.

"Perhaps we'll step through the barrier and into the hallway we cleared yesterday so that bonds might be tied?" Guiles suggested with an uncharacteristic hint of indecisiveness.

"Yes," Desini said. "The priestess hungers for what she has been denied."

"I have some tyne leaf in my pack if it please you, priestess," Guiles said.

I nodded. "That might not be a bad idea..."

Roshan squinted one eye so hard, I couldn't see her sclera. "If it be Solara's will that I bear your blessed offspring, then so shall I fulfill her desires as we fulfill our own. Or would you deny me this blessing of the Light? Do you have different ideas, noob?"

One pregnant woman and another giving off vibes? A

second child? What would that be like? What kind of fucking game world was this?

Players would live out all kinds of fantasies in Enora. Of that, I had no doubt. But those players could log out at their whim and leave what they saw as virtual families behind. I wondered what would happen if they did, disappeared for what was three Enoran days, and returned. How would that play with these NPCs?

Though I wondered if the original game developers had considered the question, I voiced a different one out loud. "If we're to be out doing our duty to Solara, who is going to be at our home, raising these children?"

"He does not desire me," Roshan said.

Priya clutched her hips. "We will all raise them. Each child born to you is a child born to all of us. And to others who come to serve Solara with you. In the meantime," she raised her shoulder in a half-shrug, "we will share responsibilities.

"Your precious leveling might come in the wilderness instead of these underground bastions of darkness early on, but it will come." Her knuckles turned white as her grip tightened at her hips. "You did not assume that our pledges to you involved only roaming around the world beating your enemies to your will, did you? Why, I pledged when you were but a... a... NOOB! For all I knew, you were *lucky*. You didn't think me so simple as to—"

I raised my hand. "Stop barking at me!"

Silence filled the room.

"Everyone but Roshan," I pointed toward the magical barrier, "out."

I found them in need of little further prompting. Priya muttered under her breath as she went. "The mere implication I would bind myself to a—"

"Priya! Stop being snarky!"

To her credit, she at least held her words until she was beyond the barrier, but I wagered with myself Guiles and Desini would get an earful.

When Roshan and I were alone, I eyed the coppery skin visible behind the slit where she'd unclasped her robe.

"Fine. No rose petals." I pointed. "But what better place than one of Enora's magical fountains?"

20

The smooth crystal shell of the fountain's edge chilled my back as Roshan curled over my lap, but I couldn't have cared less. I breathed her hair's scent deep into my lungs, reveling in it during my post-coital drowsiness. One arm hung over her shoulder, lazily cupping a breast as a fingertip on the other traced the surrounding line of her naval. Gentle ripples meandered across the water.

Roshan ran her fingertips down my arm and wiggled so her cheek rested on my shoulder.

"It fills me with gratitude that our first love happened near to these blessed waters. It feels appropriate. Cleansing, if you'll forgive my double meaning."

If she was good with it, so was I. Enora was artificial intelligence to me, but the customized rewards we'd received from the chest near the grootslang's corpse reminded me that she did give blessings. So, it wasn't that I lacked reverence. I just knew the A.I. was very unlikely to give a shit about the water.

A switch had flipped as Roshan had writhed with pleasure beneath me. I'd longed for her so much that I naturally expected disappointment. I found myself awash in the opposite from the moment I pulled down the shoulders of her shiny new robe and gorged myself with the sight of her.

Although I'd accepted the world as my own with a satisfying sense of finality, I still found myself unwilling to check Roshan's status in my interface. If an asterisk appeared next to her name when I gathered the courage, that would be bun number two in the oven. Where Priya's pregnancy had initially freaked me the fuck out, her confident words about handling children had somehow set me at ease. I had my whole life to hunker down, if I needed to, assuming we could hide. Levels would come.

That or I was really sleepy.

People in the outside world might think me psychotic, but fuck the outside world. There was no outside world. I'd spent twenty-two years there, struggling to get by after losing my parents and facing rejection over and over, just like everyone else. Earth was overrun with people so plugged into tech they didn't know how to talk to each other anymore. It'd been like that for a half-century, and I'd seen no evidence it might change.

I circled her naval again with the tip of my finger.

Coming to Enora was a blessing in that way, and my fresh start had taken on new meaning. I wanted to sweep what I hated about the old world under the rug. I'd love those who loved me, fight alongside them or lie low and have a family with them. If Enora and Takemoto thought they'd control my destiny while Enora allowed me to get Priya pregnant, if they wanted me to clear the way—whatever that meant—for new players someday, I'd have to trust the world was suited for it. What choice did I have?

It was easy to be relaxed about it when I held one of the

most beautiful women I'd ever seen warming my chest as heavy eyelids blinked me toward slumber.

I kissed her head. "You were amazing."

She slapped my arm. "Surely a virgin is not your idea of a wonderful lover." She leaned into my shoulder and raised her chin to look up at me. "I did, however, gain one stamina."

We both broke up with laughter.

I turned my gaze on the magic barrier. "We should stop defiling these magic waters and dress so our companions can return."

She rubbed my arm a few times as she nodded. "Can I ask one final thing of you, Gemini?" Her voice was soft, sweet. It sounded somewhat foreign on her lips.

"Anything I can give, you will have."

"While I would not claim exclusivity, I would want us to share a bedroll when we sleep next. Just this one time because of our bonding."

"It will be so. Desini and Priya are probably itching to get at each other by this point, anyway."

"Good!" She threw off my arm then stood. Droplets of water ran in rivers down her feminine curves.

I enjoyed the sight as Roshan pushed onto the balls of her feet and stretched. The water sloshed and rippled around her shins. Her breasts rose high and the curve of her back where it rolled into the hill of her perfect backside stole my full attention.

When she saw where I was looking, she smiled. "Let us dress. Our companions and Solara's enemies await."

Guiles and I stood at the front of our group, facing the

portal to the Plague Barrens proper. The elf had questions before we proceeded back into the world, and I didn't blame him. I was in no hurry to step outside.

"These men you killed on the road. You're certain they were the governor's?"

"You mean, like the man Priya separated from his head?" I shot her a glance over my shoulder and stretched an artificial sneer with one corner of my lip.

The half-elf scrunched up her face and stuck her tongue out as she patted a horse. It was a fine creature with strong haunches and a shining black coat. "He slit my throat in Brumhill. He held Roshan captive. What would you have done?"

"It's not like you died," I said.

"Resurrection, outside an instance, without the aid of a scroll or spell." Guiles shook his head. "The notion baffles me."

"Seems to me the one you killed is the bigger problem," Priya said.

"Why is that?" Guiles asked.

"He was the governor's nephew."

"Hmph. Your people don't do anything half way, do they?"

I shrugged in response. "We have a way of pissing the governor off, although we've never set eyes on him. The men who held Roshan at the lake were mercenaries. They went east across the ocean to fulfill a bounty for the governor. Now that I've heard your story about how he treated the serf daughters, I think he wanted something of a more exotic ilk for himself. She meant little more than coin to her kidnappers."

"Why for himself, and not one of his lords?"

"Because after we killed them at the edge of the Dark

Wood, these other men appeared in chain mail and killed Priya and me to reclaim her. They'd forced her to dress and, although they made her watch us die, they hadn't handled her roughly. She was a prize. I mean, look at her." I threw a glance over my shoulder.

"Avert your gaze, fool," Roshan muttered.

"Yes," Guiles said with a nod. "Quite lovely. But the men who took her from the inn were undoubtedly the governor's own, since they rode with his nephew. Definitely not mercenaries. The governor sent low levels because this area is full of them and he didn't expect resistance."

"Right. But I wonder why they'd risk taking her through Zhara's zone of influence."

"Again, the mercenaries were low-level cretins. Probably didn't even know where they were. If the journey was as perilous and long as Roshan describes, I'm not sure how the governor's men set a date for the rendezvous. Leira, Breeder, and I would have noticed them lurking around Brumhill if they'd waited long for Roshan and her kidnappers."

"A warlock died on the return trip, shortly before we arrived at the lake where Gemini rescued me," Roshan interjected. "Just days before Gemini found me."

"High-level warlocks can send telepathic messages across great distances," Guiles said. "He must have reported their progress."

"And since Roshan is the only eastern woman I've seen since coming to Enora, I guess it wasn't difficult for them to track us down."

"You've left no doubt as to their patronage. Thank you for sharing your story." He nodded and set his hands on his hips. Scratching his chin as he worked through something in his mind, the elf then peered up at me.

"So?" I asked.

"You're adept at making enemies. Now we know this is your fate." The elf clapped my shoulder. "The good news is, only a single mage showed up at the entrance. It's likely he was acting on a new bounty."

"Which makes sense. I did kill his nephew, after all."

I shrugged. "Like you said, making enemies seems to be my destiny."

"Again, do you do anything half-way?"

"I'll assume your question is rhetorical."

"Assumption is the tool of the ignorant, but in this case, it serves. If the second attacker from the inn received word that his traveling companion was murdered on the road, he probably visited the mage guild in Trowlsby and arranged communication with the governor. Since a bounty was placed, we can infer the governor has no legions in range. He's using locals and any wandering adventurers in search of coin. It's doubtful we'll face an army when we exit."

"Well, that's a relief."

"On the other hand, one young mage made a lucky guess where you might go and showed up outside this entrance. We should be on our guard in case others prove equally fortunate. Or brave."

"Go out armed and ready?"

"Yes. Most pursuers will stop short of the Plague Barrens and take the road east, into the rocky hills Desini mentioned. They won't expect low-level adventurers like yourselves would be so brazen as to enter the Barrens."

"Brazen is my middle name."

"What is a middle name?" Priya asked.

"Later," I said.

She shrugged.

"After they've cut to the east, they will turn north. Since

we'll follow the road through the Plague Barrens to the north before forking to the east, we should stay a few days ahead of them, depending on the size of their parties and how quickly they move. It is not unheard of for headhunters to combine resources, especially if the bounty is high."

"And you said the mage spent a lot to portal to us, so it probably is."

Guiles nodded. "When we find a place to stop, such as a place to lay your foundation—should you deem a locale in the northeast worthy—we'll have to prepare for their arrival. Running from the governor is less apt a strategy as preparing to defend against a bunch of mercenaries. It's unlikely they'll be adventurers if they come from the low-level towns to the south. If you want to establish a strong-hold, you cannot waste time traipsing across the world with your tail between your legs."

"Running isn't my thing, anyway."

"Yes, I get that impression," He nudged my elbow. "But you should consider your actions more carefully." He threw Priya a look. "All of you."

To my surprise, Priya gave a solemn nod. I would've garnered a snarky expression from her if I'd said it.

"Assuming we can stand against a parade of bounty hunters, the governor's men will undoubtedly follow after a time." Guiles clutched his hips. "No matter how we build, we'll need allies."

Desini stepped forward. "With this, I can help, if we set down roots near my former home."

"Your people?" I asked.

She nodded. "If you would accept them in your camp, they would pledge their allegiance in recompense for the gift of returning to the place they once chose for their refuge. When you see it, you will understand."

I imagined a village full of cat people running around. That idea was kind of cool.

"I can also help," Guiles said. "I know a few people." He waved his hand. "But let's set our thoughts to surviving the Plague Barrens first."

"Agreed."

The elf stepped forward and unsheathed his daggers, but I gripped his arm. "You know, there's one more thing I'd like to take care of, but I need to talk to you first."

"Is it imperative that we speak now? Your enemies gather."

"I'll let you decide."

"Which means we will speak of it now." He sheathed his weapons and tossed a length of white hair over his shoulder.

"Since you show up in my Companion tab, I can spend your attribute points."

"You mentioned the spending of points for your friends. What's a Companion Tab?"

"Why do you seem mystified?" I recalled how Roshan and Priya had inspected each other's attributes once they'd become companions the night we spent in Priya's dome in the woods. "Roshan? You have a Companion tab, right?"

She threw me a confused look. "Companion *tab*?" She blinked her eyes in succession. "No. If I focus on Priya or Desini, I can see their attributes in rows of text next to them, but I see no tab." She raised an eyebrow, her facial muscles stretching into excitement. "Perhaps this is another of your many gifts from Solara?"

"Huh. I guess so."

"Interesting," Guiles said. "Setting aside the details about your special tab, you were saying you could spend attribute points for your companions. You understand it would be inappropriate for me to ask the Chosen One for such a service."

"Chosen One? Jesus." I sighed as I considered how to best sell this idea of bonding to Guiles. "Here's what you don't know. Now that you're my companion, I need spend only six attribute points, and you'll resurrect upon death, like the rest of us."

"Yes, I recall."

"Why do you not seem surprised?"

Guiles shook his head in derision. "Don't you remember? In Brumhill, I discovered what you were by inspecting Priya and discovering she was your soul bound companion. Is it not I who told you of the way the *Shénhuà* could improve their companions?"

Shit. I forgot all about that. "Yes. That's right. Sorry."

"How does it work? You'd spend six points, and I'd become bound?"

"Right. It means that we will be forever linked, and the only way you can die a final death is by my own hand."

"Forever? That is a long time, especially for an elf."

I shook my head. "You don't get it. Even elves don't live forever. If I bind you, you'll stop aging altogether, but there are limitations."

"Such as?"

Since I wanted to be accurate, I opened the nifty note feature in my interface to which I'd pasted the message I received when I bound Desini so I could explain.

While non-players can level their attributes through labor, they may also purchase attribute upgrades from trainers in Enora. But Enoran trainers can spend only five attribute points per trainee.
Players do not share this attribute cap, but privileges come at

*a cost. While you can spend over five attribute points on the behalves of your companions, doing so will result in the companion being permanently **bound** to you.*
*In order to bind a companion to you, the companion must have a disposition of **endeared** or better toward you.*
Fallen non-players who are bound to you will resurrect at your spawn point if they are not quickly revived after a battle.
If you fall in battle, bound companions will continue to fight until your enemies are vanquished or your companions fall.
Bound creatures may not wander beyond ten miles from their binder unless given leave to do so.
If you have a foundation or pay for a room at an inn, you can leave the non-player behind at your choosing, but you will still be bound.
While bonds between non-players are broken by death, this player-to-non-player bond is permanent.
Be aware: There is no limit to the number of NPCs who can be bound to you, as long as they maintain the requisite disposition. You may bind a non-player of endeared or higher disposition without permission.
You can only break this bond if the non-player is killed by your own hand.
Binding cannot be undone.

I explained the distance rule and further that we couldn't bond until he became endeared to me. I figured that latter part was something over which we had little control, so we had time to consider all of this. For now, I could only spend five of his points.

"I'm intrigued, but we can deal with this later. Five points of Deterity would be greatly appreciated."

It seemed we would be dealing with all kinds of shit later.

I ticked up his Dexterity attribute. He showed no sign it affected him. He nodded his thanks.

"I have suffered these unspent skill points like thorns in my heel for years. My dreams have been filled with how I would spend them were it not for my inability to travel to trainers. One has to register, thanks to the former King Constantine, and to buy services as an elf who has meddled in the governor's business increases the difficulty."

"Seems I'm not the only one who makes enemies," I said.

"Bah. Even if I could have spent them, I wouldn't have had cause to use them to my benefit. Hiding out in that town, there isn't much opportunity to advance. Wait…"

I did, but when he didn't speak, I raised an eyebrow.

He tapped a finger to his chin. "It seems I've become a problem for you."

"How do you figure?"

"The rapidity with which the bounty was issued and the arrival of the mage makes little sense. He was young, and word would have to travel to him before he would arrange passage via a portal. No. I think it's more likely he was an adept of the university."

It was Guiles's turn to raise an eyebrow. Then it hit me as if he'd pushed the thought into my mind. "Oh, shit. The scryers. Because you left Brumhill. You think they traced *you* to the entrance."

He nodded. "I'm sorry. It seems much more likely than a lucky guess on such a young mage's part. Yes, I'm almost certain they scryed me out."

"That explains why the mage kept looking around for something. I didn't know what he was searching for, but once he turned my arm to stone, that didn't matter. If he was looking for you, did the Währsagers send him?"

Silence passed over us as we both considered the question.

Then I shook my head. "No, if you've been in Brumhill for many years, as you said, I doubt they're actively searching for you." ·

"*You* underestimate the ire of the governor."

"Maybe you have delusions of grandeur."

Guiles pinched his lips in a crooked slant. "Although the Währsagers couldn't use their spells to search Brumhill because of its proximity to the Tree of Solara, his men have entered Brumhill on several occasions in search of Brugh and me. Leira and Breeder protected us."

I crossed my arms over my chest to consider this new information. "The man on horseback who escaped to Trowlsby to report we'd killed the governor's men is the key here. You have to acknowledge things would move faster if he learned of his nephew's death. He was still on his horse when I stabbed him. Besides, he didn't know you were with us. Then again, if the Währsagers realized you'd resurfaced, I'm sure your bounty is worth even more."

"I'm afraid the appearance of the mage will remain a mystery, Gemini. But knowing who they chase is less important than ensuring the safety of our party and the execution of Solara's plans."

"Guiles, I know you've agreed to fight alongside us, but it would honor me if you would accept my friendship and stay with us indefinitely. You would be the perfect addition to our foundation when that day comes, and I could think of no better partner to train our people. Adventuring together, we might set right the wrongs of this region of Enora."

"Your salesmanship is strong, *Shénhuà,* but I already

planned on accepting your offer. Our destinies are inter-twined. Once we grow as companions, we should discuss how to spend my points and bind so that we may venture forth as soldiers Solara has called to duty."

Done and done.

21

The humid blackness of the Plague Barrens assaulted our senses as we gathered outside. The toppled stone of the ancient Elven structures were shadowy monoliths against a dark horizon. The glassy crunch of the black sand shards beneath my boots reminded me of the sinister place in which I stood. Compared to the rest of Enora I'd encountered, the Plague Barrens felt like a dead planet of its own. I hoped to learn more about this place someday.

But I turned my focus to a new companion since his level returned to its pre-synchronized state. I saw him for the absolute beast he was.

Guiles

Elf

Level 51 Rogue

*Strength: 14**

*Intelligence: 21**

Dexterity: 89

*Wisdom: 31**

Constitution: 51
Charisma: 25**
*Skills learned through life actions
**Elves receive a 10% bonus to Charisma gains

Combat Skills:

Ranged: 79
Unarmed: 34
Melee: 82
Ranged Attack Power: 312

Defensive Skills:

Dodge: 5

Weapon Skills:

Bow: 74
Blunt: 21
Dagger: 121
Thrown: 74

Occupational Skills:

Not to be confused with combat professions, occupational skills allow people to earn a wage, run a business, build garrisons, or create weapons, armor, and potions to supplement adventuring.

Carpentry: 21

Rank: Adept

Tool tip: Carpenters use wood as their primary ingredient in the construction of structures, wooden weapons, and furniture.

Forestry: 57

Rank: Master

Tool tip: Foresters are lumberjacks skilled with axes. They also make excellent field hands and use scythes as their secondary gathering tools.

Skinning: 38

Rank: *Journeyman*

Tool tip: Skinners remove hides from vanquished animal beings—and sometimes humanoid ones—to be used as raw materials by leather workers, clothiers, blacksmiths and other professions. Tanning is often selected by skinners as a secondary occupation to create leathers.

Cooking: 19

Rank: *Apprentice*

Tool tip: Yum! Cooks use myriad ingredients to concoct tasty dishes to feed the hungry, boost morale, and provide buffs to tradesmen and adventurers, alike.

Leather Crafting: 65

Rank: *Grand Master*

Using animal skins to craft leather armor and clothing, Leather Crafters typically outfit adventurers preferring stealthy and/or ranged combat.

Blacksmithing: 15

Rank: Apprentice

Upon viewing his occupational prowess, I realized what an understatement it had been to say Guiles would make a fine teacher. It was almost embarrassing how my new companion dwarfed me in all aspects of Enoran life. If he hadn't had such a head start, I might have taken my comparative weakness to heart, but here was a template for what I might become.

I turned at the sounds of nickering and shards crunching like low static as Priya and Roshan led the three horses—gained courtesy of the governor's slain soldiers—out of the portal. Off to the side, Desini planted kisses on Pickney's snout as she scratched the side of his head. The loving hums of the mishon words evident by a thicker accent when she spoke them to the animal brought a smile to my face.

Cloud-born flashes popped, revealing thunderheads and it was then I realized we all shared a common talent... an ability to see in the dark.

Roshan and I used Inner Illumination to view the ruins in which we stood. The elven vision shared by Priya and Guiles assisted them just enough to navigate the inky blackness and, of course, Desini enjoyed an almost feline sense of vision. I'd seen a transparent layer roll over her pupils and irises on several occasions as she adjusted to varied lighting.

Desini pointed out into the wastelands after a final scratch behind her horse's ear. "The road is just to the east. If we stick close to it, we'll be less likely to encounter trouble as the beasts of the Barrens are widely territorial in nature and tend toward seclusion. But we should be on our guard at all times. I propose two riders on horseback ride ahead of the cart. Their added agility will allow them time to react to threats and sound the alarm should danger arise."

"I like this mishon," Guiles said. "You surround yourself with intelligent, tactical creatures. Their intuition in the dungeon was strong for people of such youth. I commend you."

"I had little to do with it." It irked me to say it, but I wanted him to understand the next bit. "It seems Solara put each of these women right in my path. All I did was accept her blessings as presented." The words came like bile on my tongue. I didn't like being disingenuous with my friends, but I didn't make the rules governing NPCs. I just obeyed them to keep my XP. Besides, when I equated Solara to the A.I., Enora, it was true.

Roshan appeared next to me and torqued my ass. I jumped a little.

"My lord's humility before our sky-dwelling lady pleases me." She turned, and the lowest hem on her robe brushed the ground, giving off the illusion that she glided toward the cart.

Priya called over from her horse. "I will ride the second watch, if it's all the same to you, Gemini. I'm due sleep, and weight creeps into my bones. Perhaps you and Roshan will join me?"

I threw a glance at Roshan, recalling her request we share a sleeping space. She smiled and nodded.

"I will take the first horseback watch with Desini on the cart," Guiles said. "Would that serve?"

"Are you sure?" I asked. "Didn't you say you were due sleep, as well?"

"Another few hours won't cause any harm, and I'm exhilarated by my new surroundings. Many years in a wretched" —he cleared his throat— "in a small town of little entertainment can render any environment a welcome sight."

I thought it might have something to do with his wanting to protect us, himself. Roshan snuck a glance at me and ran a finger down her abdomen outside the pristine white robe she wore.

"Yeah. Good. Roshan, Priya, and I will sleep while you two take the first watch. We'll work out a rotation after that."

My first thought upon jerking awake was that I needed to kill and skin a few more bears. Though Roshan and Priya made wonderful bed warmers, all the wagon rocking and the resulting banging of my bones left me battered. A couple more furs would soften the blows.

But it hadn't been the road's abuse dragging me out of

my snooze. The adrenal response to Desini's cries for action beyond the slit in the tarp had done that.

Did she say—?

"Scorpion!" she repeated.

Yup, that's what I thought she said.

I practically dove into my armor as I ripped my bow from my bag and slung it over my shoulder. I counted myself lucky none of my arrows rattled free of the quiver as I withdrew it. A quick inventory reminded me of a few lost ones in the dungeon. I was down to 24. I slid between the tarp slit without bothering to secure my new belt until I got outside

"Stop, Pickney!" Desini yelled, yanking at the reins like I'd never seen. The bumping I'd experienced had been due to the horse diverting from the road.

"Whoa, boy! Ease up!" I grabbed a reign and pulled with her, urging the horse to the side of the black, rocky path. Its neighs of terror pinched my ear drums as its head reared back and shook side-to-side as if to shake off its harness. "Whoa! Whoa!"

Desini wore a piece of cloth over her head with eye slits cut into it, and my facial skin told me why. Black dust filled the air and prickled against my cheeks like a hundred tiny needle stabs. Distant screams were but whispers against the shard-blowing wind.

Invent goggles.

As Pickney finally settled, I spied the source of the horse's distress at the crest of a long uphill climb. Though the giant scorpion stood at least a couple hundred yards away, Pickney knew danger when he sensed it.

The scale of the massive beast compared to the shadowy forms standing at its base brought a lump to my throat. One tiny figure waved its arms wildly, as if trying to lure its attention. The monster lowered its head, and thrust its plated tail over its back. A long stinger impaled its target. The flailing humanoid rose flailing into the air and catapulted through the sky to a certain death.

In the distance, just leaving the road and dismounting his horse closer to the conflict, was my new Elven companion.

It would be just my luck that my trump card dies on our first day out of doors.

I suddenly had a new understanding of the need to endear my friends. If Guiles died, he'd be erased from Enora.

"Jesus wept gravy! What does the crazy bastard think he's doing?" I peered down at Desini with my question, but she was already off the bench, yanking her plate over her chest. "Where the hell are you going?"

Her tail swung wildly behind her as she twisted, grabbed her sword still wrapped in its sheath, and set off in a full sprint up the hill with its ties twisting in the breeze.

Desini tossed me a glance over her muscular shoulder and smiled. "Same place you are, my special hero. Might want to hurry, though! Things seem sour ahead!"

"Gods dammit! Just wait for your team!"

Desini lit off like a cheetah. All this time I'd fought by her side, I'd never seen her at a full sprint. Guiles had a seventy-five-yard head start, yet she might arrive at the conflict first.

"Gemini?" Priya's voice came from behind me as I tied off my quiver.

"Time to gear up, sweetness! We've got trouble, and it's apparently been decided we're the problem solvers. I need all hands on deck!"

"On deck?"

"Just come on! We've got shit to kill!" I jogged up the hill, wondering about what the climb would do to my stamina before I even reached my destination. I slipped and slid in the strange, sandy shards every few steps, and it pissed me off. Cursing the whole way, I drew close enough to assess the circumstances.

A stout woman dragged a broadsword-wielding boy down the hill entirely against his will. Every few steps, she had to stop to get a second hand on him and yank him back on track. "I will not lose your father's only son today, Yoren Hammerbeard! Come now!"

By gods Dwarves!

A slimmer girl with flowing green hair sprinted out in front of them and had just reached me as the woman I assumed was her mother yanked Yoren forward again.

"The gods as my witness, that demon spawn will fall this day!" the boy growled, struggling against his mother's will.

I slid to a halt and grabbed his shoulder. "And fall he will, Yoren Hammerbeard! But let it be by our hands!"

The boy glared suddenly in my direction, his huge, deep-set eyes burning into me. "Just killed my father, that bastard did! He will die by my hand!"

Now I know who I saw flying. Well, that sucks!

Aided by distraction, he yanked free of his mother and sped off.

So I did what first jumped to mind. I swung out with my boot and hooked his shin.

He sprawled face-first into the shards and began to curse as I set my boot on his back and bore down. Then I glared at his mother. "Those are my people up there! Sit on him if you must to keep him down. I don't have time to wrangle him right now!"

From the breadth of the kid, I wasn't sure I could wrangle him, anyway. He might snap me in half. Had it not been for the partial beard and the youthful glow of his reddened, full cheeks, I'd have easily mistaken him for an adult. Well, an adult according to J. R. R. Tolkien, but what the hell did I know, really?

The mother plopped her wide dwarven ass down on the boy, then I removed my boot. The daughter followed suit with her narrower backside. She added a slap to the back of his head. "Stay still, you bucking beast!"

Roshan zoomed passed me, the tail of her robe flapping in the wind like she was straight out of some epic film. Priya brought up the rear on her shorter legs, but certainly holding her own in the speed department.

God, they love this. What is wrong with these fucking people? Why is the gamer the only one who wants nothing to do with that scorpion? Maybe the corpse flying through the air?

I raised my head to absorb the mass of the beast again.

Yeah, definitely the airborne corpse.

As if in reinforcement of the thought, Roshan called up the hill. "Come, demon spawn! Let us decide who shall wallow in the depths of the underworld!"

"Yeah!" Priya replied.

I set off up the hill once I was reasonably sure the woman and her daughter had the boy battened down.

"Take my glory, will ye? I'll get ye for this, ya top-siding bastard!"

The closer I got to the giant scorpion, the further away from it I wanted to be. It seemed to double in size every few seconds, and by the time I was in firing range, it was two stories tall.

Plague Scorpion
Level 27 Arachnid
(Elite)
King of the Southern Plague Barrens, the Plague Scorpion boasts a stinger with paralytic venom that causes muscles to spasm and rot.
Strength: 76
Dexterity: 48
Intelligence: 14
Wisdom: 11
Constitution: 100
Charisma: 1

Its shells plated its form so tightly, I wasn't sure what effect Click or my wolf would have on the beast, and I didn't want to stop long enough to cast the Summon spell. I saved my mana for my Woodsman abilities.

Another dwarf with a shield equaling his height swung a gleaming sword at one of the beast's shell-covered front legs as Desini slammed hard into the other with her Charge ability.

Logic dictated that the monstrosity's response to her charge was driven by a game mechanic. In my old world, anyone charging such a wall of shells would have been instantly flattened and concussed.

Desini uses Charge

Plague Scorpion is stunned
Plague Scorpion
-27 HP

Fire exploded in front of the scorpion's scaly face.

Roshan spun her hands in a counter-clockwise circle, conjuring the green spirals of her primary healing spell.

Priya Casts Flash Fire.

Plague Scorpion
-36 HP
Plague Scorpion
-5 HP (Burn)

Whoa! Priya's spell left a burn effect!
Green numbers ticked off above Desini's head as Roshan's healing spell activated.

Roshan Casts Minor Heal.
Desini +15 HP (HOT)
Desini +15 HP (HOT)

Screeching to a halt on the loose shards with an arrow at the ready, I fired a Drilling Arrow at the monster's gullet, but I misjudged and it hit its chest instead, causing lack-luster damage.

You use Drilling Arrow.

Plague Scorpion
-13 HP

Now that I had a good idea of the damage the women were doing, I disabled my combat log with a quick thought to focus on the fight, leaving warning dialogues active in case the beast used a special ability of which I needed to be aware. Their flashing avatars in my party pane would let me know if anyone got low on health.

"Ye fucking ugly poisonous barb-covered spawn of hell!" the dwarf screamed as he swung his sword in a wide arc and snapped one of the protective shells off the lowest section of the scorpion's leg. The beast didn't seem to have noticed.

I liked the dwarf's word game, though. Had to give him that.

Whim Hammerbeard
Dwarf
Level 36 Paladin
Title: Paladin of the First Order of the Matron

The scorpion kicked out and slammed into his shield, hurling him ten feet backward. It could have been worse, but the dwarf rolled over the black sand then was back on his feet, executing a Charge of his own in seconds to close the gap again. When I focused on him, his health bar appeared over his head. It was below twenty percent, by my guess.

"Roshan! Heal the dwarf! Desini, don't growl! His level's higher, and he has its anger! Do as much damage as you can, and if he gets low on health, you can growl and give him a break!"

"Good call!" Guiles appeared in a sudden explosion of motion high on the creature's back. Though he was too far up there for me to see exactly what was going on, the raining yellow fluid splattering into the sand told me he'd found a soft spot.

I loosed another arrow as lightning appeared above the creature's head. Priya prepared her next cast, right on the tail of the Thunder spell. I thanked Solara it wasn't a channeled cast, or she'd have to maintain it instead of readying another one, like with her ice spell. She was on top of shit.

Wait. Did I just thank Solara for something?

Priya's head swiveled as my pride bloomed. She could cast endlessly now that dwarf had the beast's full attention and a Level 51 rogue rode its back. I'd call her off, if need be, but I doubted she'd snag its hatred from those two. She nodded in reply, snarled in her best caster's face, and unleashed more pain.

A casting disc appeared over the scorpion's head as it took three faltering steps backward.

"Uh-oh!" the dwarf yelled. "Be ye smart, ye'll take cover!" Slamming his shield into the sand with both hands, he crouched into a ball behind it as the casting dial hit the halfway point. Desini mimicked him with her own wall of protection, and Priya hustled over and jumped behind her. Roshan's gaze locked with mine.

Shit.

"Duck!" I yelled.

The scorpion swung in a full circle, lowering its tail as it swept the surrounding air. Though the shields seemed to hold their own against the wind strike, an air current lifted Roshan and me into the air and sent us sailing backward.

"Shiiiiiiiiiiiiiit!" I flapped my arms as if I'd fly. My breath ejected in a harsh huff as I slammed into the black sand with a crunch. The world tilted on its axis for a few heartbeats as I fought to force air into my lungs.

Roshan was already back on her knees, cast in a white glow from a self-heal. She pushed to her feet and hustled toward the party. She wavered and fell a couple times in the thick shards of sand, but then reached the outer range of her casting abilities and steadied. She reengaged with a minor heal on the dwarf.

Though the arachnid stood tall, its eight legs touched down on either side of its body so its belly hung near the crystallized sand beneath. When the beast reared back to peer over the shields at Desini and the dwarf, I scanned the seam where the shell split beneath its torso, searching for a weak spot.

Another casting dial appeared, and I focused.

Plague Scorpion readies Multi-sting.

A white arc of light appeared in a circle beneath the arachnid as the casting dial filled.

Eyeing that massive needle on the back of its shelled tail, I barked orders. "Everyone! Fall back! Get out of range!"

Desini's agility as she raised her shield and danced backward in rapid, leaping steps atop the blackened sand reminded me she wasn't constricted like the rest of us.

The dwarf was much less agile and, though he followed the advice, he didn't escape before the casting dial filled and the white circle vanished.

Uh-oh.

The scorpion's belly buried itself into the sand as its tail swung over its body. Its stinger—twice the length of my body—pierced the landscape, shooting up shards of sand before rising against and repeating the motion like the needle on a sewing machine until the very tip of it pierced the dwarf's shield and yanked it from the earth.

Though it didn't touch the dwarf's armor, his failure to release his wall of protection meant he flew into the air with it.

"Let go of your shield!"

The dwarf hovered and bounced before the scorpion's eyes as the giant raised a claw to attack its helpless prey instead of catapulting him like it had its last.

"I'll release me shield only when he pries it from my cold dead—" The shield ripped in half just beneath the dwarf's arms when the giant pincer closed on the metal as if it were snapping a pretzel. "Bah! Or that!" The dwarf yelled as he released the ruined shield and tumbled to the black shards.

Another flurry of motion dragged my attention to the top of the scorpion's back, near its head, as Guiles reappeared and sliced. More yellow juice dripped by the gallon down the black shells and into the sand beneath.

At least someone was damaging the damned thing.

As the plague scorpion lowered its belly and reached out with a pincer for a strike at Desini, my gaze connected with the elf's. The grin on his face was unmistakable. So rare had he shown emotion, the timing struck me as odd.

Like the less-experienced members of my party, the crazy bastard was enjoying this.

22

"Ye bastard kettle of beast blood!" the dwarf yelled as he charged, gripping his sword with both hands held high. He rolled as a pincer snapped around the spot where he'd been standing a moment before then regained his feet in one smooth motion. A flash of light surrounded him as his sword swung in a high arc before slicing the leg behind the pincer.

A gush of thick yellow grossness showered the dwarf's face, but he seemed to revel in it. "How's that suit ye, ya stinking stack of glorified spider meat?"

The pincer fell to the sandy earth, sending shards spraying everywhere. The scorpion jerked with the effort to raise it again. I saw in the dangling, ripped flesh a target. When a quick look at my mana showed my pool filled to just over fifty percent, I threw out my arm and summoned Click.

When she appeared at my feet, I cocked my head at the scorpion. "You're gonna think I only bring you around when we're in the shit! Go find something to rip off that thing, would ya?" After a shining, silvery-toothed smile and a drumroll of high-pitched clicks, my pet shot off toward the scorpion. Instead of going after the appendage as I'd predicted, she shot beneath and around the massive beast then disappeared up its back.

Changing focus, I nocked an arrow and charged a Drilling Arrow, seeking the soft spot the dwarf had created. Desini crossed my field of view and raised her glowing purple mace as she closed on the pincer.

My arrow sailed in a tracer of yellow visible even against the morning sun. Pay dirt! More yellow guts exploded from the already-open wound. The scorpion's health meter dropped five percent and the magic quality of my quiver returned the arrow to the container.

Bonus.

Priya passed, running in the opposite direction from Desini moments before.

"Where the hell are you going?"

"To get a better perspective, my love!"

It seemed she found it quickly, as she dropped her staff to the ground and reached inside her robe. I'd almost forgotten the black wand. She raised it, aiming toward the place where Desini and the dwarf held positions on either side of the scorpion's paralyzed pincer.

"Yes!" I yelled. "Desini! Get ready!" The wand probably would be resisted by the higher level elite, but it never hurt to prepare.

I aimed an Exploding Arrow at what I thought passed for a nostril on the scorpion's wide, flat face. The scorpion turned its gaze on me as strobes of light flashed from the wand, ripped across the air, then impacted the wide gash behind the scorpion's claw. Stone crept across the claw as the scorpion tried to raise it again, but the weight of the rocky appendage caused the natural weapon to topple off where we'd wounded it and disconnect in a stream of tendons and yellow muck, leaving only a bloody nub behind as the leg raised into the air.

Man! Another bonus!

The scorpion shrieked and swung around, the whoosh of its tail blowing Desini and the dwarf onto their backsides as it slammed its head on the ground. Its whole body shuddered and shook as it burrowed into the sand.

Thunder cracked and lightning slammed into the creature's back as purple light glowed around Priya's fingers. "No, you don't get to run, evil beast!" She started another cast, this time with an orange snake of light circling her hands.

The dwarf scurried up the scorpion's leg using its segments like stairs, and Desini followed. When the stinger swung around to pierce them, she swiped her shield to one side before it could stab the dwarf through his thick head.

Guiles met them in the middle of the beast's back as the neck he'd been attacking vanished into the sand.

I knew there was a metaphor in there somewhere, but I was more interested in filling the scorpion's backside with arrows. That's exactly what I did as the three met in the middle, worked together to pry up a hard shell at the center of the scorpion's back, then stabbed their blades to the hilts in the fleshy meat beneath. Click appeared in the fray and ripped away flesh. A geyser of scorpion blood sprayed into the air.

Watching the dwarf, the elf, and the mishon plunging their weapons down and covering themselves in the thick splashes of the scorpion's life force was what I imagined it would be like if Tarantino directed Tolkien. But it worked.

You have vanquished a Plague Scorpion!

XP: 13,768

Another flash of gold surrounded Roshan then funneled into the sky. Priya ran to her and threw her arms up in victory and her wand went sailing, but I just laughed.

The Light priestess was catching up to us. I liked it.

"That'll teach ye to disrespect your betters, ye stinking pile of underworld filth! Gads! Ye smell like a goblin baby's diaper, ye dead fuck." The dwarf stomped off the beast with Desini and Guiles in tow. He stopped between the party members as we closed in, as if noticing us for the first time. "Aye, thank ye for the help." He hung his head. "I'm fearin' we lost my brother, but I owe my life and the life of me kin to ya."

"We were honored to assist." I extended my hand. "Gemini Fowler."

His thick hand gripped mine so firmly, I thought bones might crack.

"I'm Whim Hammerbeard, Paladin of the First Order of the Matron and servant of the Dwarven King Dranon Stonepick."

You have discovered an advanced combat profession:
Paladin
Fierce defenders of the Light, Paladins are advanced tanks who use Light magic.

Desini bowed her head.

"I am Desini Sherre of the eastern mishon. You curse with energy born of the divine Enoran Mother."

"Pleased to meet ya, Desini Sherre. Your curses, too, are of the divine."

Guiles extended a hand and introduced himself with a curt nod.

The dwarf returned it. "Sir elf."

He went around the circle then peered back at me. "These be my kin. The Lady Gorgret Hammerbeard and her daughter Ambri. The one staring a hole into the side of your head because he desires me to cuff him one to remind him of his manners is my nephew, Yuren." The younger dwarf bowed his head beneath the heavy gaze of his uncle. "This group of brave adventurers saved us all, boy. You'd do well to kneel."

The boy glared up at me, sent a softer look his uncle's way, then ground his molars, his jaw ticking a staccato beat. Lowering himself, he tapped a knee to the sand then quickly rose again and managed to grumble, "Honored."

Tears streamed down the faces of the two dwarven women as they were introduced. The elder of the two—though she couldn't be but in her thirties, by my guess—peered at me.

I pressed my chin to my chest for a long moment. "I'm very sorry for your loss, Lady Hammerbeard. The hearts of my people ache with yours. I wish we'd come sooner."

Gorgret Hammerbeard curtsied, touching the hem of her loose green skirt. It hadn't been a gesture I'd have expected from a dwarf, but that spoke more to my own predisposition, and there was no reason I should've expected otherwise. Enora had different rules.

I was just stoked to be staring at dwarves.

The younger Ambri Hammerbeard jerked as Priya passed by me and wrapped her arms around the daughter of the slain dwarf. As she whispered words of condolence, I felt empathy flood from her. Ambri relaxed in her embrace and returned it.

Whim clutched my hand again. "I mean not to be rude, Gemini Fowler, but this is nigh a place for the children. I told my stubborn brother it'd be better to sweep around the barrens and go south before west, but I guess he paid the ultimate price for his mistake. I'll try to think kindly of him in death. He died defending his, so there's that!"

I agreed.

"I judge you're heading north to the crossroads from which we came. The east is clear, and you should be fine if'n you hustle." He turned and pointed. "The fork is there and the Plague Barrens end just beyond. I'm sure the greenery will be a welcome sight."

"It will be," I said. "Where will you all go, now?"

"I must recover my brother's body and effects. We return from parlay with an elven acquaintance of mine. We've reached a trade agreement, and I'm returning home to report to my king. South to Trowlsby, then West to the Blackstone Mountains. What of ye?"

Guiles interrupted. "If I might be so bold, master dwarf."

"Aye, ye might at that."

"Best you not have knowledge of our travels lest they be coaxed from you, if you'll grant me your pardon to say so."

"Ah. Got on the wrong side of the bastard governor, then. Bah! Worthless, foul cretin!" He spat. "That's fine. I'll keep yer secrets. I saw neither hide nor hair of ya. But know this! What ye done today won't be forgotten, and if ever my people can return a favor, we more than will. I will report your deeds to my king's ears only, but he will want to thank ye should you ever cross over to the mountains." He stuck his hand out.

The other dwarves loaded up their carts and as Yoren and I recovered the corpse of his dead brother. As they departed, the dwarves' paladin lowered his head and wiped away tears, finally given the chance to grieve the loss of a sibling.

Click, who settled on her backside at my feet, clicked what I thought might be a cheerful goodbye.

I turned to find my team in good states considering the outrageous battle we'd just had. "Who's ready to get the hell out of the Plague Barrens?"

Roshan marched past me toward the cart. "I tire of this cold, dead place!"

We all stared after her. Priya smiled out of one side of her mouth as she slipped an arm around my waist and whispered, "She is stern. Always ready to march forward. I get the impression *she* spent her life until now dreaming of days like this. Do you get that sense?"

"I have zero doubt. She's an interesting bird. Where she's a gentle soul, she also wields a certain ferocity when she perceives the goddess's will at hand. She might be the craziest one of us all."

I found it interesting I'd fallen into thinking of Enora, the advanced A.I., as Solara, when talking to my companions. Talk about adaptation.

Priya nodded, squeezed me, then released me. "No, I'm definitely the craziest one, but you'll want to keep an eye on her." As she stepped toward the cart, she smiled at me over her shoulder, and I again had a desire to try sex with her ward in view.

Then it occurred to me that the link we shared would give her the sense of my arousal, so I stifled it.

23

Any sight would've been welcome after the sea of black and ancient ruins in the Plague Barrens, but half a day after reaching the dirt fork that led to the more pronounced path leading east, the sight of grass was like a buff to my Constitution. Maybe its color was so vibrant because of a subconscious comparison to all the deadness, but the adage about the grass being greener on the other side had never seemed truer.

No grass could relieve my sense we rode under a looming cloud of danger we might never escape. While it was possible we'd already sewn a poisonous seed when we'd swiped Roshan from his grasp—both times—killing a powerful man's family tipped the scales.

More like it knocked them off the table.

Throughout the recorded ages of earth, men of means stamped out those who dared defy their wills. I doubted it'd be different in Enora. I couldn't afford to be short-sighted and brazen, anymore. My mind turned to how I'd operated when posed with a problem back on earth. I became the troubleshooter.

The nerdy superhero, himself.

If a customer's network failed, the singular priority was to get it back online. I became hyper-focused on analyzing the problem, determining its catalyst, then wiping it out with prejudice.

But the real magic came in the wake of any negative network event. I'd perform a root cause analysis to get at the underlying issue to see if a software patch was needed to ensure other customers—or even worse, the same customer—didn't experience the glitch.

In this case, things were a little backward. The root cause was me. I was the hiccup in the system. My narrow focus on retrieving Roshan had led me to a brazen solution. A very public solution. The irony that my ingenuity had led me to a non-violent way to solve the problem but simultaneously promised future violence wasn't lost on me.

Though we'd gotten out of the city, the guard who'd recognized me—the same one whose head was likely being pecked by buzzards—had no doubt reported what he'd seen before coming after us. Namely, a guy he'd seen murdered in the Brumhill Inn alive and well, riding in a cart leaving Trowlsby.

The survivor of our little conflict undoubtedly continued the narrative upon his return to the city. Not only had he seen Priya and me, but he'd also seen Roshan. As far as his people had known, Priya and the Light priestess had jumped from a castle wall built into a rock face. Though their bodies had vanished after death, the witness to our continued existence solidified the idea there was advanced magic afoot.

That was certain to get Governor Zane's attention, and the mage's appearance outside the instance proved it had. There were bounties on our heads. But I was more concerned with the stories I'd heard about Priya's former role at the university in Warrington and how they'd blocked her memory and the memories of any others who refused to comply with a king's edict. The university was under royal control. Since the faculty of the university who'd obeyed the king would've undoubtedly known of Priya's half-elven heritage and longer life span, it wouldn't surprise me if the Währsagers scoured the nether for her, even decades later.

Add in that Guiles—a wanted man—had come out of hiding to aid us, and there was plenty of trouble to go around. Our discussion about the young mage he'd killed in the Plague Barrens, and who his real target had been, nagged me. The way he'd looked around for something prior to dying, even though he mentioned outright that he was there for our heads, told me our enemies knew Guiles had joined my party.

People who resurrected upon death were unheard of. Two generations of royals had overseen the implementation of an edict that registered magic users and trainers, alike. While Governor Zane was a serious problem, I feared a larger one loomed. The king could be after us, as well.

Guiles was certain bounty hunters would be out *en masse* to fulfill the Governor's requisition for our heads. But if the king became involved? My mind reeled with the implications.

I was the root cause of a lot of peoples' problems.

So, I reverted to my knack for troubleshooting and singly decided what made the most sense. We'd evade and advance until we were ready to take on whatever came at us. Then we would take the fight to them.

A loud crack jerked me from my thoughts, followed by a hollow thump. I almost lost my seat on the saddle beneath me.

The wagon tilted sideways as the wooden wheel snapped. My gaze shot to the back of the cart as if I might find a spare.

Well, shit.

"Well, shit." Priya peered around at the wheel from the bench.

I might've laughed in any other circumstance, but when Desini's face popped through the tarp and I read her mournful expression, laughter was the furthest thing from my mind.

"How will we replace the wheel?" she almost cried as she slapped both hands to her cheeks. "If we cannot go back to town…"

Guiles didn't hesitate.

"A return to town would take days we don't have. We'll have to pack up our things and ride from here on horseback. Is your horse trained for riders?"

A tear welled and trickled down her cheek. "So easily you set aside this place where I have lived for years."

Guiles peered at me and then back to Desini. "I didn't mean to be insensitive, Desini. I was just being practical. Forgive me."

I noted how Guiles, like my other companions, was using contractions now as if adapting to my speech patterns. That thought was extinguished as Priya and I mixed our empathetic juices across the emotional airwaves at the sight of Desini's face.

I dismounted and approached the bench. She waved a dismissive hand and wiped away an errant tear. I set a hand on her back and rubbed in a circle. "We can come back for it when we've found a place to settle."

She shook her head. "It will be gone or will rot sitting here. It is done. I will tie on Pickney's bags and he will carry our possessions." She ran the length of her arm across her face and straightened her back. After huffing out a short breath, she nodded. "Don't think me weak, master."

Gently setting a palm against her full cheek, I turned her face toward me. "We'll have a new home soon and, as long as we have Pickney with us, you're only leaving wood and canvas here. We are your family now."

She cupped my face with both hands. Tears welled in the bottoms of her eyelids but didn't spill over. She nodded with a quick, wet sniff, then turned to pack up the contents of the cart. Roshan, Priya, Guiles, and I joined in.

An hour later, Desini bid a final goodbye to her beloved box on wheels. We unfastened the canvas cover and packed it in a saddlebag on her horse's back. The tightened expression of her round cheeks as she tried to suppress her sorrow led me to a silent proclamation that I'd build her a new cart someday—whether she'd need it or not. If nothing else, I could rank up my carpentry skill.

As the road narrowed and became little more than a beaten tan path, we pulled to one side. Desini suggested we enter the adjacent forest.

"If any good is to come of the loss of my cart, it's our new found mobility. We should break into the trees here and move east. Perhaps you can call out one of your pets to scout ahead. Bears and wildcats bring peril to the way leading to the hinterland hills."

"Sure. I was hoping to bond more with Wolf, anyway."

My hand glowed azure as I summoned the canine into existence. When he took a few steps forward, the horse beside me rumbled nervously. Desini's steady hand rubbed its haunches, and she made soothing sounds until the animal settled.

The wolf ignored it and came to me. Though it'd reacted well in the battle with the mist creature in the dungeon, I hadn't had a lot of time with it like I had with Click, my porcupunk friend. I scratched behind its ears and gave it a strip of deer jerky Desini had cooked from our hunt near Greycutter downs.

The wolf sat on its haunches and wagged its thick tail as it chewed the treat. I watched its status in my interface as it elevated to happy.

"You ready to run a little?" I asked.

As if it understood me, the beast perked up, jumped to its feet, and wagged its tail faster.

Pointing toward the tree line, I ordered, "Onward with you then, beast!"

The wolf shot into the woods. I decided I liked my newer pet and was glad it hadn't killed me when Click and I took on its pack during an ill-advised journey for water.

Priya rode behind me on my mount, which was easily the largest of the five, except for Pickney. Her weight against my back as she wrapped her arms around me joined with a wave of her love oozing all over me, but the conflicting empathy over Desini's loss tempered it.

"Look at it this way," I said. "The cart was a long-time friend from a life you no longer lead. For the price you pay in loss today, you gain human and elf kind who love you."

I thought for a moment she might be ready to snap, but her features softened as she gazed at me and the hint of a smile ticked up on one side of her medium lips. "You give me relief, master. Thank you for your wisdom." Scanning the sky between the high pine treetops, she tilted her head to one side. "Rain soon. The trees will provide some shelter, but a cave would be better."

Guiles's horse clopped forward to ride next to us.

"The Seran Hinterlands are riddled with caves and lounging bears who occupy them. Your tarp will continue to serve when we reach the open hills and fashion a shelter from it."

Desini nodded agreement. Priya squeezed tighter and pressed her face into my back. Someone was feeling affectionate. Roshan gazed at us, and the hint of a smile graced her full lips. I loved Enora.

We rode into the trees single file, and I kept an eye out for the wolf. But after a couple hours, I had an urge to check my map for the little blue dot that represented him. I had to zoom out to cover a wide swath of the surrounding forest to find him. The new distance meter I'd found in my interface options placed the wolf two miles ahead of us.

"What the hell is he doing?" I asked myself aloud.

Guiles answered.

"He is a wolf. He is prowling. Perhaps he hunts prey."

"I fed him. Besides, Click didn't do that. She took the lead, sure, but she never went off like that."

"Then perhaps you should train your animal," Guiles said. "What did you think, a wild beast would bend to your every desire without first knowing you?"

"Click did."

"Then summon Click, imbecile." He jerked the reigns on his horse and shook his head. "By the King of Ninn, you prattle on like a spoiled Elven child."

What's up his ass?

But the elf was always right. If I wanted an animal that behaved like Click, then I should summon Click. I raised my hand as the horse slipped around a patch of thick oaks and made its way down a gradual incline of moss-covered rocks and mud. The cast failed because the horse was in motion, which kind of sucked. I yanked the reigns and we jerked to a halt.

A moment later, my porcupunk appeared beside the horse.

Wolf has been dismissed.
Click has been summoned.
Click's Disposition: Happy

Happy right out of the box. Good shit.
A rattle of clicks emanated from my porcupunk's throat.

"Hey, babe," I said. The animal peered around as if searching for a target. "Nope. We just need a scout. Think you can handle that?"

Priya leaned to one side behind me.

"Hey, Clicky-poo. How's the world's greatest porcupunk today?" She kissed the air and Click bounced happily on her hind legs.

"Hello, beast," Roshan said. Though there was no smile in her voice or on her lips, a memory of how she'd stroked the little flesh hairs on the back of the animal at Priya's dome in the Dark Wood reminded me of her affection for my pet, even if she didn't always wear her emotions on her sleeve.

I contrasted the two women. Where Priya was my snarky, energetic elf, Roshan was more reserved, perhaps a tad formal in her mannerisms and speech. Desini was too complicated to think about at the moment. It seemed each time I thought about all she'd been through, I could go off in my own head for hours. The mishon's baggage made me wonder if Priya wasn't better off by not remembering her former life. I'd guess being the head of the university in Warrington was a lot to lose.

"You are flooded with complication today," Priya whispered.

Somehow, Guiles's Elven ears picked it up. "Just because you can't draw on your spirit pool yet doesn't mean some meditation wouldn't suit you, Gemini." He turned his head. "Roshan."

"Yes, elf?"

"When we rest, begin meditation training with Gemini. It will aid him when he reaches Level 20." When her only response was a curt nod, he added, "And the way you've been leveling, you won't be far behind him. You possess a strong spirit, *human*."

Roshan's lips tightened, but the dip of her dimples told me it wasn't out of irritation. My team was bonding in their own ways, and I liked it. I liked it a lot.

Click rattled off a chorus of high-pitched drumbeats between its teeth and looked back at me over her shoulder.

"Yes, young lady, scout ahead."

She sped off as rain began to pitter-patter against the leaves overhead.

"Listen to the elf," Roshan said. "We will have to train your wolf." She muttered an addition, "Mangy beast."

"Why do I get the impression that people don't like my wolf?"

"Again," Guiles said, "You must train the beast in order for it to comply. It is not about liking or disliking. Don't project your own shortcomings onto a stupid animal."

While I might have usually told the elf to go and fuck himself, my mind reigned me in with realization. Guiles was speaking as a strict teacher would to a student. I'd agreed that he would be my mentor, and that meant I'd need to stifle my ego.

"Yes, master," I said. "Your logic is true."

I pulled the reigns to the left and my horse skirted a narrow pine. I'd never ridden in my previous life and wondered if it was as easy as in Enora, if this horse was just that well-trained, or if it was a simple game mechanics. At this point, I was thankful not to be on foot and even more grateful mount training wasn't required, like in so many other games I'd played. It was always so ridiculously expensive.

Clicks echoed through the woods from beneath the tattering of rain, then my pet came tearing through the underbrush.

Guiles shot her an inquisitive gaze.

"I'm pretty sure that's a warning bark." Between the trees down the hill, I spied an opening into grasslands. As we hustled down the incline, the sound of trickling water rose into the air, a sound previously concealed by the rain beating the forest's leaves.

"Let's dismount and inspect," Guiles said.

Priya grabbed my arm for support as she slid off our mount behind me. If my first days in the Dark Wood had taught me anything, it'd been to be cautious of my footfalls. Just to play it safe, I ripped out my daggers, switched to assassin class, and activated stealth.

Guiles shot me a look, and I recalled how on the night of our first meeting, he'd recommended that I remain a woodsman until I reached Level 20. I assumed the strange gaze was about that.

"I don't want to make a lot of noise."

He shrugged. "Acceptable. Just be ready to use your

ranged skills and make sure you account for the global cool-down."

I mock bowed. "Yes, oh wise one."

Priya, Guiles, and I stepped to the edge of the clearing then shrouded ourselves behind trees.

By my count, five hulking creatures surrounded two smaller humanoids with such green skin, they almost blended into the lush grass on either side of the river behind them. Long beaks jutted from the taller creatures, and their bodies were covered in thick feathers with the consistency of felt.

I could just barely make out what one of the bird creatures was saying over the tympani of light rain dancing on the leaves.

"This is Swisa Tribe land. You hunt Swisa fish."

Though the strange creatures had thick shoulders, their strong biceps led to tiny wrists, and long necks rose from barrel chests to tiny heads.

Unknown Swisa

Level 16

The Swisa are a territorial humanoid race evolved from creatures of flight. Though the avian hybrids no longer take to the air, they are known for hollow bones and fierce dispositions.

Outside the Plague Barrens instance, my interface had returned to the simpler display of creature stats. But I didn't need to inspect the smaller creatures to know what they were. Their rounded heads, green flesh, and pointed ears told me what I needed to know, but I checked anyway.

Unknown Goblin

Level 14
Known to reproduce like rabbits, goblins are tribal creatures.

A small stick with a line dangling from it hung over the shoulder of the bald goblin on the left. His companion had long yellow hair and stood behind him, her shoulders hunched and head lowered.

"I haven't caught anything. We didn't know it was your land. We were just fishing. Your people took our cave and drove us away." He held up two fingers. "Twice. How far do we have to go to leave your territory?"

Hmm. For a goblin, he sounded pretty sharp.

"Do you understand their words, Gemini?" Desini whispered.

I nodded and held up a finger, wanting to focus on the conversation.

She nodded compliance but whispered a final thought. "These are the ones who drove my people from the plateau."

My body conjured a new flood of adrenaline with the news.

"You can go to moons for all we care. This Swisa land. If you leave, you live." The Swisa raised an orange claw to indicate the female goblin huddled behind him. "But we see this one. She scouts Swisa plateau. She sees our home. Must not know. Must die."

I focused my inspection on the Swisa again and found what I wanted.

Alignment: Neutral Evil
Neutral Evil are honorless creatures with no qualms about killing the innocent if it furthers their own agendas.

I understood languages of neutral beings and higher. Because these Swisa were *Neutral Evil* in alignment, their language came off choppy, like broken English.

The bird-like bully raised a three-toed, orange, rippled foot then kicked the goblin backward, causing it to roll over its companion. They both tumbled hard to the ground. The female goblin shrieked in surprise.

My head thumped with anger. These bird fucks were at least four times the goblins' sizes.

"Yes," Priya said without my having spoken a word. "We should help them. Poor things. They can't be five-feet-tall and those... those things will hurt them."

Guiles glared at her, leaned toward us, and whispered, "You know they're goblins, right? They aren't exactly—"

Desini cleared her throat gently, but there was nothing gentle in the harsh whisper that accompanied it. "I suppose I am just mishon to you, elf? What does being a goblin have to do with tolerating injustice? Are goblins not creatures born of Solara's grace?"

Guiles gaze trailed up to the high tail wagging back and forth over the Desini's shoulder and sighed. "Are not the Swisa the same?"

"Hmph," Desini said. "Mighty elves. So superior. So crafty and intellectual."

Mentor or not, I agreed with Desini. That was bullshit, and I let him know it. "The Swisa are the ones causing the conflict with their territorial crap. The goblins were just fishing. I don't like bullies."

"Perhaps you forget our peoples' first tenant," Priya said.

I hadn't forgotten—Protect the weak.

"Yeah. So why are we standing around talking?" I asked.

Guiles rolled his eyes in that way he did.

"So, we're doing this?" Priya asked, a sneer crossing her angular features.

I nodded and flashed my teeth. "Oh, yeah, m'lady. Like I said, if there's anything I cannot stomach, it's a gods-damned bully. Even less, five of them picking on two people —goblins—half their size."

Guiles rolled his eyes again and faded into stealth mode. Without a word about strategy, he stepped into the clearing like a blue ghost and paced toward the ruckus by the creek.

I sheathed my dagger and shrugged off my bow. My global cool-down dial ticked.

"I will charge the one who speaks then draw the rest to me." Desini's mace glowed to life as she ripped it from her belt with a click. She smiled a mouthful of sharp teeth at me, her cart forgotten for the time being

"Let's kill some bullies."

24

I picked at bloody feathers pasted to my gear and flicked them aside as I meandered toward the goblins. They'd taken refuge behind a boulder at the edge of the wide shallow creek when bones began cracking.

The fight hadn't even been close. Crimson splatter painted the rocks, the grass, and Desini's face, although the light rain worked to cleanse her smooth cheeks. Her sheer ferocity during the engagement lent little wonder as to what inspired her. These Swisa stole her peoples' second home after they'd suffered the Plague Barrens and lost many to find it. But her sheer ferocity might also have been born of her despair at having lost her home on wheels.

I wasn't sure Roshan had cast a single heal, but I definitely saw the curved white arcs of her Smites. Her prowess as a healer of an inferior level in the Plague Barrens rendered discussions of mana pool conservation and when to use offensive abilities moot. She'd obviously gauged the lopsided battle and made the educated decision to inflict pain.

Hell, it probably felt grand to inflict pain for once.

In the meantime, we'd left quite the mess, and two green people were staring up at us wearing taut expressions of fear as if they were next on our hit list.

Click sniffed one of the corpses, climbed onto its feathered barrel chest, and squatted.

Nice.

Roshan stood with her hands on her hips, chin raised in high satisfaction over the dead beasts at her feet. Guiles patted them down for loot. Desini wiped beast kin blood off her mace with a rag that usually dangled from her pocket. Priya accompanied me to the boulder, which was wetter on one side where it lowered into the water.

"Hello." I raised my hand in greeting but stopped at a distance. "You're safe now. You can come out."

The bald goblin wearing the reflective sheen of rain on his forehead didn't hesitate. He stomped forward a few steps, his face tight.

Charney
Half-Goblin
Level 14
(No Class)

"Safe? You call this safe?" He gestured around at the hairy feathers. "Now we have to go even further south! They'll hunt us down like squirrels and bash our brains in or rip our guts out!"

Priya frowned at the mention of squirrels.

"Charney!" the female goblin barked, stepping out from behind the rock. "They would've killed me, idiot! Would you rather these people just continued on their way instead of helping?"

Charney seethed. "At least it would mean an end to our

problems. First, they kill everyone. Next, they chase us from our cave. Then, they pursue us all the way here. It's like they've got it out for us." He wheeled around. "And what did he mean, he saw you at their place? You been sneaking off again?"

The female goblin set her hands on her hips. "Someone has to scout the enemy. You sure weren't doing it."

"Scout? What, did you plan on a two-goblin raid to claim their territory?"

The female goblin wore dingy shorts and a ragged shirt opened below the neck. She'd probably spun the garments herself. A silver medallion hung on a leather rope around her neck with a star at its center. It was something akin to a Star of David with rough edges.

"Human!" Charney barked. "Stop looking at my sister's boobs!"

"I was checking out the medallion." My gaze shifted between the two goblins.

The female flashed me a bashful smile. She had an ample bosom with plenty of green cleavage, but it was *green* cleavage. She was a *goblin!*

"Sure, that's what you were looking at." Then he muttered, "Freaky humans."

The urge to bully this guy inflated like a balloon inside me, but I suppressed. Thankfully, the female paced over and bowed her head, buying him some time with distraction.

Lucias
Half-Goblin
Level 1 5
(No Class)

"Thank you for helping us, sir..."

"Oh, it's not 'sir.'" I flashed my best smile, trying not to grimace with irritation at her brother. "I'm Gemini Fowler." I introduced the whole circle.

"I am Lucias. This is my brother, Charney."

Charney shot me a sneer in greeting.

"I gathered. Nice to meet *both* of you."

I extended my hand. Lucias stared at it for a breath and then clasped it. Her whole hand and wrist disappeared in my grip. Charney stepped forward and glared at our hands as if they were an offense to his existence. I released Lucias's cute little fingers and maintained my smile despite her ill-tempered sibling.

"You'll forgive my brother, won't you? I'm sure you understand, humans don't take to our kind. You can see why he'd be... hesitant."

Guiles cleared his throat. "I'm not sure 'hesitant' is the word I'd use."

Charney shot Guiles a glare. The elf raised jazz hands and shrugged, despite his ability to slice the goblin thirty-seven levels his junior into ribbons without releasing a breath.

"What is *that?* And is it with you?" Lucias pointed behind me.

I didn't have to turn to know what he pointed at. "That's Click. She's my porcupunk."

Lucias tilted her head to the side for a few beats while she stared at the porcupunk. Click did that for which she was named, in greeting.

"I see why you named her that, but it's still weird. She's kind of cute, though. Is she friendly?"

I nodded. "Very friendly, as long as you're being friendly. Otherwise, she's about as fierce as they come."

"That's a useful dichotomy." She eyed me up and down. "For an adventurer."

Desini clicked her mace back onto her belt then flipped her shield onto her back. "Charney, why have the Swisa come so far from the plateaus? It's still another day's travel from here, yes?"

"What? Oh, right. Those bastards think they own the entire world." He pointed at the surrounding ground where the spears they'd tried to fight us with lay. "They were hunting. The ones who return with big game are highly respected by their people, and there's an abundance of wildlife out here."

My head swiveled, taking in the miles of grassy hillside surrounded by trees, except to the east.

"Don't worry, human," Charney said, "they're mostly night creatures."

"I wasn't exactly scared," I said. "As you saw, I have friends."

"Must be nice," Charney said.

"You are such a downer," Lucias said. "Cheer up, brother. It's our lucky day."

"Hmph." Charney paced back over to the creek and peered into the water.

Lucias cocked her head in his direction. "Charney is a little shy. He's looking for fish."

"Didn't strike me as shy," I muttered.

"Well," she raised her shoulders and smiled up at me again. "He's kind of protective, too. I'm his only surviving family."

"Well, we gotta eat!" Charney replied from the distance. "It's been two days!"

"Days?" Roshan asked. She pointed toward a rock next to the creek. "Is that not your bow?"

Lucias nodded. "It's his bow, but he shoots like shit."

I chuckled before I could stifle it, and Charney shot me a look over one shoulder.

Roshan huffed, stepped around a Swisa corpse, and grabbed the other spear leaning against the boulder.

"Silly goblin," she muttered as she marched toward the creek.

Lucias peered up at me.

I smiled. "Sorry."

She shrugged and watched Roshan walk to the creek. "He is a silly goblin, but he's all I have."

The mage kicked off her sandals and teetered down the bank. The bottom foot-and-a-half of her robe sloshed in the slow-moving water. As she turned in our direction, a subtle white flash illuminated her irises.

Inner Illumination?

The spear plunged, then Roshan barked, "Ah!" When she raised it from the water, a medium-sized fish with pink flesh and silvery scales jiggled on its end. Jerking the spear in a practiced motion, Roshan sent the fish reeling off the spearpoint to the bank near Charney, where it flipped and flopped on the rain-soaked earth.

"Well, that's useful," Lucias said, a smile crossing her goblin lips.

"Roshan is full of surprises," Priya said.

"Ah!" the Light priestess exclaimed again. Another fish, this one bigger than the last, appeared at the end of her pole. The pink, fat fish landed right next to the last so they flopped next to each other in their dying dance. Their death throes made a smacking sound contrasting the pattering of the sprinkling rain.

We were all soaking wet, but no one seemed to notice.

The goblin stared at her in disbelief, his pole hanging over his shoulder and his mouth hanging open.

Roshan approached him then offered the spear.

Charney gazed absently down at it.

"Now you will eat, goblin. Probably twice, considering your small belly." Roshan stomped back up the bank and stood next to me. She whispered, "If he knows how to make a fire."

Desini crouched, bouncing in place. Her tail waved in wide strokes behind her. "The sight of these Swisa bring out my hunger for blood. Long have I desired to return and reclaim the lands of my people from these swine." She stood and kicked a corpse.

We were corpse kickers, it seemed. We did a lot of that.

Lucias's chin dropped. "You're one of *those* mishon?" She clapped a hand to her chest and grasped the medallion. "I'm sorry."

"Yes. The plateaus this beast spoke of were my home. We have come to reclaim this land."

"Um, have we?" I asked.

Desini peered up at me and nodded. "Yes. This is why I brought you here. You need a place to set your stone, and I know where."

"I recall the suggestion. Well, I'm glad we got that worked out."

Roshan nodded agreement. "I, too, am glad we have freed ourselves of uncertainty."

"How's that?" I asked.

"To support your quest to serve Solara in ridding this world of evil demons, stability would be of great aid." She ticked off answers on her fingers. "We can build our family in service to the goddess." She ticked off another finger. "Then I can build a monument in gratitude to Zhara near the home Desini has offered us." Then another. "We can search the surrounding areas for opportunities to level in preparation for our war against evil, while protecting our new home." She shrugged as if she'd spoken the most obvious things.

"Zhara?" Priya asked.

Roshan nodded. "Yes. It is she who taught me to meditate and channel the Light in a more efficient way as you fornicated with our man. This deserves thanks."

Priya sighed.

"Fornicate?" Lucias stared at me with one eyebrow arched high and a smirk at the corner of her mouth.

Ugh.

"Fair enough," Priya said. "Monument. Whatever."

"I'm glad you have this all worked out." I made sure my tone bled with as much sarcasm as possible.

Roshan nodded curtly. "Yes, noob. This is why we are your beloveds. We work things out. You listen."

Aside from corpse kicking, I also sighed a lot.

Guiles chuckled.

"The fuck are you snickering at?"

He waved a hand and headed to the creek, apparently preferring the company of a crotchety goblin to a quick-tempered student.

"Wow," Lucias said, focusing hard on me.

"What now?" I asked.

"You're a Level 18 Woodsman. That's so hot." Her gaze traveled the full length of my form.

Considering the way I often unleashed my gaze upon the women in my party, I decided Karma was real in Enora.

"I knew you must be adventurers when I saw how you" —she flashed a look at my shoulders— "man-handled the brutish birds."

I jutted my chin toward Guiles. "He's a Level 51 rogue."

"Fucking hell, you say?" Lucias turned and peered after the elf.

"I think I like this one," I said to the women surrounding me. "She has my kind of command of the Common tongue."

"I also think she would make a fine companion." Priya threw Lucias an expectant gaze.

"Wait, what?" I asked.

Priya raised one shoulder. "I would like very much to keep her."

Lucias's black eyebrows furrowed. "I'm sorry, keep me? What are we talking about, again?"

"Yeah," I said. "What are we talking about?"

"Don't you *feel* me like that," Priya replied.

"Feel you?" I asked.

"Our bond? I can feel your... well, whatever that emotion is. I don't like it."

"Don't misunderstand, hon. People—and probably goblins—rarely accept such forward offers without having gotten to know someone first. It's a little uncouth. I'm afraid your social skills could use some—"

"Some *what?*" She glowered at me. "Do you not remember when you rescued me, how Roshan said she wanted to keep me?"

"Oh, that."

"Yeah," she mocked, "that. How is this different?"

"Well, maybe she doesn't want—"

"I'm in," Lucias said.

All heads swiveled.

"What?" I croaked like a frog that'd been stepped on.

She shrugged with both shoulders high and hard. "What else am I gonna do, run around with this one" —she tilted her head toward her brother behind her— "and constantly listen to his belly aching?"

"Love you too, sis... Bitch."

She continued as if he hadn't spoken. "I could use a break from his brand of monotony. Besides, where some mishon were lucky enough to fight their way out of trouble and escape, those assholes you just laid out wiped my whole clan off the face of Enora. If you'll put a hurting on them, I'm totally in."

Why is it a goblin is the only person I've met in this world who actually talks like a real person?

A smile crept across my face as the answer came on the wind. *The developers left their imprint. That shit is gold. Funny stuff.*

"How's your brother going to feel about this?" I asked.

"It doesn't matter. I'm the female and the oldest."

"Right!" Charney barked from the creek side. "By how many minutes are you the oldest?"

"I'm still the female, dip-wad. So, I'm in charge."

"I wasn't aware goblins were a maternal society." As if I knew anything about goblins. I hadn't even known Enora had them.

Lucias shrugged. "Someone has to get it right." She eyed Roshan. "Judging from the gumption on this one, I'd say you got it right, too. As I see it, your women outnumber you. And they speak freely, so you can't be all bad. What do you say? We gonna do this?"

"Yes!" Charney yelled.

We turned to find him holding up the spear, a jiggling fish impaled on its end at his eye level. He raised the spear and shook it. "I was celebrating the fish, not answering the question."

The way he wielded the weapon with both hands

compared to how Roshan had easily stabbed single-fisted was comical, but I didn't think Charney was the type to take any jabs from me. I remained silent despite the strong temptation.

"Hey, the one with the weird eyes isn't so bad, at least. And we'll eat tonight—that's an improvement. I'll follow your lead, sis."

Lucias shrugged as if this had already been established —a forgone conclusion. "Glad you're in, Charney."

"Bite me, witch." Charney grabbed his crotch.

I shook my head. We were adopting goblins now. *Goblins.*

Lucias sighed, allowing a moment of silence to pass.

Roshan filled it. "Who has strange eyes? Does the little green one speak ill of me, when I fill his belly?"

I threw her a wan gaze. "Your sexy eyes make me drool."

She blushed, and the goblin's comment was forgotten. Or, more likely, she let it go. She stepped close, pressed her lips to my cheek, then whispered close to my ear. "I shall feed these hungers, as well."

When can we start?

I poked Desini. "Which way?"

She pointed northeast across a set of high hills. "That direction. But before we leave, perhaps we should allow our new companions to eat. I spy a cave on this side of that hill, with the flat black rock. We could make a fire and rest our behinds."

My ass was chapped from the horseback riding and I'd just as soon stand, but the idea struck me as sound.

"Besides, I believe we have business we should handle."

"Business?"

Desini nodded and smiled. "I have leveled, if you recall."

"I'm short a few points, too, babe." Priya raised a hand.

Roshan nodded. "I, as well."

Lucias folded her arms across her chest, pushing up her ample half-goblin bosom. A strange sensation crept across my abs.

Green. Small. No.

"Points? What language are you people speaking? Have we switched from Common?"

I waved a dismissive hand. "It's nothing. Let's check out the cave, build a fire, cook the fish, and eat. I'm starving."

Chaney yipped another celebration as he flipped a large pink fish onto the shore.

Lucias spread her full goblin lips. "Looks like there will be enough for everyone."

"Bonus," I said. "I haven't had fish in a while."

"I dislike it. I will stick with our reserves," Roshan said.

"But you're the one who made it possible," I said. "How is it you're an expert spear fisher and don't like fish?"

"Just because I can teach a goblin to fish doesn't mean I have to eat it." She turned, grabbed the reigns on her horse, then led the animal toward the cave. Her staff bounced on her back as she strode away. "Come, tank. I long to nourish myself and then drive these dirty birds from your home." Roshan thrust a hand out behind her, and Desini jogged to catch up. They held hands as they walked away.

Priya stepped next to me. "Seriously, I love that woman."

I nodded. "Me too."

25

The journey would've taken half a day on foot—longer on goblin strides—but horseback carried us to the valley in a few hours. Lucias rode with Desini, and Charney—who had to be coaxed onto the back of a horse—rode with Guiles. The male goblin went to great pains not to put his hands on the elf, gripping the saddle beside his hips the whole way.

My breath hitched in my chest at sight of the landscape. As the sun set to the northwest, it painted an orange hue across the strange, glowing pines forming a perimeter around the hillside. In the last hour of our journey, just as the light transitioned to dusk, I spied a herd of wild cattle with strange spiraling horns better suited for rams. The scene made me feel small.

Priya's arms locked lazily around my waist, and soon she snored against my back. For someone who didn't need much sleep, she sure enjoyed it. The random moans told me she was dreaming pleasant dreams, but I noticed the slumbering emotions didn't reach me.

NPCs who dream. Weird.

If I suddenly panicked, would she shoot awake, or was sleep a barrier to the Elven bond in both directions? Either way, her slumber was a nice respite from the constant *sharing*. I needed to ask Guiles if I could turn the bond off somehow next time I had him out of Priya's earshot.

Roshan spoke from her mount next to me as she extended her finger toward the herd. "You have such wondrous creatures in this land. To think how my fortune changed so I might encounter them is a blessing."

"You say that as if it's my land. You forget, I got here two weeks ago."

Roshan's lips parted as if she'd say something, then a long moment passed as she pressed them back together and stared into the distance. When I thought perhaps she'd left the topic behind, she spoke again. "I knew when I warmed to you in our first hours that the union was Solara's will. You were a special being despite your horrible threadbare clothes. But I underestimated the goddess's will. Even during our time apart, I held no doubt you would come for me, Gemini. But what I've learned about you, about Priya, and about Zhara since we left Trowlsby has lent further insight about the extent to which the goddess desires me to do her bidding."

Mystified by the onslaught of formal words and having to play them back in my tired mind to grasp their meaning, I found myself without a response. My nod was likely imperceptible because we bounced gently above the hoofs packing holes in the wet grass of the hillside, but when she reached out and I squeezed her hand, the fullness of her smile tugging at the skin near her temples showed she understood me.

Born to agnostic parents, I explored churches during my teenage years, but it never took. When I was younger, the impression there might be something bigger out there seemed to tick at my brain, but after my parents died and I took a more introspective look at what my life might be without them, the theory of a supreme being seemed more pliable than plausible.

Enora offered an interesting duality. On the one hand, all these races seemed to accept the existence of a higher power without question, much in the way some people of my old world did, though they often used different names and rule sets to define the being they credited with the creation of the world. I wondered if continents other than Rubal and Lau believed in different gods or called Solara by a different name.

The major difference between here and earth? I knew a higher being ruled this world. These people with whom I'd surrounded myself were right, but I had a scientific explanation for that they'd deemed supernatural. What a brain fuck.

Enora *was* the unseen ruler of Enora. What they called her was irrelevant.

God was real. Or goddess. Whatever.

Every night in Enora, I'd lain on my furs puzzling over my strange new life, but my early worries that it might seem artificial because I was forced to fake a belief system had already begun to fade. I knew I'd learn to merge the two things—engaging my companions on their terms, while accepting the underlying truth.

I was also well past belief that all my encounters in this world were random.

Roshan's well-timed scream in the woods. Zhara's quest leading us to the underground mini-dungeon where we found Priya and made an enemy of a dark underlord whose minion we imprisoned and later had banished beneath the soil. Priya becoming pregnant because Zhara cast a spell to make it so. Zhara telling us to seek out a vendor on the road to travel north to retrieve Roshan, leading us right to Desini, who we found in need of aid.

Then there was Guiles. I didn't need to get myself started about the stroke of luck riding that horse in front of me, drawn to Brumhill by the cover of Solara's Tree of Light, or whatever the hell they called it.

I was finished accepting anything as coincidence. Evolution or not.

Zhara might not have known Enora as an A.I. She might actually have been a guardian of the tree created by developers as part of the world's lineage, but she knew Lucera—who she might see as a simple woman from a village at the far southern edge of the Dark Wood.

The range of Zhara's influence was a mystery, and while I couldn't be sure she wasn't just an extension of the A.I. whose role was to ensure I helped prepare the world for an influx of adventurers six Enoran years from now, I had strong suspicions and a lot of supporting evidence.

But each encounter had become my own and been shaped by my words and reactions to situations. Each battle had been decided by how we fought our enemies. Someday, I might try to figure out why events unfolded as they had. Maybe my former girlfriend, Katelyn, would show up as a player, and I'd ask questions. But for now, I rode with an elf, the pregnant half-elf child of an immortal, an Asian-like priestess, a cat woman, and two goblins.

How cool was that?

I'd been a networking engineer just months ago, Earth-time. My life had been total shit!

"It seems this world has a lot in store for us, and I believe none of it is a coincidence."

Easing her horse closer, Roshan's expression softened as she raised my hand to her lips and kissed the back for a long moment. "Solara rewards the faithful."

The customized gear rewards after defeating the grootslang proved her words true. I nodded.

Nokuro Takemoto had reasons that stretched far beyond altruism for giving me a six-year head start in this world, and my illness had presented him and his niece an opportunity. Enora had spoken through Lucera's body as if a beta tester might have screwed things up—acted in a way that threw the world out of balance. I thought it might have something to do with the blight in the east and the demon invasion. Not to mention the Plague Barrens.

I didn't know if Enora wanted me to stop the governor, the king, or the dark underlord Caym. But I looked forward to finding out just how I was to pave the way for new players. Meanwhile, I planned to build a foundation to ensure they stayed the hell out of my way, when those entitled earthling assholes arrived.

How about that? You think of yourself as an Enoran.

26

My suspicions about Desini's appearance in my life only deepened as we peered down at the flat, rocky plateaus that formed steps leading to the wide mouth of a cave. Grass blanketed a long and sprawling expanse in front of it, stretching a hundred yards in each direction, and the valley was framed by high stone walls washed dark gray by a renewed downpour.

The natural stairs led to a valley at their foot. They could be navigated by an adolescent child as if they were designed by nature for bipedal habitation. Two foot-worn paths wound at the feet of the natural walls and out of the valley in the north and the west. The sprawling area was otherwise surrounded by the high stone, leaving those paths the only entrances and exits.

Though we didn't care to lie on our bellies on the rain-soaked pine straw on the southern ridge, we crouched low on our haunches as we surveyed the encampment from the shadow of the high trees. My butt cheeks were raw from all the horseback travel, so the posture worked.

Inner Illumination revealed every detail of the village

below under the cover of night. The sheets of rain blanketing the valley had apparently driven the inhabitants into the small square thatch structures I couldn't quite call houses. Light twitched in the glassless openings where one might have otherwise placed windows, leaving me to wonder how they controlled the rain pouring through them.

Despite the incessant prattle of the rain and the way it dripped from the needles and leaves above, a strange warmth mixed with its cooling wash made me wonder if I might catch a cold.

Wouldn't that be some shit in a game world?

Neither Lucias nor Desini knew whether the bird-like Swisa were capable of night vision, but judging from the three campfires atop the plateau, two torches mounted on either side of the cave mouth, and an orange glow shimmering on the floor of the entrance from inside, I guessed the answer was no. Still, we stayed low.

Lucias explained the setup, drawing a spiteful glare from her brother. Her knowledge spoke to how many times she'd been there. "The chieftain lives inside the cave. I've never seen him exit without at least two spear-wielding armored guards."

"What kind of armor?" I asked.

"Probably coelophysis scales."

"Are there dinosaurs in the area?" I recalled my encounter with a young coelophysis in the woods my second day in the world. The heavy, thudding footsteps of its pursuit as I hurled myself wildly around trees still echoed in my ears. I'd snapped awake a few times with it thumping in my ears.

"They go out on extended hunts. The dinos are more common in the woods close to the coast, about a day's journey to the east."

A sigh of relief might not have displayed strength, so I nodded instead.

"About ten birds patrol the valley, but fewer in the rain." She pointed down to the bottom of the natural steps. "See those winding paths?"

"Do they always walk the same patterns?"

"Best I can tell. I don't remember seeing any of them deviate."

Deviate, she says.

"Where did you learn to talk? Your vocabulary is better than mine."

She raised a shoulder and dropped it. "I was born a slave, like the rest of my clan. When I was too young to work the fields around the keep, I was a chamber servant with my mother. Mostly cleaning. The lord was well-educated, as were his children. One of his daughters warmed to me before she was old enough to know better. I was a plaything, of sorts." A thoughtful frown crossed her face as she scanned the perimeter of the valley below.

"Tell me the lord wasn't the Governor of Knall."

"Governor of Knall?" Slapping a tiny hand over her mouth to keep her laughter muted, Lucias's oversized peppers goggled at me. "You ascribe such value to my life, Fowler."

"Sorry, just curious." And thankful the answer wasn't *yes.*

"The guards only patrol at night. The line-of-sight on the plateau is a distinct advantage. Though it wouldn't be considered high ground from here, I've never seen weapons capable of the range to attack from the cliffs on any side. Invaders would have to enter through those narrow passages or scale the cliffs, and then they'd be in a low-ground position because the defenders would wait atop the steps at the center of the valley."

I leaned toward Desini. "I see why you would want to recoup this place."

She nodded.

Lucias continued. "The paths into the valley between the cliffs are highly visible in the daylight, so guards are stationed in the rocks above. I don't know how many because it's too easy to conceal oneself there. I've spotted two in each pass." She leaned in, and her voice took on a conspiratorial tone. "But the Swisa are sneaky buggers."

"A fact with which I am too familiar," Desini said. "They caught us unaware and drove us out with superior numbers. We only lived here for two years, but this place's seclusion made it the perfect home. Its loss was devastating to those of us who survived their invasion. They burned all we had built as they drove us out. This is why my people have returned to nomadic traditions."

"Where are they now?" Lucias asked.

Desini shrugged. "They migrate from place-to-place just to the north of these hinterlands. They change camps seasonally to follow the blooming fruits of spring, the wheats of summer, gourds of fall, and greens of the southern winter. I will find them easily enough when the time comes."

"Mobility makes for good security." Charney had actually settled on the wet pine straw despite the soaking it'd taken. "If you're always moving, you're hard to find."

Lucias shook her head. "Hmph. Charney thinks we're better served by heading south and finding a quiet spot in the Dark Wood to live. But mobility sure didn't help us when those bird shits showed up today." She adopted a mocking tone. "My brother fancies himself something of a special one because he has a pool. He claims the place calls to him in his dreams, or some nonsense of that order."

"You mock that you don't understand, sister."

A strange emotion crept into my bloodstream, and I peered over at Priya. I didn't have to shake my head to communicate for her to leave the topic alone, for now. We were getting pretty good at this.

After I gulped hard enough to swallow a stone, I inspected Charney.

Charney
Half-Goblin
Level 14
(No class)

I'd learn more later, though it was very strange Zhara's woods—which were at least a week's trek south of here by horse—called to him. For now, I wanted to know more about the place below us because Desini's impatient fidgeting was gnawing at me.

Unfortunately, Roshan wasn't the kind to save things of this nature for later.

"Yes, I sense the Light in him. Hmph. A goblin."

A big rain drop slipped past the overhead tree cover and smacked my forehead as I turned to regard my first teacher in Enora. I was reminded of the strange warming sensation I'd been experiencing since we got here.

Since Charney sat next to me.

"You what?" Charney's thick black monobrow dipped above the bridge of his nose.

"Shit, I do, too," I said. "I'd wondered about the strange warmth. Its Zhara's gift, right? The ability to sense light in others?"

Roshan nodded, and her lips parted to speak, but she wasn't given the chance.

"Wait, did you say Zhara? The tree woman from Charney's dreams is...?" Lucias glared at her brother. "You mean she's real?"

Charney shrugged. "Even I wasn't sure I believed it."

"Unbelievable. She'll be wound up in my business for the rest of my life." Priya formed her patented scowl. The difference between hers and Charney's was she was hot as fuck. He was a goblin.

Charney shook his head. "Your business? What the hell is going on around here? I'm getting a little freaked."

Roshan patted Charney on the shoulder as if she were scraping mud off a leaf. "It is fine, little goblin. You should rest easy as you wield the blessing of Solara's Light to guide your way." She sighed. "I suppose I will call you brother."

Charney scrunched up his nose. "It's not nice to call people *little*."

Priya elbowed me and cocked her chin like she was loading a weapon.

I smirked.

Roshan shrugged with infinite indifference at Charney. "You are not people. You are a goblin. How am I to know your social rules, little one?"

"Look, lady. I don't know if you're just fucking stupid or are trying to be funny, but—"

I ripped a dagger from its sheath. "You will measure your tongue, or I will slice it from your gullet."

Roshan's glare met my sudden utterance, but it was the reflective glow of Guiles's against my night vision spell that snapped me to attention.

He spoke low. "Your temperament toward our new ally shows you could use some meditation."

"Sorry, I'm just feeling a little impatient."

Roshan pushed Charney's shoulder. "You will forgive my betrothed. He is protective, for he loves me."

Charney pushed himself up without another word then stepped off into the thicker trees down the hill.

Lucias leaned in and shoved her shoulder against my bicep. "My brother can get a little mouthy. It's confusing for him. We've always known he had... some weirdness. I just didn't know the extent. I still don't."

"I'll talk to him later," I said. "Roshan is just... special to me. All of my people are."

Priya nodded. "But she is especially so, and with good reason."

My head jerked up. I searched her features and emotions for jealousy, but the half-elf wore an understanding smile inside and out. Desini's longing gaze returned to the valley below.

I sighed. "Lucias, I want to take that place away from those bird dudes. The *Swisa*."

A wide smile crossed the goblin woman's lips, revealing perfectly square, clean pearly teeth. Her huge irises gleamed purple in the light of my spell. Her little button nose was adorable. My gaze dropped.

Goblin boobs. Green. No.

Priya smacked my shoulder and whispered.

"Insufferable."

"I was hoping you'd say that." Lucias leaned into me again and pointed down the hill. It took a moment to realize she was replying to my sentiment about wanting to take the valley. "I've fantasized about the day we'd drive these bastards from their home like they drove us from ours. You see that little 'U' shape cutting into the cliff? To the left?"

"That narrow dip where that trail runs into the wall?"

"Right. There's a small monument to their ancestors there, molded in clay. Ugly thing about eight feet tall. Gives me the creeps. They sometimes commune there, and their women take the children daily."

Roshan spat. "Bird worship." Her hand jerked side to side. "I'll hear not of such blasphemy. I will go and talk to the other goblin." Rising from her crouch, she stepped off, her sandals sloshing wet pine straw as she descended.

Lucias watched her go. "I kind of like her, I think. She reminds me of someone."

Her brother, perhaps?

I shuddered at the thought. "We all like her."

Then Lucias returned to the subject at hand. "Anyway, if the Swisa were drawn to that monument, they'd be isolated from the trails, right? Caught in the recess?"

Scanning the curves of the cliff faces surrounding the valley, I saw the goblin had a good point. The closest trail was to the west, the farthest far to the north. The recess at the foot of the cliff to our left where Lucias indicated the monument stood was the lowest point in the valley.

"It couldn't be more perfect." I wrapped an arm around her shoulder and squeezed. "Perfect."

Priya smiled at the goblin when she lowered her pudgy cheeks and blushed.

Yellow. She blushed yellow.

"He has that effect on women." She absently rubbed her flat belly, reminding me of yet another situation I would have to deal with someday soon. The list was growing long, but at least the job at the bottom of the valley appeared tenable.

I brought my arm back to my lap. "So you think their reverence for that idol could be used against them, that we could draw them them into the corner there. I assume that doesn't mean you want to force them uphill and out of the valley through that western trail."

"They killed my people. If we play it right, the women and children will be separated from the warriors, and we can minimize casualties, though I'm uncertain they deserve as much."

Desini crept toward me in her crouch and set her hand on my knee.

"I agree with the goblin, master. They are evil creatures who deserve no compassion, but the invading party that drove us out was not composed of women and children. The blood of my people once washed this plateau, but we need only the blood of their males to cleanse it from the rocks."

It didn't surprise me when Priya agreed. "Sounds like death to me. Let's burn them down."

I was really wondering about these dark streaks and thought maybe it was a good thing Roshan had walked away.

The natural steps ascended to the outer walls of the cave and wrapped around into shadowy areas the torches' flames couldn't reach. It was the perfect hole in the Swisa's defenses to exploit.

Lucias proved quite the tactician. Between her, Guiles, and me, we'd developed a plan within an hour. Priya just wanted to burn feathers and Roshan didn't trouble herself with the details. Charney added the random sentiments as to our questionable sanity from time-to-time.

If Priya was snarky, Charney was a belligerent asshole. Aside from his near-fatal snap at Roshan, I kind of liked him.

Though we discussed our mini-invasion from multiple angles and debated the best way to accomplish our goal, I won the day by explaining a recurring theme in earth warfare—cutting off the head of the snake and watching the rest scurry and slither away.

The range from the cliff to the cave rendered my Woodsman class useless. The casters lacked spells that could travel that far. Creeping quietly and low to the recess in the cliff, we peered down into the place we'd trap our prey. The stony ancestral idol sat in the corner below.

I pointed down a group of rocky outcroppings. "Priya, do you think you and Roshan could make that climb?"

She raised an eyebrow in confusion as she peered over the ledge. Then her cheeks spread in a devious smile and she nodded. "It's perfect, Gemini."

Desini set a hand on my back. "I have rope to ensure their success in both directions."

"Rope? That's even better." I sent party invites to the goblins and a second party box appeared on the opposite side of my interface.

Raid Group Formed
Charney has accepted your party invite.
Lucias has accepted your party invite.

I asked Roshan if she saw the goblins in her interface. She confirmed. At this range, I didn't expect them to take damage, but gone were the days I got caught with my pants down.

Guiles and I descended the long way around and down the hills to the western entrance, enabled our stealth, then went to work. The others stayed on the cliff and prepared for their parts in the deadly dance to come, save one. Her part would come last.

It took more than an hour to navigate around from the high cliff, down the valley through the trees, then around to the western passage. The journey reinforced my speculation that this valley was an amazing place to hunker down, if one knew how to defend it.

Lucias's reconnaissance proved accurate as we found only two guards manning the narrow western pass into the walled-in valley. We spotted them snoozing up in the rocks, so we entered stealth, climbed up the narrow paths between rocky footings to ensure they never left their slumbers. That cleared the way for our final act, which would follow shortly.

After we followed the path to its outlet, we split up at the mouth inside the valley, where our boots transitioned from stony dirt to lush grass.

The stack of stones chipped and carved in the shape of a bird creature stood in the recess cut into the corner of the cliff wall. Hidden in its shadow, I cast my gaze skyward. High above the sheltered torch sitting atop the statue, I could almost see the pink in Priya's cheeks as she raised a thumb. When I returned the gesture, I peered right through my hand, marveling anew at the stealth effect.

The first risky bit was to extinguish the torch burning beneath the stony shelter atop the statue. Guiles told me that passing in front of a light source around watchful enemies could break stealth and, though the chances were slimmer beneath the cover of night, I wasn't taking any chances.

I cast a quick glance over my shoulder and scanned the village on the plateau above the coast. It seemed clear. The torch thumped to the wet ground. The rain would do the rest and, by the time anyone noticed their religious symbol cast in darkness, I'd be gone.

I wrapped around to a hill ascending in the dark eastern corner of the valley behind the natural steps then climbed until I slid into the shadows alongside the cave at the top.

The torchlight danced in the breeze as I peered around the corner to find two bird-man guards standing on either side of the cave's mouth. The glowing outline of Guiles's narrow form hunkered on the opposite side.

[Party:] [Guiles:] Took you long enough.
[Party:] [G3m1n1:] I don't have speed bonuses. Bite me.
[Party:] [Guiles:] Too scrawny.

I eyed the closest guard.

Unknown Swisa
Level 15 Guard

We unsheathed our daggers and eased below the torches, sneaking up on our targets. The black eye icon on my HUD blinked red as I passed beneath the flames, so I stepped quickly out of the aura of light and froze, waiting for it to turn black again.

As planned, we took a quick peek inside the cave mouth to ensure there were no unplanned arrivals as we worked. Once we determined the way was clear, I nodded at him and held up three fingers, then two, then...

We ambushed the Swisa, aiming for the openings between their chest armor and helmets that rode up high in the backs of their necks, as directed by Guiles.

You use Spine Snap.
Critical Hit!
Mortal Wound!

Swisa Guard
-67 HP
-9 HP (Bleed)

Clamping my free hand around its beak, I followed the attack with a smooth slash across the bird-man's neck, then slammed a dagger into his chest. The feathered humanoid's armor clinked quietly, like bamboo wind chimes, as I eased its weight to the ground and scanned both directions to ensure no one had heard.

But with the steady pitter-patter of the rain falling all around us, I'd had little to worry about. A quick glance at Guiles confirmed the elf had also accomplished his task. No surprise, since he was a fucking Level 51. One stab had undoubtedly done the job.

We dragged the bodies into the entrance of the cave and waited for combat mode to end so we could stealth naturally and spare ourselves the cool-downs of Shadow Merge.

We crept along opposite walls, extinguishing the torches on the interior rocky bulkheads. We'd left the ones under the rock overhang outside the cave burning, lest the darkness raise villager suspicions, but if we were right and the bird people didn't possess night vision, a dark tunnel would prove a useful ally.

The cave split after a minute of careful pacing. Guiles and I stopped and peered at each other. Since I had no idea as to the sensitivity of Swisa hearing, I gestured with a finger at the elf, then at myself, and finally at the right-hand passage. Party chat might have been easier, but I didn't consider it until after he'd acknowledged the sign language.

He nodded and fell in behind me as I crept along. After a final curve in the tunnel, yellow light reflected against the dirt-packed floor and rocky walls. We lowered ourselves to a crouch as we eased forward. I peered into a wide, oval room with crystal stalactites hanging from a high ceiling.

As we'd feared, armed soldiers filled the area, some sitting along the walls with their spears propped next to them, others leaning with their weapons in-hand. In the center of the room, an empty, wide stone chair of stacked stones perched atop a platform. Behind it stood a high wooden totem of a swisa.

Guiles waved a hand to get my attention. He leaned against the left wall pointing off to the right side of the oval room, but I couldn't make out what he gestured toward.

> [Party:] [Guiles:} *Chief is right there.*

I slid quietly over to his side and took a peek.

A much taller, broad-shouldered Swisa with a long, curved orange beak sat on a natural step that led to another tunnel behind him. Adorned in the same black armor as his guards, fashioned from scales, his arms were wrapped around the waist of another Swisa I could only identify as a woman because of her bare chest, her featherless breast cupped in one of the leader's hands.

Behind him a shadowy figure stood outside the light of the torches, just inside the far tunnel. A head dress with a white feather circled the crown of its narrow head, and as he stepped forward, a staff with a bird skull perched at the tip of its shaft clanked on the stone surface of the inner sanctum.

It leered through slits in our direction.

Unknown Swisa Shaman
Level 17

> [Party:] [Guiles:] *That's not great. When we get outside, he goes first. For now, we go for those two.*

He gestured to the guards closest to us.

> [Party:] [Guiles:] *After, we must move quickly. Remember to*

watch your stamina. One strike, no more. Conserve until we're at their monument outside. Also, remain attentive of your footing on the plateau. Its grass will be slick.

"I get it," I whispered as the suspicious gaze of the shaman tickled a nerve in my temples. "Relax."

If only I could take my own advice. My heart thumped against my ribs like I'd been fed an IV drip of amphetamines.

I conjured up an image of Desini's face as a reminder of how her people had suffered at the hands of these feathered shits. That so steeled my resolve that I found my feet inching forward without thought.

When I ambushed my guard, I failed to land a critical strike, but my intent was to garner attention, not kill a single bird dude. Besides, when I ripped my dagger out of the back of his neck, I didn't need my interface to tell me the eruption of blood meant he wasn't long for Enora.

An uproar of squawks filled the room as my stealth broke and the Swisa guard crumpled. Armor rattled, spears clanked. Guiles and I were already well on our way back down the tunnel when commands echoed behind us.

"Intruders! Bring to me! I want alive!"

I tripped after just a few steps, but Guiles grabbed my arm and helped keep me upright as he dragged me forward and back into a steady stride. "Relax, huh?"

Despite the tension, I laughed through my heaving breaths. "You can stab me in the temple when we've set our bind point somewhere closer, deal?"

Guiles sprinted past me and gave a laugh of his own. "You've got it, Shénhuà!"

His good humor reminded me who I was running with. The rogue elf could likely take out this tribe himself, but suggesting it might have been insulting and, since he'd volunteered to mentor me, he likely saw this as a good training opportunity. I knew better than to get cocky over a perceived advantage though, and I steeled my mind.

The squawking Swisa filled the cave, their utterances of rage bouncing off the stony walls as if screamed through megaphones. The pattering of their clawed feet smacked the earth as Guiles and I burst out into the night.

Avoiding the path leading down the center of their village, we turned left toward the southwestern corner of the valley. I measured every footfall on the ground in front of me as we reached the steps. Guiles set our pace, and I got the idea he was taking it easy on me.

The squawking echoes ceased as the guards rushed from the tunnel and their feet sloshed in the grass behind us, but neither of us risked a look back. Although the dark tunnel had bought us some time, speed was paramount from what Lucias had told us. Despite their broad shoulders, the bird creatures were fast. Hesitation could cost us.

Though it seemed like minutes, we were down the steps in less than one, hauling our asses toward the small monument I'd passed on my way in. When we reached it, I ventured a look back to find a black swarm of enemies charging down the steps in our direction.

I eyed my HUD, hoping we'd run far enough to meet the objective we'd planned from above. My ears pulled back as my lips turned up. "I'm clear? You?"

Guiles nodded and, though I huffed and puffed, he replied as if we'd been out for a stroll. "I'm out of combat mode. Wait until you see the color of their irises as we discussed."

What is this, Bunker Hill?

As they reached the recess in the corner of the valley,

Guiles and I shared a final glance. As the first Swisa stepped up to the monument, we each selected a target and cast Shadow Merge. Because we wanted to maintain stealth, we didn't attack when we returned from the void behind our targets. Instead, we soft-stepped around the onslaught of coming enemies, and exited the recess.

[Party:] [Guiles:] *Priya, proceed.*
[Party:] [Priya:] *My pleasure, brother.*

A trace of purple light crackled above, then a shimmer of white light burst across the sky in multiple directions before expelling fingers of lightning that zapped the bird men below, causing each to convulse for three seconds. None of them resisted.

Priya's casting meter blinked on my interface as she channeled the follow-up spell. Ice rained down to slow the electrocuted birds. By the time they recognized the trap and tried to distance themselves from the two casters on high, their feet dragged as if they were players in a macabre slow motion stage play.

Red text popped up over multiple Swisa heads as the spells rained down their furies. But then green text and a matching glow appeared over one bird man.

Someone is healing.

I watched the cool down on Shadow Merge because I didn't want to break stealth until it was available again, but we had to keep these birds trapped in the corner. Time seemed to fly in contrast to the creeping movement of the impaired bird men, but there were still five seconds remaining on my cool down timer. Roshan's meter filled on my HUD, then a smite bolt slammed the furthest swisa from the idol, bringing him to one knee. When another smite struck the enemy next to him, I realized she was tapping the row closest to us, using them as barricades around which the back rows would have to navigate to escape.

Brilliant!

Priya cast Ice Storm again, bringing her mana down to 35%.

Knowing I'd only have to survive in the open for a few seconds, I finished Roshan's first kneeling target with a Spine Snap.

You Spine Snap Unknown Swisa.
Mortal Wound!

Unknown Swisa
-82 HP
-22 HP (bleed)

Eighty-two damage was a new record, but I didn't have time to enjoy the accomplishment.

The bleeding damage would have to finish my first target as I wheeled then slammed my dagger into the side of the neck of the closest bird.

Guiles ambushed another at the rear and called out.

"Over here, birdies!" The birds turned to find the elf shoving his shoulder into the monument. The stones began to teeter and rock as rain matted the elf's white hair to his cheeks. I'd never have thought his rail frame could move the stones, but when I'd questioned it during the planning phase, he'd merely pursed his lips and asked if I knew my role in the endeavor.

Long, anguished squawks filled the air as the Swisa charged toward him, but then the statue's top stone toppled, slamming onto an encroaching head. The swisa's skull cracked and it thumped to the ground though my interface reported his death before he landed.

A taller form stepped out from behind the monument bearing a tall black shield with a wide silver curve painted into its face and a long, glowing, one-handed mace. Boots clanked on stone, and a tail waved high.

The harbinger of revenge.

Desini.

"Come, you odorous feather-wearing cowards of the night! Hence approaches your rightful death!" Desini roared with a rage I'd never heard before. The ear-splitting sound bounced off the recessed walls, and the Swisa cowered, but then charged.

Not missing a beat, Guiles activated Combat Flurry, finished off a bird, then sprung another ability I hadn't seen before, where he attacked, vanished, appeared behind another bird, attacked, vanished, and then repeated the move.

Guiles executes Shadow Dash
Stealth cool down removed
Critical Hit!
Mortal Wound!
Fatal Blow!

Unknown Swisa
-121 HP

Unknown Swisa dies.
Critical Hit!
Mortal Wound!
Fatal Blow!

Unknown Swisa
-119 HP

Unknown Swisa dies.
Critical Hit!
Mortal Wound!
Fatal Blow!

Unknown Swisa
-127 HP

Unknown Swisa dies.

He zipped through the nethers to each bird with such blinding speed, the rest of the group hardly had time to react before Fire Flashes started and the burning sticks from above whistled down into the valley.

I want Shadow Dash!

Desini swung wildly at the few birds who reached her. She made easy work of them and straightened. A wicked smile stretched her cheeks.

Then her glare shot over my shoulder and she peered through slits. Another bird man hustled in her direction, but she raised a boot and slammed its heel into his face, dropping him with barely a notice. I turned to see what had captured her attention.

The leader of the bunch who'd been groping a bare breast in the cavern above stomped off the final stair and pointed his mace in Desini's direction.

"Should have known! Stinking kitty! Come forth, kitty! Claim prize!"

Desini marched forward, her singular focus burning lasers into the enemy she'd longed to send to hell. As she passed, she didn't spare me so much as a glance as she said, "He is mine."

I didn't bother answering.

As the shaman stepped forward with his staff held high, I sensed his intent from the way his gaze cast upon his chief.

Oh, no, shammy bitch. No heals for this battle.

I prowled into the nethers and took up position behind him. Guiles was soon at my shoulder. I counted down from three again, and this time, when we attacked, it was as a team. We both activated Spine Snap, we both scored critical hits, then we unloaded flurries of stabs until blood erupted from wounds across his back and torso. He crumpled to the ground with a final, ear-shattering screech.

The leader swung around, spied the dead shaman, then met my gaze.

I smiled.

The boss looked to Desini, who marched toward him with a purpose, then back at me.

"Oh, yeah, bud." I thrust out a crooked finger. "You are all kinds of fucked."

"Ahhhh!" The boss screamed as he charged our tank with his sword clutched in both hands above his head.

Desini braced herself with one foot set in front of the other and her weight distributed to her hind leg. Feinting with her shield as the blow came down, she twisted and spun aside. As the boss's sword splashed into the wet ground, she used the momentum of her spin to swing her mace in a wide arc. The spikes slammed into the boss's back and sent him lunging forward, though somehow he maintained his footing.

He seethed, and clouds of mist sprayed from his nostrils. The rain's tympani grew louder as patter became downpour. Distant thunder rumbled.

It was like a scene out of an interactive theater experience.

Desini spun her mace in a few tight circles. "You will have to do better, bird. I grow bored with you, already." She raised her voice, speaking to the few remaining soldiers near the monument struggling to get to their feet. "This is the one you call a leader? This slithering snake of—"

The boss charged, this time lunging with his pommel at his gut and the sword aimed at Desini's chest. Parrying the weapon with her shield as she pivoted, she swung the mace easily around and caught the leader on the side of his head.

"Ooooh! That's gotta sting!" I yelled, taunting the boss.

Guiles joined in. "Indeed. This creature of shadow might best find a smaller cave in which to crawl so that his life might be spared."

Desini shot him a glaring reproach.

Guiles waved a hand. "I hadn't considered my words."

The boss stepped forward and bellowed, "Your people never take land, mishon. You must to kill us all!"

"Then I will kill you all, bird shit." Desini zipped across the distance, lowering her shoulder before slamming it into his chest. The boss thudded to the ground under the impact of the Charge ability. Instead of standing above him and readying her defense, like usual, Desini dove on top of the beast and pinned him down. "This is for my sister, you filthy scum!"

Sister?

She slammed the mace into the Swisa's beak. Crimson splattered as it snapped off and fell to the ground. Desini tossed the mace to one side, balled up her fists, and pummeled the leader of the bird people. Bones cracked. She grunted with each brutal haymaker. Blood splattered in droplets as she raised her fists for each swing to mix with the driving drops of rain.

Then she raised one hand, stretched her fingers, then four curved claws popped out.

Oh yeah. He's done.

Gross, wet sounds emanated with each swing of her wide, arcing hooks. Her enemy gurgled blood and spat it out its nostrils beneath where its beak had been. She sliced until his body quivered.

"Perhaps we should pull her off?" Guiles asked.

The remaining soldiers lingered near the broken monument, uncertain. Some of their shoulders slumped, Others grasped the dinosaur armor covering their chests, as they watched my tank pummel the ever-loving shit out of their leader.

"Usually, I might agree with you, but in this case?" I shook my head. "No. Let her send a message to the rest. She's earned it." I leaned closer. "Besides, do *you* want to step into those claws?"

If we would truly establish our own place here, I wanted there to be zero doubt among these people that we would fight for it. Desini represented people the Swisa murdered and drove from their land. She was a symbol of an important lesson. My party and I might face enough challenges here without these beasts returning, thinking they might find weakness... or mercy.

Guiles considered me and, just when I thought he would dissent, he sheathed his daggers and bowed his head slightly. "In this, the decision is yours, Shénhuà. It is mine only to advise."

When we looked back, it was over. Desini stood, her back and shoulders expanding as she huffed for breath while peering down at her dead enemy. Her frame was a thing of magnificence, a strong, feminine structure of low hills of muscle rolling out from beneath hard steel half-plate.

What few bird men remained stumbled away from the monument. They gazed down at their fallen leader and stopped.

Maintaining my grip on my daggers, I pressed my fists into my hips and raised my voice above the rain as Guiles scanned the steps behind me, watching my back. "Your leader is dead! Many of your tribesman are dead! My people up on that cliff stand ready to wipe this whole village from Enora's memory. You are beaten. But if you drop your weapons, gather your women and children, and leave peacefully, I will allow you to take provisions for your trip to find a new home. I am returning this place to the people from whom you stole it."

A large bird man stepped forward and raised his spear. Guiles vanished and reappeared behind him. The Swisa crumpled to the ground.

Nice touch, elf.

He vanished again and prowled around unseen as spears rattled to the ground in surrender.

"You have twenty minutes to gather your things, head west, and keep walking until three nights have passed. My companion will follow you in the shadows. If you stop before the third coming of the moons, or if ever I see you in this region again, your clan will be annihilated. Leave us in peace, and we will not hunt you."

Desini clipped her mace to her belt. "Pray to your ancestors with thanks that my master has deemed you should live this day! If the decision were mine, you would die where you stand!"

The Swisa stared at us, and though their narrow faces

didn't show much in the way of expression, I sensed their obvious defeat in the way their heads hung. They passed around us in a wide arc, their heads lowered and throwing the occasional glance at their unrecognizable boss.

They were out of the valley with many minutes to spare and, when the rain calmed and the next day's sun shone in my new home, I planned to burn their thatched remnants to the ground.

28

Inside the cave, I peered at the tunnels leading away from the central room where we'd found the soldiers, their now-dead leader, and the shaman.

"How far do you think these go?" Priya asked.

Desini cleared her throat. Her face was red as if she'd painted it in blood. I'd never seen her look more like a warrior. Ferocious. "They wind for miles into the earth. At the far end are hot springs that bring warmth in the cool months. It is exquisite down there. I will take you some time." She peered at Roshan. "Glowing crystals surround the springs. You would like it very much, priestess."

Roshan gripped one of Desini's bloody, gloved hands. There was something sweet about that. "I would enjoy it even more if the two of us go alone the first time, so we might become better acquainted."

Priya stepped away from the tunnel's entrance and circled around the empty stone throne in the center of the great oval room. She gestured with one open hand. "Your chair, my lord."

I eyed the seat, breathing in the dank scent of the area,

still coppery with the blood of the two birds Guiles and I had lain to rest here. I squeezed my eyelids together, inhaling in that odor, forcing it into my lungs, knowing there would be so much more of it in what promised to be a bloody future.

Surrounding me were a mishon, two elves, two goblins, and my human healer. I wanted to mark this moment in my mind because, for all our struggles as individuals and those we took on as a team, this marked a new beginning. I wanted it to mean something.

I'd been in Enora for eleven days, but still felt at times like I hadn't had a moment to stop and gather my thoughts. Sure, there were nights in our furs when I asked myself metaphysical questions or subjected myself to queries about expectations of me from inside and outside the game.

And I still sweated fatherhood.

But now I stood at a pivotal moment in my new time-line, surrounded by people who respected me—well, except for the goblin fuck, but he'd learn—and as I peered from the chair to Priya then back to the chair, it all became clear. Clear like when I traversed fiber optic cables to enter this world when I'd experienced that ultimate moment of epiphany as I transitioned between life and digital. A moment I couldn't remember, except that sense of under-standing for which I grasped in vain given my all new context.

Lucera.

Zhara.

Roshan.

Enora, herself.

Guiles.

Desini.

Priya.

Goblins.

Baby.

"That's not my chair, Priya Skyy."

Priya peered up at me, a slight curve on her lips, her facial muscles relaxed.

"Who else's chair would it be? It is you who is Shénhuà, yes? It is you who brought us here, right? I couldn't imagine who, but the immortal brought to bless us by Solara—"

"It's you."

Priya did a double take. Her voice squeaked.

"What?" She took a stumbling step backward, her gaze moving around the semi-circle we'd formed. The goblins moved in from either side, closing on us to complete the group as Guiles took up a spot in the center. "Why would it be my seat?"

"You were born of Solara's energy and are the daughter of the Guardian, the Matron of the Dark Wood. You wear the magical ward of protection and once led the university in Warrington. Besides, if the Shadow Coven Prantu mentioned comes to contact us, it is you they'll come looking for.

"I'm Shénhuà, and I accept that role. But you—an immortal born of an immortal and who breathes the magical energy of this world—are the mother of the *Shénhuà's* child. The chair is yours. From here, we build your influence and retake what the governor, the king, and the king's grandfather have taken from this world. We will balance Enora, together."

"Don't hold back or anything," Charney muttered. Lucias elbowed his ribs and muttered something too low for me to hear.

Priya shook her head. "No. I don't want it."

I shrugged. "It's is Solara's will."

Priya jerked and stepped backward. "Speak not blindly of the will of our goddess!"

"You've been with me since the day we met and have never left my side. You struggled with me through all of it. We rescued Desini and Roshan, liberated the roads of the bandits. We conquered the first tier of the Plague Barrens Gates. *We*, Priya. Not just me. Considering your unique qualifications and all you achieved since we met, setting aside a past that you don't even remember," I thrust out my finger, "that's your chair."

Priya turned to Guiles. "Talk sense to him."

To my utter surprise, Guiles stepped forward and knelt. "As is the will of the mystic, I pledge my fealty for as long as I shall live to the immortal daughter of Solara. May you be forever happy and contented in service to the Light."

Roshan knelt next to him.

"What the hell are you doing?" Priya asked.

"Even if it is Gemini who leads us, he chooses you to claim our seat of power, governess. Who am I to argue with this simple wisdom? My life is yours, Priya Skyy."

"But I betrayed all of you on the road! How can you trust me?"

I took a knee.

"No," Priya muttered, taking another step back. A tear streamed down her cheek. "I don't want it."

"Solara commanded Zhara to send you forth into the world, Priya. They waited for me to come. They waited for Roshan. Then they gave us Desini. Then Guiles. Then the, um, goblins."

"Gee, thanks," Charney muttered.

I continued as if he didn't exist. "It's you who was always there. It's you they sent us to. You who we are to help bring the world back to what it once was."

And I'm not going to be tied down to this place when I need to be out there gaining levels and living my destiny.

I was a sneaky bastard, but sometimes you played your hand, and other times, you hedged your bets.

"We all waited for *you*, Gemini!"

I shook my head. "Only to fill a role."

"Oh?" She thrust her hands on her hips, but without the usual conviction. "What role is that?"

And hence, came the hook... the role I decided I would best serve in Enora.

"I'm your protector. Your soldier. I'm going to build you a stronghold. I'll lead our people to bring you success in battle, and I'll be at your side when we return the Light to this dark, dark world."

God, I was a freaking cheeseball.

29

We stood in the plateau's center beneath the sunny morning sky, surrounded by my companions. Guiles wore a rare smile as Desini's arm hooked through mine. Priya leaned against Roshan wearing the red robe she preferred over the new one I forced her to wear in battle. Roshan grasped the ruby she'd pried from the undead warrior's sword in the Plague Barrens. One thumb rubbed its smooth surface as she gazed into it. The goblins stood further back, the looks of uncertainty adorning their faces revealing the familial resemblance I hadn't seen before. Smoldering ashes pushed the scent of burned huts around us.

I held out my hand, palm up. The stone with the glowing rune etched in its face pulsed blue. From our stepped-off measurements, we stood in the exact center of the plateau.

"Any idea what it will do when I drop it?" I asked Guiles.

"It will create a foundation, but I don't know exactly

know what it means. As I told you in the Plague Barrens, they are quite rare. A thing of lore, really."

I peered at Priya. She winked at me and patted her stomach. Her warm sense of comfort washed over me. Desini squeezed my free arm.

"Are you all ready?" I asked.

Nods all around, except for the goblins, who backed slowly away.

I drew a cleansing breath, peered around the walled-in valley, and committed the high, vertical rock faces topped by trees and the surrounding green of the natural steps to memory. I wanted to mark the moment.

The scent of the grassy earth wafted from around my boots as I turned my hand over and dropped the glowing stone to the earth.

Or the Enora.

Whatever.

The ground rumbled, my feet slid back and forth in my stealth boots, and a gap burst open to swallow the Foundation Stone.

THE END

Thank you for reading book three of Enora Online.

I'm hard at work on Book Four, and I've got some surprises in store for Gemini and his band of crazy noobs. That'll be out later this year.

Be sure to join my mailing list at enora.online so you'll be the first to know when it's coming, and to get a chance to read it early!

OR, if you'd rather, click the Follow button at Amazon to get updates from them at https://www.amazon.com/Arlo-Adams/e/B07NCBNDWQ.

You can also follow me on Bookbub.

Thanks for reading!

JOIN ME!

If you're into Social Media, I tend to spout insanity now and then.

    facebook.com/authorarloadams

    twitter.com/ArloAdams

www.ingramcontent.com/pod-product-compliance
Lightning Source LLC
Chambersburg PA
CBHW051627180726
48284CB00006B/1630